MURDER AT THE MANSE

ANDREA FRAZER

Murder at the Manse

ISBN 9781783751563

This edition published by Accent Press 2014

DRAMATIS PERSONAE

The Guests at The Manse

Enoch and Aylsa Arkwright – a successful scrap-metal dealer and his wife

Bradley and Fiona (Fudge) Baddeley – an articled clerk, and his wife, a charity worker

Mark and Madge Berkeley-Lewis – bank clerk and his wife

Persephone (Percy) and Lloyd Boyd-Carpenter – author and her husband

Freddie (Fruity) and Edwina (Teddy) Newberry – a professional gambler and a croupier

Lewis and Suzanne Veede – a third-generation baker and his wife

The Staff at The Manse

Jefferson Grammaticus – part-owner

Jocelyn and Jerome Freeman – part-owners

Beatrix Ironmonger – housekeeper

Antoine de la Robe – chef

Dwayne Mortte – sous chef

Steve Grieve – barman and parker of guests' cars

Chastity Chamberlain – chambermaid

Henry Buckle – gardener

Market Darley Police Personnel

Detective Inspector Harry Falconer, Detective Sergeant 'Davey' Carmichael, PC Merv Green, PC Linda (Twinkle) Starr, Sergeant Bob Bryant, and Dr Philip Christmas, Police Surgeon

Others

Alison Meercroft – owner, DisguiserGuys Fancy Dress Hire

Céline Treny – her new assistant

A SHORT HISTORY OF THE MANSE

The Manse is situated about three miles or so down a roughish road, which bears off to the south-east from the road between Shepford Stacey and Carsfold. It was once the residence of the incumbent vicar for the fair-sized village parish of Magnum Parva, a bustling community through which the River Darle wended its lazy way.

The road to it was of a roughish nature, because the village was no more. It was the great fire in the early nineteenth century that had been the catalyst in its demise. A small outbreak in a thatched terraced dwelling had quickly spread to its neighbours, for the houses were built close together, separated only by winding lanes, and it soon spread to most of the homes in the village, and even the church.

At the time it was high summer, and the Darle was low on water, so the bucket chain faced an impossible task. The fire soon spread out of control and burned for two days, at the end of which there was precious little village left, with the exception of The Manse, through the grounds of which ran the river had acted as a firebreak and kept the building unscathed, while the reverend gentleman's parishioners were all left virtually homeless.

Village businesses had perished in the blaze too, and the place was a site of smoking devastation. Some folk stayed on, as some folk do in even the most impossible circumstances, too shocked to leave the place that has been their home, but there was no chance of rebuilding the village. Too much had been destroyed to make that viable, and its population seeped away, to stay with relatives or friends, and to make new lives for themselves elsewhere.

The Manse remained empty. The Church of England

refused the funds to rebuild the church because it no longer had a congregation, and the incumbent was sent elsewhere to pursue his calling.

Nature gradually reclaimed what had been its home before the existence of Magnum Parva, and only The Manse stood to mark the passing of such a thriving community. The unstable remnants of the church, the businesses, and the homes slowly crumbled to the ground, and although traces of old walls existed over a wide area, it was now just a large piece of rough woodland, but with some quite well-grown trees, given how long ago the fire was.

The Manse stood empty for some time, until the Church tried to find tenants for it. Over a period of three decades or so, four families tried to live there, but the woods were too immature at that time to hide the evidence of what had happened in the surrounding area, and all four families found it desolate and depressing, none of them staying for more than six months.

During the First World War, the War Office requisitioned it and equipped it as a convalescent home for wounded officers, and for a few years, the building was a-bustle with patients, nurses, and doctors, enlivening its interior again after so many years. With the end of the War, however, it did not take long for it to empty again, and begin another long vigil, waiting for life to return once more to its empty echoing rooms.

Ironically, it was another war that peopled it again, this time the Second World War, when it was cleaned up and used to house evacuees from London, being run almost in the manner of an orphanage, with some paid staff and a number of volunteers to provide the necessary security and affection that the move had denied the children from their parents.

When the evacuees were dispersed back to their homes in various parts of the capital, the building dropped out of use once again, lonely, unloved, and uncared for by anyone.

The Manse was not to blossom again until 1965, when an enthusiastic lady bought it and refurbished it as a girls' school, dividing and sub-dividing the bedrooms until there was not a room above ground floor level that boasted more than one window. Some of these had been partitioned right across the pane, to provide bathrooms, staff bedrooms, extra classrooms, and the like. The children were confined to dormitories on the second floor, and these dormitories may have had more than one dormer window, but they had a much greater number of beds.

The main teaching was carried out on the ground floor, where the administrative centre of the establishment was situated, and these rooms, consequently, were left more or less alone, to have as many windows as they had been blessed with when The Manse was built.

The school survived until1989, when things in the country began to take a turn for the worse financially, and parents began to pull in their horns, saving by not spending on anything which wasn't an absolute necessity. The final closure was in 1991, when the tiny cell-like rooms walled by plasterboard divisions, and its corridors ceased to echo with girlish laughter, and the occasional squeals of a hair-pulling, biting, scratching fight.

In 2008, the Church placed a lacklustre advert for its sale in the *Times* property section, its wording totally without hope or encouragement. It caught the eye, however, of one Jefferson Grammaticus, who was just contemplating early retirement, and wondering what he would do with himself if he wasn't prosecuting criminals and sending them on holidays of varying lengths at Her Majesty's pleasure.

Over the next few days, an idea began to form in his mind, and finally he made two telephone calls, to Jerome and Jocelyn Freeman, his old friends since they were all at university together, over thirty years ago. Having put his seed of an idea to them, and having received an enthusiastic response, he plucked up the relevant edition of the newspaper, and picked up the telephone to make a third call.

Prologue

Late May

Chastity Chamberlain, chambermaid of The Manse, stood behind the reception desk in the large reception hall and frowned. This was not supposed to be her job. Jefferson Grammaticus had promised he would have a receptionist in place for the grand opening weekend, and she would not be disturbed in her chamber-maidenly responsibilities, but here she was anyway.

As usual, Grammaticus had made one of his pie-crust promises, and as far as he was concerned, her duties could go hang, as long as he had someone to man (or woman) his precious reception desk, and welcome his very first guests.

Not, that is to say, that they were exclusively his guests, for he had the twins Jocelyn and Jerome Freeman as equal partners: it was just that he had taken it upon himself to represent the face of the hotel, and now he'd imprisoned her behind this ruddy desk to smile like a hyena at anyone who had an enquiry, or wanted information which she was barely able to give, having prepared for the room-keeping aspect of the hotel's running, and not that of a mindless robot who just greeted people and directed them to various rooms and features in the grounds. She gave a tiny growl as she thought once again, 'This is not my job!'

She would have a word with Grammaticus – 'the Squire', as he liked to fashion himself – on Monday and state that she must return immediately to the post for which she had been hired. If he wanted to run the business as he planned to, then she could no more waste her time standing here than she could fly.

Ruminating on her sorry situation, after such high hopes of a low-profile position in the hierarchy, she started slightly as the jingling of one of the internal telephones disturbed her silent fuming. As she snatched at it sullenly, the other internal phone rang. Intoning crossly into the first, 'You'll have to wait. I've got the other phone to deal with as well,' she addressed herself to the second instrument, repeating her abrupt remark, then suddenly became aware of an urgent squawking coming from the first call answered.

Lifting the first receiver to her ear, she snapped, 'Yes, what is it?' knowing that this was not the recommended way to greet a guest, but not really caring at the moment. She was instantly deafened by a wail, and an unidentifiable voice which informed her, fairly incoherently, that someone had the audacity to be dead in the billiards room.

Stunned, she transferred the second in-house telephone to her ear, as the sound from this one had turned into a high-pitched squawking that also sounded urgent, leaving the caller from the billiards room with an abrupt, 'Please hold the line.' For a moment she was unable to comprehend what had been said, and hoped that the other telephone might expose the last few seconds as an auditory hallucination brought on by her ire, but her hope was to go unfulfilled.

'It's chef! He's been poisoned. I think he's dying. Get an ambulance before it's too late!'

As she listened, unbelieving, to the announcement of a second calamity, there was a bumping sound, simultaneous with the wail a cat makes when it has been accidentally trodden on, and one of the guests suddenly appeared at the foot of the grand staircase in a tangled heap that would only be good news for a contortionist.

Dropping both telephones and staring in incomprehension at the figure that had suddenly adorned the bottom step, she opened her mouth and screamed.

Chapter One

Jefferson Grammaticus stood in the entrance hall of the recently and expensively refurbished building with his business partners, Jocelyn and Jerome Freeman, looking around him with smug satisfaction. He was a burly man, not tall, but with the sort of personality that makes people think, in retrospect, that he possessed at least three more inches than was his given lot. His curly hair, still with no sign of grey (*or dye!*) was cut fairly short, and he sported a beard, which was much in keeping with the style of hotel that he had spent what seemed like an eternity planning and creating.

There were still builders in evidence, compiling a snagging list, and the decorators still had some work to do, but that was all small fry compared with what had been achieved. A few more weeks and the new boutique hotel 'The Manse' would open its ornate Edwardian double doors to a discerning public, whom he hoped would pay dearly for the sort of all-round time-travel experience that this establishment intended to offer.

Add in the acres of manicured grounds that had been recovered from a veritable jungle, the newly built and aged gazebos, summerhouse, folly, and lily pond complete with ornamental koi carp. As the cherry on the top of the cake, which he hoped would prove as irresistible as a real cherry-topped cake, would surely be the murder mystery weekend – period costume hire included.

The script and parts were already being written by an author whose acquaintance he had made in his previous life as a barrister; the costume-hire company, unknowingly, had signed a nicely loose contract, allowing him to pull out if there were insufficient guests – he *always* read the small print, even if no one else did – and keeping the guest numbers low, while maintaining high prices, should create a clamour amongst the 'right' sort of people, to grace the establishment with their company (*money*).

A small but eye-catching advertisement about the incredible offer for their opening weekend would appear shortly in a few select newspapers and periodicals, from whence he fully expected the first drops of the cataract of money (which he firmly believed would drench the establishment eventually) would fall, and ensure its place in exclusivity and uniqueness in the minds of 'those in the know'.

Slipping seamlessly from his daydream to reality, he surveyed the grand staircase with a loving look, caressing it with his eyes as he would with his hands the body of a lover, turning his head first to the right, then to the left, to admire the huge marble fireplaces which adorned each side of this entrance space. By golly they were impressive, and he drifted off again, imagining a cold winter's day with both grates blazing merrily with piles of logs, the sofas and chairs that would soon adorn this space, filled with contented guests deciding to stay on, just for a day or two more, because of the impeccable taste in which it had been decorated and dressed, and the seamless and courteous service that came with the surroundings.

Abruptly changing season mentally, he saw, in his mind's eye, croquet on the lawns, and afternoon tea being served, either in the cool of the summerhouse, or out on the lawn itself, the cooing of the woodpigeons adding that *je ne sais quoi,* to the perfect setting in which to be an English country gentleman (or lady).

He could even see the ladies' parasols drifting lazily down the lawns to the tea table, set with exquisite porcelain, one of the footmen drifting down after them with a silver tray and the matching silver tea service, the kettle with its own little oil-burner to keep the hot water hot for a refill of the teapot.

As his thoughts conjured up a footman, he turned to his two partners, who were also gazing round with bemused expressions and money in their eyes. Jocelyn and Jerome Freeman had been, respectively, an accountant and a surveyor until the three of them had all taken early retirement in their early- to mid-fifties to take on this project.

All three of them had worked hard at their careers, achieving success and a good wad of money to supplement excellent pensions. It had seemed like a marvellous idea to give them a new lease of life, and not leave them to rely on cocktail parties, endless restaurants, golf, bridge, or any of other of those little deaths that lead one ever more swiftly on to the grave.

The Freemans were identical twins and, although born in Africa, they had been educated in England, eventually ending up at the same university as Jefferson, where they had become firm friends for life. They were tall, with close-cropped wiry hair and very dark skin, and had thought it a fine joke to insist that their visible role in the running of the hotel should be as liveried footmen. Slaves may have been free men by the era the hotel was to set itself, but people of their colouring had been highly sought after as footmen, especially if a matching pair could be found, and they were both keenly looking forward to the arrival of their uniforms.

Jefferson was to be front-of-house, greeting guests as they arrived and making sure their every whim was catered for during their stay, and waving them off for a safe journey home, hoping to see both them and their wallets and credit cards again soon. In anticipation of his role as the hotel's genial host, he had grown the aforementioned beard, and acquired a wardrobe full of hairy tweed suits and waistcoats suitable for the winter months, and a number of lighter ones, still with 'country gentleman' waistcoats, for the warmer seasons of the year.

With the work nearing completion, the staff interviewed

and hired, and the furniture arriving in ten days' time, they were like little boys with a new toy, and all desperate to get into the dressing-up box.

The staff would arrive a week in advance of the first guests, to allow them to get used to the layout of the building and grounds, and the demands of their various roles. Training would be strict and exacting – none of this 'have a nice day' nonsense and 'in a minute' sloppiness. Immaculate and prompt service, with a smile, would be a large part of the appeal of the place – the hotel where service was still given the highest priority, and where the guest was always right, and his every need catered to.

A voice from the open double doors shouted, 'Chandeliers, delivery, and fitting thereof,' and the three large little boys turned as one, with eyes sparkling with as bright a light as that which would soon be reflected and refracted from the myriad crystals that were now to be hung throughout the building.

'Bring them straight through here,' called Jefferson, and rubbed his hands together with glee, as he contemplated the extra frisson of elegance that French crystal would add to the establishment. 'Have you got the wall sconces as well?'

Cherubs! He must have cherubs – putti, if you like, but they were essential to the look that wasn't quite wholly English, but included a whiff of the exotic European. He should have lived in Edwardian times, he thought. What a hit he would have been in one of the classier hotels in London. What a hit he would be now – there was no doubt in his mind whatsoever that this would be so.

Early June

Aylsa Arkwright stared for a moment at the small but attractive advertisement in *Country Life*, and put the magazine down on the coffee table to think for a moment or two. It looked perfect to her, but she knew it would be useless to approach Enoch with the idea: far better to present him

6

with a *fait accompli*, and a reasonable explanation for why she had done what she had done.

This would take some thought, and not a little cunning. Fitting a cigarette into her long ebony and mother-of-pearl holder, and lighting it with a gold lighter, she rose from her recumbent position and walked through the open French windows to take her sneakier side for a walk round the substantial area of the garden, to see what occurred to it.

Her husband Enoch, a rather dour man who obstinately preferred work to pleasure, and was loath to be dragged away from it, replaced the telephone back in its cradle on his desk, and gave a lupine grin. What a deal he had just done! What a corker! Who said there was no money in scrap metal? Well, he'd shown 'em over the years, and would continue to do so for some considerable time to come.

He was the top man, and he would celebrate tonight with a bottle or two of champagne with dinner, not that it would be drunk in the confines of a restaurant. Aylsa's cooking was good enough for him, and although he'd down the champagne with pleasure because he got it from a contact at a rock-bottom price, there was no need to go throwing money around in a fancy restaurant just because he'd just clinched a corker, now was there?

He'd give his wife a ring a little later, and ask her if she could produce something a little fancier than normal, as he had some good news to share, but he'd make her wait until after they'd eaten, in case she got any ideas about trying for a late booking at that slimy Froggy's fancy French restaurant 'L'Etoile'. The prices in there were enough to give a man a severe nosebleed. No, he wasn't going to be caught by that old trick – the 'it'll keep till tomorrow in the fridge' trick. In fact, he was going to be caught by a totally new one, but of this, he had no idea whatsoever at the moment, and carried on with his afternoon, in blissful ignorance of the fleecing that he was going to undergo later that day.

Aylsa, meanwhile, had not wasted the forty years she had been married by not picking up a trick or two. His phone call about something a little special for dinner had alerted her to the fact that he was in an unusually good mood, which probably indicated that he had made or put through a good deal that day, and that could only work in her favour, but she'd have to play her cards carefully, lest he suss her out.

When Enoch arrived home that evening, he found his wife draped pathetically on the sofa in her silk dressing gown, an expression of woe on her face lifting slightly to a small smile as she caught sight of him. 'Hello, darling,' she greeted him in muted tones, as he bent to plant a perfunctory kiss on her cheek, while he sniffed the air like an elderly Bisto kid.

'I can't smell anything cooking,' he barked, his good mood slowly evaporating. 'Why can't I smell cooking? I said I wanted something special, because I had something to tell you.'

'I know, my treasure,' she cooed, looking into his eyes pitifully. 'Tell me your news. I'm sure it'll perk me up. I've been feeling so seedy and exhausted for the last couple of weeks.' (She couldn't make the period too long, or he'd wonder why she hadn't mentioned it before.) 'Have you been *very* clever? Oh, do tell me: I can't wait any longer. Have you made an *awful* lot of money, my clever, clever bunny?'

She knew that Enoch could resist anything but flattery, and she was right. With a small rise to kiss his cheek, and a hand intertwining with one of his, he was hers, bait taken, hook, line, and sinker.

Later, over coffee and brandy at L'Etoile, she showed him the advertisement which she had prudently clipped from the magazine and placed in her handbag, explained how woozy and tired she had felt of late, and he walked, metaphorically, off terra firma and down into the jaws of the trap. She had caught her bear. He might be a grizzly to others, but to her, with the right handling, he was her teddy bear, and he'd just come up trumps again by promising to book a room for the opening weekend of The Manse first thing in the morning.

Céline Treny, idly studying the 'situations vacant' column in the local paper while trimming her cuticles rather untidily with her teeth, suddenly sat upright in her chair, and stared at one of the job advertisements. Why, that looked like exactly what she was looking for, and its location was perfect, so there would be no trouble with the non-existent rural train and bus services. It was only fifteen minutes' walk from where she rented her share of a flat, and any travel during working hours would be in the company vehicle, so she didn't even need a car, which was very lucky indeed, as she couldn't afford to run one. In fact, she was beginning to wonder how on earth she had ever done her job without benefit of wheels.

She knew what was in the offing, and she had found the perfect passage for a mole. She would dazzle them in her interview and get the job, and then she would see. In fact, everyone would see, and that would be that.

Freddie Newberry, known as Fruity, had positively goggled when he saw the name in the chat room on the internet. By Jove! He could hardly believe his eyes, as the memories floated back. It surely couldn't be the same person, could it? He'd have to get his twinkling fingers on the keyboard and make some enquiries.

When he proved to be correct, he began to twirl the ends of his moustache with his free hand, then brushed his hair back off his forehead, so that he would look his best, even though the person with whom he was communicating could not see him, vain old codger that he was. His slightly watery, gooseberry eyes widened in anticipation, as he considered the rekindling of a friendship hailing from some time back, and what a time it had been!

Later that day, a pair of slightly slanting, dancing, brown eyes happened upon an advertisement in *The Times*, and positively twinkled with merriment. Wouldn't that be fun! It would take a bit of wriggling and conniving to get it organised, but one must have faith, mustn't one? With an outstretched hand, a finger depressed the button that switched on the computer, and then eyes gazed hungrily at the screen,

9

willing everything to connect up with as much speed as was technologically possible.

Edwina Newberry, aka Teddy, woke at 1 p.m. on the dot, made her morning ablutions, dressed, and came downstairs to find her husband poring over the small ads section of the *Daily Telegraph*, with a look of fervour on his face. 'What gives, old stick? No racing paper for you today? I didn't know you were planning to take a holiday.' Fruity was a professional gambler who made a living from betting on the horses, and any deviation from his perusal of form, track conditions, and current odds and tips, left him momentarily out of touch, and vulnerable to losses instead of gains.

'Nothing of the sort, lollipop. I was just considering the idea of a few days away from the madding crowd: give the two of us a little break; a little luxury.'

'Ooh-er,' replied Teddy with pleasure. 'And when would this little break be? And where?'

'There's a fancy new boutique hotel opening, out in the countryside not far from a little town called Carsfold. It's going to specialise in the Victorian/Edwardian era in style and service. They've got their grand opening coming up, with a very special offer, on a first-come-first-served basis. There's going to be a murder mystery dinner with period costume provided, and the author of the mystery will be in attendance too. What do you think? I thought it'd be rather fun.'

'In the countryside, Fruity? Won't we be terribly bored? I mean, Brighton is a rather happening place at the moment, and I haven't got over that weekend when you took me to Newbury. You were at the races, and I was left to fend for myself in a tiny town that only had one department store. I thought I was going to die.'

'Don't be so negative, Teddy. The ad says there's loads to do, and it promises a real taste of the Edwardian country house, with tea on the lawn, cocktails on the terrace, and this murder mystery thingy thrown in as well. It won't be crowded because they've only got ten guest rooms – ahem, ten 'luxury guest suites'. It should be rather exclusive, in my opinion. Go on! We've never done anything like that before. Why don't we give it a try?'

'Is it dreadfully expensive?'

'Not as expensive as it's going to be for any follow-up weekends, and I've had a couple of really good weeks. Let's just do it. You can get a few days off, and just relax and read all those books you've been meaning to get round to. Or we could go out in a boat. The river Darle runs through the grounds. And there's a ha-ha to fall down, a summerhouse to take tea in if we want to, a folly, a gazebo to canoodle in, a lily pond with a tiny island and ornamental fish, and an oriental bridge.

'It seems they've got some fancy French chef, and a reputable company providing all the costumes, which are included in the price. Eh? What do you say? Shall we give it a go, old girl? Go on, be a sport. Let old Fruity have a taste of the high life.'

'Oh, go on then. We haven't really done anything other than work since that Caribbean cruise in January. It'll give us a little lift. I'll just get my diary, so that I can note down the dates, and I'll arrange time off when I get to the casino tonight.' (*Teddy was a croupier in a gay casino on the seafront.*)

Suzanne Veede (known as Sue), thirty-nine years old, still pretty and with a good figure, assistant to her husband Lewis (Lew) who was a third-generation master baker, and bored out of her mind with her life, looked down at the tray of pastries she was putting on displaying in the window of their shop, and clenched her teeth, to stop herself from screaming. If she had to look at one more cream horn, she was going to go insane and beat the next customer she saw to death with a loaf tin. She had to do something; had to have something to look forward to.

Turning the '*Open*' sign to '*Closed*', she marched through to the bakery at the rear of the shop, put a hand on her husband's shoulder to gain his attention above the noise of the machinery, and drew him into the little lobby that housed the cloakroom.

Before he could open his mouth to ask what she thought she was doing, she launched into her desperate off-the-cuff plea. 'Lew, I'm going mad. I can't cope any more without a break, even a little one. I haven't had any time off since last year, and I'm losing the will to live. I covered for you when you were away on that un-leavened and sour-dough course; now it's my turn to do something.'

'Like what?' Lew was surprised, but cagey. He couldn't close the shop for a week, or he'd lose a whole mess of customers, who were surprisingly fickle these days, and two weeks out of the game and you were in the gutter, such was the competition in these hard times.

'It's a weekend I've seen advertised. It's not cheap, but it looks like just the sort of thing to distract and amuse us, and I've got a real yen to go. I know you can't close up, but my parents could cover the shop, and maybe your father would come out of his precious retirement for a couple of days, just to let us catch our breath.

'If they won't help, I'm going to go on my own. I am so sick of the smell of yeast and *crème patissiere*, and I'll probably run away to sea if you don't take me away from all this.'

'Hold your horses, honey. If it's that important to you, of course we can go. I can't speak for your parents, but the old man won't give us any trouble. He'll be in his element, being back at the helm of a bakery for a few days and, to be quite honest, I was feeling rather flat and stale myself. Show me the advert.'

Sue excitedly fetched the newspaper through from under the counter, and pointed out the advertisement, which she had ringed in red ballpoint pen.

For the next few minutes, the only sounds were, *'How much??'* and the, inaudible to the human ear, whining and whimpering that a desperately pleading look would have made, were it capable of sound. Then, after an exceedingly long silence which was, in fact, only ten seconds, he capitulated, and said:

'Oh, all right, then! You mind the shop and I'll go and book it. We could both do with some down time.'

Sue positively skipped back into the shop, punching the air with her fist and muttering, 'Yes! Yes! Yes!' returning only to her normal sensible demeanour as she turned the '*Closed*' sign back to '*Open*', and opened the door for an elderly lady, who was staring through the door in astonishment at finding her favourite bakery closed at this time on a weekday.

Chapter Two

Friday 18th June – morning

It would not be too much of an exaggeration to state that the staff and owners of The Manse were running around like blue-arsed flies, on this, the morning of their first day of business. Although check-in today was not until after four pm, things were by no means all prepared and raring to go.

Persephone (Percy) Boyd-Carpenter (author of tomorrow night's first mystery for The Manse) was incarcerated in the office locked in a battle of wills with the computer. She had uploaded all her character parts, and that of the between-courses narrator – a part to be played by Jefferson Grammaticus, in fine pompous form – had turned the printer on and, she firmly believed, put the two machines in communication with each other, but every time she pressed the print button, it produced half a hotel brochure, with tonight's menu right in the middle of it.

With a cry of 'Damn and blast you, you cyber cretin!' she fled the office in a rage, in search of her husband Lloyd. At seventy-one years of age, he wasn't very computer-savvy, but he might just know a trick or two that she didn't about those two machine-creations of the devil

Beatrix Ironmonger, housekeeper of this establishment, was in her quarters on the top floor, a grimace of fury on her stern countenance, her free hand running through her bleached topknot of curls in impatience, as she engaged in a telephonic battle with yet another supplier who had not delivered.

This time it was the butcher, who was supposed to have

delivered at nine o'clock sharp. 'I don't care what troubles you have your end, Mr Catchpole, I am only concerned with the problems that I have this end. We are expecting a full complement of guests this afternoon, and we have not a scrap of meat to serve them. Were they all vegetarians, I would, no doubt, not be in this position, but they are not, and so I *am*. I want that meat here within the hour, or we look for another supplier – one who can deliver on time – for what will be quite a nice regular little earner, might I add. Do I make myself clear?'

Slamming the telephone back in its cradle, a sensation of softness made itself known at her ankles, and her expression changed immediately to that of one smitten with adoration. Her darling silver-spot Bengal cat, Perfect Cadence, was winding herself round her owner's feet, making little 'meep' noises and purring.

'Hello, my darling little precious,' she crooned, bending to lift the animal into her arms, where it proceeded to lick her cheek. 'Does Mummy's ickle baby want a little snackie-poos, den? Come with Mummy and we'll see if we can find any of those delicious dried whitebait for a beautiful girl, shall we?'

Carrying the cat in her arms like a baby, she went into her small food preparation area, laid out a few choice mouthfuls for her darling, then returned to the telephone, two more names on her list yet to tick off, in more ways than one. As she walked, the chatelaine chain that Jefferson Grammaticus had lovingly assembled for her, to add an historical air to her presence, jingled softly as it dangled from her waist. She already found the sound comforting, as it confirmed her status here in this establishment. It was the sound of security and respect, and she sat down with a little flourish of her right leg, to set off its jingling once more.

'Is that Mr Dibley? Oh, Mrs Dibley! Would you be so kind as to fetch your husband to the phone – The Manse here. There seems to have been some sort of hitch with our order and, as I hope that this may be the first order of many, I should like a word with him with the utmost urgency. Thank you so much.'

We shall not eavesdrop on the rest of the conversation, lest we are shocked by Mrs Ironmonger's language. Suffice to say that the bread order was loaded and on its way within half an hour.

Mr Connor, the greengrocer and fruiterer, could hardly believe his ears at the tirade that assaulted them when he answered the telephone. 'Yes, Mrs Ironmonger …Yes, Mrs Ironmonger … Sorry, Mrs Ironmonger … It wasn't a case of being dilatory or forgetful, I was … If I can get a word in, Mrs Ironm – Mrs Ironmonger, I insist that you listen. The exotic fruits have only just been delivered to me, and – I didn't see the need to telephone, as that would only waste more time. As we speak, my assistant is loading the van for delivery, and your order will be with you as soon as is humanly poss – Yes, I realise it's a substantial order, and will be a regular one. Should there be any delay in the future, I will not hesitate to phone you straightaway, so that you are apprised of the situation… Thank *you*, Mrs Ironmonger. Good day to you!'

'Who does that bloody woman think she is? The Queen of England?' shouted the beleaguered tradesman, driven to fury by the way he had been spoken to. 'If I didn't have a living to earn, I'd give her her bloody exotic fruits, and they'd have a bloody hard job getting them out again if I shoved them where I'd like to!'

Hurling the telephone into his display of bananas, Mr Connor treated himself to a marathon swearing session, making squeezing, choking movements with his hands, imagining the housekeeper's scrawny throat between them, peppering his swear words with 'the bloody foul-mouthed bitch – I'm going to kill her'.

If he had but known it, there were two other tradesmen feeling exactly the same as he did, and with similar thoughts about what to do with their diverse produce, these variously involving a very long French stick and a string of sausages.

Beatrix Ironmonger – courtesy title Mrs, as no one really

knew her marital status, and she had no intentions of enlightening them – smiled as she finished her third and last phone call. The thrust and parry of her verbal tussles had put her in fine fettle for the day, and she felt ready for anything now. Perhaps she'd go down to the kitchen and see if she couldn't tease Chef into a bit of a tizzy: but first, a nice cup of tea, she decided. He always jumped in such a guilty fashion when he heard the tinkle of the keys and accoutrements that accompanied her wherever she went – unless she used a hand to still them! Then, she could make him jump out of his skin.

There was no need for her input, however, as he was managing very nicely on his own. The chef, Antoine de la Robe, gave a Gallic shrug of such immensity that Dwayne Mortte, the sous chef, thought he was going to turn himself inside out.

Chef was a large man with a shiny bald head, with just a tiny white arrowhead of carefully shaped and gelled hair sticking up from the centre of his upper forehead. A mirroring arrowhead hung from his chin, making it look as if he were wearing directions. His eyebrows were black, furry caterpillars, and his build, on the generous side, hinting at his profession. His arrogance was beyond belief, but whether this was just part of his character, or the resulting artistic temperament for one of his culinary talents, it was difficult to decide.

'The deliveries will be here in a minute, Chef. No point in getting all bent out of shape, is there?' soothed Dwayne.

'What are you tocking about, ziss bendink? I don't bend nussing, you silly boy,' shouted Antoine, still unwinding his head from deep between his shoulders.

'Forget it. Surely there's something else we can get on with while we're waiting. Why don't we start on the soup?'

The chef's voice rose to an ever higher pitch of indignation. 'Ze soup? Ze soup? You theenk we start on ze soup?' By now he was shouting at the top of his voice.

With no clue as to what exactly he had done wrong,

Dwayne pushed on bravely in the face of the birth of a first-class Gallic tantrum. 'Why can't we do the soup?' he asked, not comprehending the consequences of his innocent question.

'Where do I get ze *legumes*, idiot boy? Where do I get ze *oignon*, ze *pomme de terre*, ze *carotte*, ze *celeri*? Where I get zose from, *hein*? You tell Antoine, and 'e will start ze soup. Also, where I get ze bones for ze stock, and ze *poulet* for ze *saveur*? *Tiens*! I cannot do nossink wizzout zese sings.'

By now, he was nearly apoplectic with rage, and was making little jumping movements, accompanied by punching movements with his fists to display his anger, not only at the lack of deliveries, but at Dwayne's lack of comprehension about what was needed before he could commence making the soup.

Luckily for Dwayne, he was not 'quick' enough to understand Antoine's thick accent when the chef was having a conniption, and was, therefore, unmoved by the whole episode, reacting only when he heard the honk of a delivery van outside the kitchen door, standing cannily to one side as Antoine leapt to open it and hurl himself through it, already raining down abuse.

Hearing only, '*Espece de vache ...*' and understanding that this would take some time, Dwayne swiftly closed the door and disappeared down a passage to seek another exit. He felt a fag break coming on, and thought that a bit of peace and quiet was his due, after the hysterics of the last few days. Chef wasn't the easiest of people to work for, and he'd worked for some right arseholes in the past. Mr de la Robe, indubitably, took the proverbial biscuit.

Jefferson Grammaticus was also discovering that his every wish could not be fulfilled, discussing, as he was, the water in the lily pond and the water in a smaller ornamental pond about two hundred metres away, and not being told what he wanted to hear.

'I'm sorry, Mr Grammaticus, but it don't matter 'ow much

19

you arsks me, I simply can't get that there lily pond to feed t'other. It goes against nature, that does.'

'What on earth are you talking about, man? All I'm asking is for you to connect the two with a pipe and let the one feed the other. Where's the problem with that?'

'Well, it might look as if there's a slight slope to that there ornamental jobby with the benches and willow tree, but if you take the trouble to hexamine the ground, you'll find that that's an optical delusion.

'I got one of those doo-hickeys with a bubble in it – what's that called now? I misremember. Anyway, I'll just grab it and you come along-a me, an' I'll show you why you can't have your way on this one.'

The two men walked, stopping every twenty metres or so to check the flatness of the ground, and, sure enough, the slope that appeared to fall from the smaller pond, actually rose, the false impression provided by the undulating surface of the surrounding lawns.

'I don't believe it, and this, on opening day. What the hell can we do about it, Henry?'

Henry Buckle, head gardener and groundsman stropped his stubbly chin with the fingers and thumb of his right hand and stared off into the distance, lost in thought. 'We'd 'ave to fit a pump,' he offered at last. 'That's the only way water's ever gonna run uphill, cos, as I said, that's against nature, that is, Mr Grammaticus, sir.'

'How soon can you get your hands on one? The price doesn't matter: it's time we're short of, not funds.'

'I could probably get one from Market Darley today if I went to collect it in the truck, but fittin' it's another matter. And where are you going to put it? You can't just 'ave a pump sittin' in the middle of the grass, can you? That doesn't fit in with the image you described to me for this place.'

'Oh, damn and blast it! There's always got to be a fly in the ointment somewhere. Is there any way you can get some water into the little pond temporarily? Then we could arrange to have the pump fitted when the opening weekend is over, and work out some way to disguise it then. We're not taking any other bookings for next week, while we assess our performance to see if there are any services that can be improved; any little wrinkles to be ironed out – that sort of thing.'

'I can shove a sheet of plastic in the bottom and fill it with the hose, if I start filling it now. Then we'll have to do something as soon as the guests leave. And water don't just flow by magic, yer know. It needs pipes, and a pipe is what you're goin' to 'ave to sink in the ground for that there pump, and a return one, if you want the water to circulate round and pour over yon thingy you've put in. What the hell is it?'

'It's a small waterfall. I must have been out of my mind – not thinking straight – and I just had this vision of the two pools, and a small cascade of water at the far end of the lily pond, where it could be seen from the island. The sound of falling water is so relaxing, I suppose I got a bit carried away. Oh, bum, Buckle! I'm an arse! And I don't want you agreeing with that, either. Get off and see what you can do, and see if you can think of any way to disguise the pump – a clump of well-grown shrubs round it – something you can get from the garden centre without too much trouble should do the job. Now, be off with you, Buckle, before I can spot any other balls-ups I've made.'

'Good day to you, Mr Grammaticus, sir.' Buckle doffed his hat in an ironic execution of the outmoded fashion of bidding good day to a member of the gentry, and strolled away, his bandy legs swinging like the bottom half of John Wayne in search of a horse.

Halfway across the lawn he turned, and called out to Jefferson Grammaticus, 'Spirit level – that be the bugger! Friggin' spirit level!'

Jocelyn and Jerome had made a wise choice in opting to be the modern-day equivalent of those Georgian prestige members of staff – tall, black footmen. Even in their everyday clothes, they made a striking impression, with the darkness of their skin, the broadness of their shoulders, and their impressive height. The fact that there were two of them made them an even more arresting sight.

At the moment, they were in their respective rooms, each trying on one set of their new footman's uniforms. From the top down, these consisted of white wigs (not powdered with arsenic these days, fortunately), turquoise jackets with a discreet amount of silver frogging, navy blue knee breeches, white shirt, white hose, and black patent leather shoes with polished steel buckles. With the addition of white gloves to complete the outfits, they considered they would be a real vision of loveliness.

Jocelyn was the first dressed and, after a narcissistic gaze of admiration in his pier glass, he wandered through into Jerome's room, to see how his twin was getting on. Fine, as it turned out, as he was just adjusting his wig, and repeating recent history from the adjoining room, by glancing, with admiration, at the reflection in his own cheval mirror.

'Yo, Bro!' Jocelyn greeted his brother, walking with mincing little steps across the room. 'Don't we just look the bizz?' he enquired, and Jerome turned to face him. There followed a moment when they used each other as mirrors, their grins wide, at the sight presented to each of them. 'Ain't we just peachie, Massa?' asked Jerome. 'I ain't so sure this freedom business was such a good thing if you could look this good.'

'Don't be daft. Footmen weren't slaves; they were honest-to-God servants, just like all the other staff.'

'I know, but you get my drift.'

'I sure do,' replied Jocelyn twisting round so that Jerome could admire the view from the back, an action that drew a wolf whistle of appreciation. 'Now you turn round for me. Oh, man, that's beautiful. Do a little walk and a twirl for me,' he requested, sighing as he viewed the vision of sartorial elegance in movement. 'My turn now, so that you can see too,' he stated, and began to walk sedately round the bedroom, a haughty expression on his face.

'I think this could turn out to be a lot of fun, you know,' he said, reverting to his normal public school-educated accountant's voice.

'And, as part-owners,' replied Jerome, also in his everyday voice, 'if there's anything too onerous, we can pass it on to one of the other staff. I assume that if this weekend is a success, we can assess staffing levels for full running, and decide whether we need anyone else on board. I'm of the opinion we're going to need a few more.'

'Me too.' Jocelyn was before the cheval glass again, examining his appearance with a self-satisfied expression. 'I know Jefferson wants real fires in the winter months, and cleaning those grates out, humping coal all day long, or even logs – they're heavy enough – then just getting the whole thing alight in the first place, that's a dirty role we have no one to fulfil at the moment. Me? I ain't doin' it.'

'Me neither. Then there's all the heavy cleaning,' suggested his brother, getting into the swing of the subject. 'Chastity can't manage all that on her own. She's got all the rooms to do on a daily basis, so she's not going to have the time to dust skirting boards and wainscoting, polish mirrors and silver and brass, and scrub the floors, not to mention all the wood that'll need waxing. And there ain't no way one little old man from Carsfold's gonna be able to cope with the sheer physical labour of keeping the grounds in immaculate order.'

'I'm sort of assuming that, once Jefferson gets a measure of just how much work is involved in providing the sort of service and surroundings he's hoping for, he'll realise that we must have more hands on deck.'

'Well, if he doesn't, it's our place to point it out to him. Apart from the fact that we might be called upon to hump baskets of logs around – I mean, in this gear? – we don't want the current crew trying to jump ship, now do we?'

'Nope, but there's plenty more where they came from, and they're not going to break the bank, are they?' On which cryptic comment, Jocelyn closed the conversation, and returned to his own room to change into something a little more practical for the intervening hours between now, and when the first guests arrived. He and his brother were both looking forward to their new role in life, seeing it as more of a game than a position of service, because of their financial stake in the venture.

A voice followed him through the door. 'And your hose are crooked,' followed by a cackle of laughter. Jocelyn, knowing his brother's sense of humour, didn't know whether to examine his back or his front in the pier glass. A blush showed against his dark skin and he shut the adjoining door with a little more force than was strictly necessary.

Chapter Three

In the entrance hall, the sound of raised voices carried from the first floor. 'I can't manage all these bedrooms on my own. It's not just a case of running a vacuum cleaner and a duster over them, and straightening a duvet. There're no fitted sheets, and it's taking me an age just to get the bedding sorted in one room.'

'Well, I don't see why I should help you. I'm supposed to be the housekeeper here. Chambermaid does the bedrooms.'

'Have you seen how many sheets, blankets, and eiderdowns there are, not to mention pillows and cushions? It needs an army of chambermaids, not just me.'

'I've said I'll help you this once, but don't expect it on a regular basis. You knew what was involved when you signed the contract.'

'But this is the first time we'll be open.'

'Then you should consider yourself lucky. The work'll be even harder when we have change-over days.'

'No! It couldn't be! I mean … how?' Chastity's voice now had a tinge of hysteria in it.

'Because you'll have to strip all the beds, and take all the bedding and towels to the laundry before you can even start making them up again. I'm not getting involved in this every time a room needs changing, I can tell you. I've got my own work to do, without doing yours as well.'

'Well, how am I going to manage?'

'Haven't you done chambermaiding before?' asked Beatrix Ironmonger, inadvertently inventing a new word, her dull blonde curls bobbing in her indignation, her chatelaine chain's appendages chiming in sympathy.

'No, I haven't. I thought it would be easy, and now I just don't know how I'm going to manage. I feel like a Victorian domestic servant.'

'That's exactly what you've been employed as, and you should have realised that when Grammaticus offered you the job. That man's no pushover, and he wants his pound of flesh out of all of us. And don't forget all the downstairs cleaning as well. I expect Chef'll get his sous to keep the kitchen spotless, but you can't bank on anything these days. Then there're the log fires in the winter ...'

The sound of a wail of despair was accompanied by that of hurried footsteps along the first floor landing, and a deep voice intervened on Chastity's woes. Jefferson Grammaticus had entered the scene, and was soon soothing her with soft promises of hired help from the nearby villages, assuring her that he couldn't expect her to do more than was humanly possible (although, of course, he did).

His reassurances were interrupted by the ting of the reception counter's bell echoing round the entrance, and he abruptly wound up his soothing and bustled off to see what needed his attention now. He'd been run off his rather small feet already today, and it was only two o'clock. What would it be like when they were fully booked and up and running? He'd have to get his little black book out again and see what he could do, for it wasn't as if paid help were expensive. He'd just have to choose wisely.

A woman stood at the counter, drumming the fingernails of her right hand on the counter top and looking around in admiration. They really had done a good job of bringing this old ruin back to life, she thought, as she waited somewhat impatiently to be attended to.

The sound of dainty footsteps twinkling down the stairs – for, for all his bulk, Jefferson was light on his feet, and a wonderful ballroom dancer – caught her attention, and she wheeled round to see the be-whiskered figure of a veritable Edwardian gentleman tripping his way towards her, a smile on his broad breaming face, a hand extended in greeting.

'Good afternoon. You must be the delightful Ms Meercroft to whom I spoke on the telephone. I am Jefferson Grammaticus, at your service,' he broadcast in a hearty voice, all the while pumping her hand as if he expected cream to pour lavishly from her mouth.

'Absolutely correct, Mr Grammaticus, and please call me Alison, as we're to be partners in crime, as it were.'

'Oh, jolly good! Jolly droll that, Alison, and you must call me Jefferson. Have you got the gear with you?'

'Yes. It's all outside in the van, if you can get someone to give me a hand, and show me where to put everything. I've brought all my own rails, as agreed, so I just need a room, and somewhere for the guests to try on their costumes, preferably with mirrors on hand – for checking out the effect. Unless they'd rather do that in their rooms,' she added, remembering that all the costumes would be worn by residents.

Alison Meercroft was proprietor and manager of the Market Darley fancy dress shop known as 'DisguiserGuys', and had been persuaded to dress all the hotel guests in appropriate period costume for this opening weekend. Should this prove to be a success, her services would be retained for any future events, and for guests who may wish to adopt period costume for the duration of their stay.

Future events were covered by the same deal, and she wholeheartedly hoped it would be an enormous success, for she needed the business. She had had to invest quite heavily in extra rigs for the period, and had taken on an assistant to help as dresser, and to keep the shop going should she, Alison, need to visit The Manse during business hours.

Meanwhile, Jefferson Grammaticus had put the index finger and thumb of his right hand into his mouth, and produced a piercing whistle, which had both Messrs Freeman arrive at the trot. 'Yass, Massa?' queried Jocelyn facetiously, and immediately received, in reply, a stern look from both his business partners. 'Sorry! Just trying to lighten the mood, dispel a bit of the tension around here. I can't help it if I sometimes speak in bad taste.'

'Alison, may I introduce you to my co-owners in this venture, Jerome and Jocelyn Freeman. Don't ask which is which, because I've known them for over thirty years, and I still can't tell. Gentlemen, this is Alison Meercroft of DisguiserGuys, who will be taking care of our costume needs throughout this grand opening weekend, and, I sincerely hope, for some long time after that.'

After hands had been shaken and 'howdy-do's exchanged, the three of them went outside to the large van that was parked just outside the entrance doors and began to gather armfuls of rich clothing from out of its rear doors. On the way back in, Jefferson yelled, a sort of yodelling sound, and Beatrix Ironmonger and Chastity Chamberlain appeared at the head of the staircase at the point where it bifurcated.

'Can you two come down here and give us a hand with the costumes. We need to get the rails into the billiards room and hang them all in there.'

'We're too busy!' stated Mrs Ironmonger, preparing to turn on her heel and leave.

'Oh no you're not,' shouted Grammaticus. 'You get yourselves down here and get these clothes hung up this instant. If you've got too much to do before opening, we'll discuss it after everything's ready in the clothing department. NOW!'

The two women trotted down the stairs in mute but sullen obedience, their expressions wooden and fixed. They would do as he asked – no, demanded as his right – and, if the rooms weren't ready when the guests arrived, it would be his business and reputation at stake, not theirs.

Mrs Ironmonger opened the doors to the billiards room while Chastity received mobile hanging rails from Alison Meercroft, lining them up at the back of the room, where the rich jewel-coloured silks and satins of the ladies' clothes would catch the light and look their best.

As Mrs Ironmonger began to hang the garments from the pile under which Chastity seemed to have disappeared, Jefferson's voice could be heard from just outside the door, addressing the bringer of all this extra work for the two hard-pressed women.

'Alison, you didn't forget to bring the masks and wigs, did you?'

'Of course not, Jefferson! They're the real fun of the whole thing, aren't they? I mean, the clothes make you feel completely different, but you still basically look like you. But add a wig and a mask, and you can be anyone you feel like being. I've done my best to make your guests look like they're attending the Carnevale – have you ever been to Venice for Carnevale?'

Without waiting for an answer, she swept on, regardless. 'I went one year, just to get a look at the costumes. Oh God, they were to die for! But the things people got up to when they were masked! You might get a bit of that going on here, if they swill enough wine,' she said disapprovingly

Jefferson smiled a success-anticipating smile, and said he didn't mind if they decided to go in for a full-blooded orgy and stripped naked to go midnight bathing in the river, so long as they paid for breakages and collateral damage, refrained from swinging from his French chandeliers, and didn't frighten the horses.

'What horses?' Alison asked, momentarily puzzled at how animals had suddenly entered the conversation.

'Just a figure of speech, my dear: no real horses to worry about – unless any of the male guests fancies himself as a bit of a stallion, eh?' Jefferson was feeling very high-spirited in his excitement, and had totally forgotten about the high standards, both of service and behaviour, that he expected from his establishment, which would put it up there with the most exclusive boutique hotels, in the perception of future guests.

Alison could feel herself blushing as she reached into the van for the great bag of wigs, and the other, of masks. She

29

hoped he had been kidding with his suggestion of the possibility of events at this hotel bearing any resemblance to the Bacchanalian rompings in the Pearl of the Adriatic. Surely he was only pulling her leg. If not, it didn't sound like her sort of weekend at all.

She didn't mind the thought of beautiful surroundings, fine food and wine, coupled with superb service: it was the other sort of service that now played on her mind, and she dismissed it as fanciful on her part. Not in this quiet part of the English countryside, at any rate, but the man's eyes had been full of silken sheets and sex, and she gave a reluctant little shiver in response.

At this point in the shouted discussion, Beatrix Ironmonger appeared through the door of the billiards room with her hands on her hips and a sour expression, clearing her throat to attract attention. Turning, Jefferson took one look at her and burst out laughing.

'It's no laughing matter, Mr Grammaticus, and you know it!' she spat.

'Don't get your knickers in a twist, Mrs Ironmonger.' At this point, he was moved to a further gale of laughter, eventually continuing, 'You won't be required to do any wenching. Your duties are strictly those of a housekeeper in this establishment.'

'And glad I am to hear it,' she replied. 'And I hope that pertains for young Chastity, too.'

'It does, indeed, my dear Beatrix, if I may so address you. Now, come and take these bags of wigs and masks from Alison, and get Chastity to help you set them out on the cover of the billiard table. And then, would the two of you be so kind as to go up to the attic floor, to the room where I store surplus props, and see how many hand mirrors you can rustle up. If the women are going to be wearing wigs, we'd better be prepared for them to be able to examine their rear view, as well as their front.'

'If you give me a bucket of sand, I'll sing you a desert song,' was her parting shot, as she disappeared back into the room, to alert Chastity to the next task on their list of chores. 'And get someone else on to the bed-making, or you'll have nowhere for your swanky guests to sleep tonight, unless they fancy a bare mattress.'

As Alison Meercroft took her final leave of The Manse, promising to return that evening with her new assistant to help guests choose their outfits, she found said new assistant standing just inside the foyer, reading the staff list (for the convenience of absent-minded guests who hadn't brought their information brochures downstairs with them.

'What are you doing, Céline? Thinking of doing a bit of moonlighting?'

'Ze sought nevair crossed ma mind. No, Ah am jost 'aving a look at 'oo works 'ere. I see zey 'ave a French chef.'

'But of course, Céline. Nothing but the best for Mr Grammaticus, or so I've heard.' She still found it difficult to think of him as Jefferson. He was definitely a 'Mr' to her, with his imposing presence and slightly intimidating personality.

'Ah should sink so too. Ze best chefs in ze whole world are French, *n'est-ce-pas*?'

'Anything you say. Now, let's get back and see if we can't get a bit of work done in the shop before we have to come back here again, later.'

'Can't Ah jost go 'ome for a leedle rest?' pleaded the Frenchwoman.

'Absolutely not! What a lazy lot you French are! If you're going to live in England, you're going to have to learn to work like a native, not skive off at every opportunity that presents itself.'

'*Espece de vache*!' muttered Céline.

'I heard that!' retorted Alison.

'Yes, but you don't know what it means, do you?' Céline whispered very quietly to herself.

In the end, everybody had to pitch in to get the rooms ready to be occupied – everybody, with the exception of Chef – and

Jefferson had to admit that he had been just a little bit light on the numbers he had thought would be able to manage the day-to-day running of The Manse.

When he had broached the subject of pitching in with everybody else, he got a very dusty and uncompromising answer.

'Ah am ze great ,ze only, ze magnificent Antoine de la Robe, and Ah do not do ze work of little girlies. Ah am no maid of ze chamber. Ah am an artiste. Ah create flavours that cry on ze tongue and sen' ze stomach to 'eaven. Ah do not tuck shits.' His final pronouncement was that he would rather disembowel himself with a melon scoop than stoop to manual work of the traditionally female kind.

Jefferson's last task was to gather his staff together to explain the intricacies of the murder mystery dinner to them, for they too had to get in character. They met in the staff sitting room, most of them looking hot and bothered after having to work so hard pitching in with bed-making and the like, but he quickly quelled their protests.

'We'll have none of that for the moment. I understand your frustrations, and I promise you that I will contact an agency for extra help immediately. I fear, however, that we shall have to manage this weekend on our own, and I realise that the extra work involved will require a little bonus.'

The angry muttering subsided, and was replaced with various expressions of avarice and greed. 'You will be required to act your own parts in this little drama, but that is more to do with costume than acting skills.' Mrs Ironmonger, who had raised her hand in protest at the thought of playing a part, lowered it again.

'The mystery script that Persephone has been kind enough,' (and been paid enough, he thought) 'to produce for us is set in nineteen-twenties Venice, at the height of the Carnevale. The exact location is a private dining room in an *hotel* that is holding a masked ball. The guests, of course, will be in character and costume.

'All I require of you is the impeccable service that I hope

will become a trademark of this establishment, with the addition of large white aprons for the ladies, and a long black skirt if you have one. The barman – that's you, Steve – will wear a white shirt and black bow-tie, but you already have a supply of those for your everyday work.

'Jocelyn and Jerome, I have something a little special for you, which I shall show you forthwith. Steve, do you know when the Bellini was invented – er, scrub that. I'm sure none of the guests is going to quibble about a slightly out-of-era cocktail if it's free gratis. Now, off you go. We've only a short time left before the first of our guests arrive and we'll be open for business. We'll meet back here when everything's locked down for the night, and share a little champagne to celebrate all your hard work, and our first day's trading. Now, scoot!'

In the billiards room, Jefferson Grammaticus proudly displayed the special costumes he had actually purchased, rather than hired, for Jocelyn, Jerome, and himself. For the twins, he had chosen jesters' costumes in gaudy turquoise with a darker blue, to echo the colours of their everyday uniforms. As they would be wearing jesters' hats, with the addition of a mask, this would make them easier to identify in the heavily disguised party that would populate The Manse tomorrow evening.

For himself, he had chosen an outrageous outfit, part jester, part something extremely sinister, in red and white, and he felt he would strike just the right note, with Death himself on the prowl within their fantasy. This ensemble, however, was safely secreted in his room, so that everyone would be subject to the same surprise, guests and staff alike, when he made his entrance just before the meal.

'Lawdy, Lawdy, jest look-it all this fahnery. Ain't we gonna look a coupla han'some peacocks in this get-up?'

'We sure is gonna look a coupla fancy n …'

'Don't use the 'n' word – either of you – and stop messing about with those phoney slaves' accents. You spent decades being well-spoken, respectable members of the community. I don't see why you have to degenerate into a comedy duo, just as we're about to launch our business.'

'We do this *because* of all the years we had to be sober and serious, Jefferson,' explained Jocelyn.

'And don't worry: we wouldn't even think of doing it in front of anybody but the staff here. We're not going to let you down: we're just enjoying a little freedom. It's been a long hard road to today, and we're naturally excited.'

'Sure are, honey-chil',' agreed the other. Even now, Jefferson couldn't be sure who was who, unless he debagged them, for Jocelyn had a small birthmark on his left buttock.

'Shut up and go try on your costumes,' ordered Jefferson, smiling as the two of them capered from the room like a couple of women about to try on new party frocks.

As they raced each other up the stairs, Jefferson heard a commotion from the kitchen, and speeded his steps to see what was afoot; no doubt another Gallic outburst of temperament. Antoine cooked like an angel, but maybe hiring him had been a step too far. He was far too prone to tantrums, and was liable to throw the first thing to hand when he was in one of his furies, and there were a lot of sharp objects in a kitchen.

The force of the large man's fury was like a tempest, encompassing everything and everyone with which it made contact. Currently, Dwayne Mortte was in the firing line, receiving yell after yell of contumely as Antoine battered the hell out of a piece of veal on a chopping board. It could not have been more than a millimetre thick, so hard had he laboured at it with his little wooden meat hammer.

'What the hell's going on in here?' yelled Grammaticus, in a voice that would not have disgraced a parade ground, and certainly stopped Antoine's tirade immediately. 'What is it now, Antoine? A fly in the soup, or something equally world-shattering?'

Antoine drew himself up to his full five-feet-nine-and-a-half, and glowered at his boss. 'Whah you bah all zees wop food for me? Why Ah gotta lotta stuff for wop deeshes? Ah

34

am French, an' Ah cook French food.'

'I ordered, what you refer to as 'wop' food, because the murder mystery dinner for tomorrow night is set in Venice, and I rather thought it might be a good idea for our guests to eat Italian food – get them in the mood, as it were. Tonight you cook French. What's the problem?

'*Zut alors*! Zees eez *incroyable*! 'Ow can I cook wop sheet, when mah reputation is for the fahn deeshes of Paree? *Nom d'dun nom d'un nom*!'

'Shut up, Antoine, and remember our little arrangement. French tonight, Italian tomorrow. Do I make myself clear, Chef?'

The Frenchman crumbled, and mumbled, '*Oui, monsieur*!' then more quietly, '*Merde*!'

A swoosh from the kitchen doors announced the arrival of Chastity Chamberlain, who broke his mood by gushing about the fabulous costumes that DisguiserGuys had just delivered, a dreamy look in her eyes. She was at that ball in Venice, and she was the belle of it, in her head.

Successfully distracted from his previous grievance, Chef threw his hands in the air, and declared, 'DisgeezerGeez? Eet eez Ah oo need a disgeez – Ah, oo am on ze run from a derahnged charactair. Ah am pursued wherever Ah go. Zere eez no peace for me in zis world.'

'Oh, give over, Chef! Your histrionics have got you into trouble more than once in the past, and I'll have none of it here. Calm down and stop making such a drama out of every little thing. Wear a disguise if you want. I don't give a rat's arse if you dress up as Lucrezia Borgia, as long as you turn out your customary fabulous food, and don't poison the guests. There now! Get on with your job, and let me get on with mine.'

Grammaticus turned on his heel and smartly exited the kitchen, running into Steve Grieve, who was scuttling off to the bar with an armful of assorted bottles of such delights as angostura bitters and Worcestershire sauce. 'Bellini, Mr Grammaticus!' he stated, stopping in his tracks, and setting his burden down on one of the sofas.

'Bellini what, Steve? I've got a hundred and one things to do, so make it quick.'

Steve bunched his eyebrows together in thought, and cast his gaze about a foot above Jefferson's head, then began to recite as if he had learnt it by rote, 'The Bellini was invented between 1934 and 1948 by Giuseppe Cipriani, founder of Harry's Bar in Venice. It is a mixture of Prosecco and peach puree. Its unique pink colour reminded Cipriani of the toga of a saint, in a painting by the fifteenth century Venetian artist Giovanni Bellini, hence its name.

'I looked it up, guv, on the internet, in the office, before I went down the cellar. That Mrs Boyd-Carpenter's in there – the office, I mean, not the cellar – and she's in a helluva funk with those machines of yours. But anyway, that particular cocktail's right out of our time scale, sir. Sorry to be the bearer of bad news, like.'

'As I said before, Steve, if it's free, guests will forgive anything, especially something as heavenly as a Bellini. Do you know how much those things cost in Harry's Bar?'

'No, guv.'

'Well, I do, and I'm sure some of them will too. Take my word for it, there will be no complaints about complimentary Bellinis. And don't call me 'guv'. If you *must* use anything other than my name or sir, would you please address me as 'squire'.'

'OK, squire, guv.'

Jefferson sighed as the barman collected his cache of bottles and strolled off to the bar, whistling.

And there would be no complaints about the way they were mixed either, he thought, as the whistling disappeared in the distance, or any other cocktail that was ordered. Steve had been an excellent barman in some of the best hotels, and was a demon mixer of cocktails. He knew, off by heart, the recipe for just about any drink that could be ordered, and, in case he came across one he didn't recognise, had a reference book to provide him with the necessary details.

So good had he been in the past, that when he hadn't known the ingredients, various managements had allowed him to serve the first drink free – an incentive for him to learn a few more recipes, and for the customers to find the most obscure cocktails that they could.

It was just a shame that he had to part from so many bars at such short notice. Grammaticus was sure, however, that that would not be the case with The Manse. Steve would settle here, and stay for many years – if he knew what was good for him.

Jefferson mounted the stairs two at a time, almost twinkling on his size seven feet, at last having found a moment in which to try on his own special costume for tomorrow night. On the way he stopped by the twins' rooms, hardly at all out of breath at the two flight climb. Sounds of great merriment were coming from Jerome's room, so he assumed that they had tried on their finery, and were now admiring themselves and each other. It was weird the way they used each other as a mirror.

'Oh, my God!' was his initial reaction, for they had also donned their hats and masks, and presented a very macabre sight. 'You two look absolutely terrifying!' he exclaimed.

'Terrifying handsome, I'd say,' retorted Jerome.

'Devastatingly handsome, in my opinion,' Jocelyn stated. 'Ain't we just a pretty pair?'

'Grotesque!' was Grammaticus' final word on their appearance, as he closed the door and headed for his own room, rubbing his hands with glee. This was just going to be such a hoot!

Chapter Four

Jefferson, suitably attired in his summer 'squire's uniform', stood behind the reception counter and examined the register. The rooms, as well as having numbers, were colour-coded in their decoration and accoutrements.

The hotel boasted ten exquisitely appointed bedrooms, and Jefferson hoped that his guests would avail themselves generously from his exclusive cellar, contents provided courtesy of an old university friend, now a fine wine dealer, and at bargain basement prices. He was also aware that a few too many 'nippy-sweeties' could cloud the mind with regard to one's actual room number. Each room, therefore, had its own colour, and they ran thus: room one – pink walls, curtains and bed throw; room two – yellow; room three – blue; room four – green; room five – dove grey; room six – white/gold; room seven – mauve; room eight – peach; room nine – beige and tones of light brown; room ten – cream.

Guests turning up at the reception counter to be reminded of their room number had only to state the colour of their room to identify it, and a list of guests and their rooms would be quickly accessible under the counter should anyone not familiar with the computer system be on cover duty at the time of the enquiry. To make doubly sure of a quick and efficient issue of keys and/or reminders, little blocks of colour were affixed in the top right hand corner of the wall-mounted box that held the hooks for the keys, with the numbers in gold upon the glass cover of the box, locked, of course, for maximum security.

For this first weekend of business only six rooms had been let out, leaving the four smaller rooms free for 'experimental' occupation. The twins were to take the cream and light brown rooms, numbered nine and ten, and Jefferson Grammaticus and Beatrix Ironmonger were to take the green and the dove grey rooms, respectively. Between them they represented the most OCD tidy of guests – (Beatrix Ironmonger) – through 'normal' occupation – the twins – to the untidiest occupant on the premises – Jefferson Grammaticus.

It had seemed quite a good test of how long it would take to service the rooms on a daily basis with guests of different habits, test the rooms for noise levels, comfort and genuine all-round pleasantness, and really get to know their hotel. The four staff involved in this experiment would all carry pagers, so that they could still be available if needed, twenty-four hours a day, a practice that would be extended to other staff if it proved useful. Apart from that, all rooms were, of course, connected to the internal telephone system within the hotel for room service or assistance when necessary.

These rooms had already been taken over by their prospective staff occupants, to spare at a time when the guests of the paying sort arrived, as had the yellow room, to be occupied by Lloyd and Persephone Boyd-Carpenter, the latter being housed in a guest room because of her status as author of the murder mystery script. Jefferson rather hoped that when he had half a dozen or so such scripts in the bag, he could stop according this non-profit making largesse, and get down to the real business of letting the whole bang-shoot to a bunch of 'wallets'.

Jefferson was just beginning to get jumpy at the non-arrival of guests – he had secretly expected his privileged little band to be queued up outside waiting for the minute they could commence their stay – when the first couple breezed in at thirteen minutes past four, and they didn't so much breeze as blow in, like the precursor of a storm.

'I told you that short-cut was a bad idea. They always are, especially if they're yours. Why you can't just stick to the main roads and arrive in decent time, I shall never know.'

'The map was wrong! It should have worked perfectly. I knew exactly where I was going, and we ought to have been here dead on time,' the man grumbled, glaring at the woman at his side. He liked to get value for money, and was not impressed that they had arrived thirteen minutes after first check-in time. That was thirteen minutes of the hotel's facilities that he had failed to enjoy.

'You took the completely wrong road out of Castle Farthing. I told you so, but would you listen? – no.'

'It was that diamond-shaped Green that fooled me. You can hardly blame me for that. It was very confusing,' the man parried, his whole compact frame quivering with anger.

'Of course I can blame you. I had the map, and you simply wouldn't listen to me, which meant that you got yourself right over to the west to that tiny little place called Fallow Fold. Enoch, at Castle Farthing we were only about seven miles away. By the time we got to Fallow Fold, you'd more than doubled that. Why do you always think you're right?'

'Hindsight is so easy, isn't it?'

'It has nothing to do with hindsight. I had the map in front of me. You must've gone round that green three times before you took the wrong turning. Why you won't invest in a sat nav I have no idea. You're just so mean over the little things I sometimes don't believe you can be for real.'

'Oh, shut up, Aylsa. This place is spanking brand new. It wouldn't even have been on a sat nav.'

'But Lower Shepford would have been, and, from the direction we came from, the brochure said to turn left down the first turning after the one for there, which was an un-made-up road, and it would take us right to the doors, but no, you have to go your own way, as per bloody usual.' At this point the woman shook her head of strangely coloured beige curls, and stamped a tiny foot in frustration.

Jefferson, having spent the last minute or two totally mesmerised by their already in-progress mobile disagreement, finally cleared his throat loudly and unveiled his 'mine host' smile. If they were all like this, it promised to be a very unexpected weekend. He had hoped to attract a rather more select class of guest.

Maybe he should have listened to Jerome and Jocelyn, who had warned him about the very low pricing for the opening. Jefferson had said it would be an excellent way to get a real snagging list, and no one could complain; the twins said that anyone who had any experience would know what he was up to, and would avoid it like the plague. He'd just get the riff-raff who thought they were pushing out the boat financially, and would be as picky as hell.

If these two were anything to go by, it looked like he owed the twins a drink.

'Sir, Madam, may I assist you to check-in? Your luggage can be taken to your room while we complete the formalities, and I acquaint you with the timetable for this very special weekend. May I take your names, please?'

'Mr and Mrs Enoch Arkwright,' declared the man in a thick Yorkshire accent.

Jefferson scrutinised them as he spoke. Both were short; probably in their early sixties, but spry – they obviously kept fit by sparring – and both wore that slightly discontented look that people who feel they are always being taken for a ride financially, habitually wear. Value-for-money wasn't in their vocabulary, because they had spent most of their lives diddling others, and didn't see how anyone else could act any differently.

Sir had on a light grey safari suit – how long had that been in the wardrobe? – he was obviously a man who did not wear formal clothes for his everyday occupation. Madam wore a flowing silk dress printed with large pastel-coloured, slightly out-of-focus flowers and dainty gold sandals. He mentally dubbed them 'Mr and Mrs Chalk-and-Cheese', and rang the bell for one of the footmen to collect their cases.

As Jerome approached to heft their bags in his large, strong hands, their mouths fell open in unison, as they surveyed his uniform. If the outfit had this effect on unruly guests, Jefferson had already judged them worth every penny he had paid for them.

'I've put you in the pink room; that's room number one.' That should please the old curmudgeon. 'The rooms are colour-coded for your convenience ...'

But he never had the opportunity to finish the sentence, for Mr Arkwright cut right across him with his own candid opinion. 'Pink's for girls, women, and pansies. Me, I'm colour-blind, so I couldn't give a monkey's if it's done in tartan, so long as the bed's comfortable and the towels are fluffy.'

'Typical! You would be bloody colour-blind, wouldn't you? And you probably chose to be at birth, just so you could be extra irritating and ungrateful throughout your whole life,' thought Grammaticus, and summoning up his professional smile again, this time with a little more difficulty, he handed them a glossy brochure outlining the timetable for the weekend's activities and the amenities available, and got on with getting them to sign in, with a slightly sinking heart. He then rang the bell, and the other twin trotted into view to show them to their quarters, as the first one reappeared on his way down the grand staircase.

'Did you realise you had coloureds working here?' Enoch Arkwright hissed into Jefferson's right ear in a hoarse whisper. So he could distinguish that, could he? Bloody little tit! And it was obviously not the hideously expensive footman's uniform that had caught *his* eye, but the fact that the footman was dark-skinned.

Glancing at the register to diffuse the anger that had begun to course through his body, Jefferson spoke in a voice that really projected – the voice he used to use in court – and addressed the unpleasant little fellow. 'Mr and Mrs Arkwright, may I introduce you to my two business partners in this new leisure venture – Messrs Jerome and Jocelyn Freeman, my fellow investors.' That cut his cackle, and caused Mrs Chalk-and-Cheese to hide her mouth with the back of her right hand, as she gave an amused little smile at her husband's obvious discomfiture. Indeed, as the Freemans came closer, Enoch Arkwright's brows knitted furiously, and he stared open-mouthed at them, as if he'd seen twin ghosts.

Checking the register – old-fashioned and nosy, of course – he noticed that the man was a scrap-metal dealer. Well, that explained a lot!

Jefferson also indulged in a little smile, as he watched the three of them begin to mount the stairs, turning left as the staircase bifurcated, but was interrupted by the sound of the arrival of more guests.

A man with rather long salt-and-pepper hair in a suit not dissimilar to Jefferson's breezed through the doors with a woman, rather younger than him, (*and playing on the age difference with her hair, make-up, and clothes*), on his arm. The man wore a bow tie, as if this were habitual, and his partner had certainly pulled her costume from the dressing-up pile.

Although she was a large woman, she wore a rather short, hot-pink skirt, the hem of which stopped well above the knee, but also dipped unexpectedly at the right front and left back corner, as it were. Her top half, generously upholstered, was squeezed into a blouse in bright shades of crimson and mauve, with batwing sleeves, and she had the best part – God knows where the worst part was! – of a hairpiece, not quite perfectly matched to her not quite natural colour, on top of her head.

Her shoes had heels so high that Jefferson rather doubted that her toes reached the ground at the front, and so many buckles and straps that they looked more like instruments of torture than shoes. She tottered along beside her partner in a Chinese foot-bound shuffle, a large and obviously designer handbag dangling from her free hand, her face a mask of thick make-up, gone slightly blurred in the June heat.

Both smiled as they approached the check-in counter, and Jefferson's smile was even larger than the beam he had intended, due to the fact that he would really like to turn his back for a moment or two just to have a giggle. He'd have to get those prices up *tout de suite* on Monday. And how dare the man dress like him! It had taken him ages to come up with the garments that would project his image, and here this chap was, just swanning in, in a pastiche of one of the hotel's owners. Damned cheek! Well, the fancy dress would soon settle his hash!

'Frederick and Edwina Newberry, sir,' announced the man in a hearty voice, extending his right hand to Jefferson across the counter. 'Pleased to meet you. I assume you are Mr Grammaticus? We'd like to book in, if it's not too much trouble, old bean.'

'How dare he!' thought Jefferson. 'He's trying to 'out-squire' me. Well, I'm not having that!' Summoning up his plummiest courtroom voice – the voice he used when he was trying to convince the jury that the man that stood before them, with the bloody axe in his hands, was actually completely innocent – he asked if they would be kind enough to sign in, while he summoned a footman to escort them to their room.

'I've put you in the blue room,' Jefferson projected, beginning to sound a little like a member of the outer circle of the royal family. 'It is situated in the back left corner of the hotel with sweeping views down across the lawns to the river. I hope you find it convivial and welcoming.' He'd show him who was the squire around here, Jefferson internalised, taking a silk handkerchief from his breast pocket and waving it towards Jocelyn and Jerome, who were now stationed, one each side of the staircase, like alternatives to decorative suits of armour.

'Oh, jolly good show, old chap. Quite Georgian, if yer know what I mean,' he commented, thus further annoying Jefferson, he was stealing all of his own lines, and seemed to be starting at the very beginning of what he had scripted, to reinforce his character.

Damn and blast the man! He'd have to find time to confer with that old Boyd-Carpenter bird, see if she could furnish him with a few more phrases to bulk out his fictional persona. He didn't want the weekend to deteriorate into a competition to see who could sound the more proprietorial and genial.

'If you would just fill in your details in the register, the footmen will take your bags and show you to your room,' he requested, handing the blasted imposter a Mont Blanc pen from his own pocket; petty, he realised as he did it, but it soothed his feeling slightly to see the man appraise it with a discerning eye.

'Jolly nice pen,' commented Newberry. 'I should keep a keen eye on that when there are a lot of guests around. So many imposters and bounders around these days, yer can't trust anyone unless you've known them years, and sometimes, not even then.'

As Jocelyn led the way, Jerome following behind carrying their bags, Jefferson waved his silk handkerchief across his brow. He'd have to be on his toes with this chap around. He was certainly not top drawer, but it looked like he was a good blagger, and he didn't want to be left looking like a comedy squire in his own establishment. He had to hand it to him, the man was good. It was his vowels that let him down – just a touch of the northern about them; a certain flattening that occurred when his attention was distracted by the unexpected.

As the four figures took the left bifurcation of the stairs, he noticed Newberry lift a hand to his head, and give something a minute wiggle. Good God! Praise to the heavens! The man wore a 'rug'. He should have noticed when he signed in, but was too disturbed to exercise his usual almost scientific powers of observation. Vanity was the man's Achilles heel, and Jefferson would be sure to give it a prod or two during the course of the man's stay here.

He was saved as squire-in-chief. All he had to do was use the word *syrup*, or point out a particularly nice rug, with an appropriately accompanying knowing look, and he'd won the game hands down. Glory be! Grammaticus felt a wave of relief wash over him, as he filed away this devastating piece of information – devastating for Squire Newberry, that is.

From below the counter, he reached for a glass of iced mineral water, took a sip to refresh his acting, and resumed the alert but confident pose he had decided was to be his character's stock-in-trade. A quick glance at the register had confirmed that the man had stated his occupation as 'professional gambler', which didn't surprise him in the least. His stay here would no doubt be some sort of gamble, although at the moment, Jefferson didn't have the faintest idea what sort. That he was up to something not on the agenda, he was sure – absolutely sure. He had a feeling in his monocle, which dangled from a fairly wide black velvet ribbon attached to his lapel by a small fourteen carat gold pin.

The next arrivals were suitably over-awed by the establishment, already commenting on the parking service offered by Steve Grieve, and dazzled by the rich appointments of the entrance hall, the whole scene being set off by the arrival of the footmen, back one each side of the stairs.

The woman was the first to reach the counter – late thirties, Jefferson thought, and perspiring in a somewhat unladylike way. Where she should have glowed, she perspired, and in some unfortunate areas, she positively sweated. She wore only a hint of lipstick and mascara, and wore her copper-coloured wavy hair caught on the top with a velvet band of some kind.

Her husband followed in her wake, tugging two enormous suitcases, and muttering as he dragged. 'It's only a bloody weekend, Sue. Why have you brought everything in your wardrobe? I expect to hear the kitchen sink clank inside one of these any moment now.'

'Don't fuss so,' she instructed in a low hiss. She then turned on Jefferson Grammaticus one of the most devastating smiles he had seen in a very long time. It positively lit up what had appeared, at first glance, to be a fairly ordinary countenance, with only a small crowning of the nose and upper cheeks with light freckles, to distinguish it from any of

47

thousands of other female faces.

Dear Lord, she was exquisite, and he really hoped that the man that accompanied her was aware of what a rare jewel he possessed, for she had a face that, if it would not quite launch a thousand ships, would happily get nine-hundred-and-ninety-nine into the water without too much difficulty.

This last thought hit him as he noticed a slightly chipped front tooth in her smile, and realised that there was always a serpent in Eden, and nothing was ever really as perfect as it appeared at first glance. For a moment, he cursed his observational powers, realising that those other nine-hundred-and-ninety-nine men launching ships would never have noticed such a minuscule imperfection, and would forever hold her memory dear.

'Good afternoon. We're the Veedes,' she introduced them, and Jefferson had to fight to stop himself from wincing. No doubt the other nine-hundred-and-ninety-nine men, like he just had, would certainly have noticed her broad Black Country accent, which was echoed by her husband, who identified them individually as Lewis and Suzanne, 'But we prefer Lew and Sue – more friendly, loike. (*Author's note: I shall not be trying to reproduce their pronunciation, as I shall more than likely end up in a severe sulk, and quite possibly with a stress-induced fainting fit.*)

Lew, usually the quiet one of the couple, was inclined towards loquacity, brought on by the grandeur of their surroundings, explained at length that he was a third-generation master baker with his own business, ably and efficiently assisted by his lovely wife, Sue, and that this was his first break since he had been to an un-leavened and sour-dough symposium several months ago. Sue, he pointed out, unable to stop the flow now that he had got underway, had gone even longer without a break, so they really considered that they had earned a little luxury and rest, and with efficient and trustworthy people manning the barricades back at the business, both in the bakery and in the shop, they had decided that they could at last afford the time.

How did the man manage to breathe? Though his ears, maybe? Jefferson had switched off when Lew got as far as 'third-generation master bakers', and brought himself back into focus, as the baker cleared his throat self-consciously, at the end of the rather long speech he had just undertaken. He really was a man of few words that weren't closely associated with 'yeast' or 'flour', and had surprised himself by such a lengthy explanation of their circumstances. He really would have to catch himself on, and not be so over-impressed. This was supposed to be to relax them, not to reduce him to a quivering heap of jelly with a severe inferiority complex, and a substantial hole in his bank balance.

A couple of minutes later he found himself trotting off behind one of the two liveried men, glad to be rid of the weight of his wife's luggage. As Sue had gazed first on the two uniformed honeys, Jefferson had seen a look in her eye that he had not seen since a very dear female friend of his, after over twelve months on a strict diet, had viewed a double chocolate fudge dessert with ice-cream and extra-thick double cream.

Sue Veede was practically drooling, and as she walked away from the counter, he could smell the sex oozing from her pores. Jocelyn and Jerome had better watch themselves: she might be into double helpings!

As she sashayed behind her husband's retreating figure, the cases bobbing along behind her in the firm charge of Jerome Freeman, Jefferson cast a glance at the entrance, which was empty, and checked the kitchen, from whence he could hear the beginnings of a ruckus floating on the air. Oh, sod it! What was going on now?

On the threshold of the kitchen, he got an earful of Chef in full flow. 'Why Ah 'ave a blerdy cat in ma *cuisine*? Ge' the fockin' theeng outta here. How do Ah cook with a feelthy animal in ma *cuisine*, *hein*?' He stood with a boning knife in his right hand, slowly transferring it to his left, and back again. Dwayne Mortte was crouched out of general sight, behind the side of the large refrigerator, looking terrified.

'What the bloody hell is going on in here? I spoke to you earlier, and said I wanted no more stupid behaviour. What, in the name of Christopher Columbus' dick, is going on now?'

It was only after his rather coarse question that Jefferson noticed Mrs Ironmonger sitting quietly in a wheel-backed chair in her black uniform, almost invisible in the steam and gloom of the room. 'It's my Perfect Cadence,' she explained, in quiet, reasonable tones. 'She wandered out through here to find her way to the garden, which is really terribly intelligent when you come to think about it, because there's no cat-flap for her convenience. Obviously, I came with her, she not yet being able to manipulate a door handle, and then this Froggy freak started to have a hissy fit.'

'You should have let her out of the window in your room, Mrs Ironmonger, as agreed when I said you could bring your little kitty here in the first place. You know very well that there is a hotel rule forbidding children or pets, and I can't be seen by guests to be condoning one of my staff flagrantly breaching this rule. It reflects badly, it makes me look a fool, and I won't be a party to it. Do I make myself clear?'

'I'm sure I should have complied with that request, had I not been downstairs doing work that isn't actually mine, because you have left us understaffed. If you would only fit a cat-flap in my personal window, I should keep my little darling within the confines of my room, and not let her roam the hotel in general to get her exercise.'

Jefferson would have loved to fit a cat-flap in her 'personal window', but he had the idea that they may be thinking of two entirely different actions. 'I take your point, Mrs Ironmonger, and I shall order the services of a glazier as soon as is humanly possible. As for you, Chef, shut the fuck up, or I'll fillet you with your own boning knife. I've just about had enough of your histrionics for one day. Do I make myself clear? To both of you?'

'Yes, sir.'

'*Oui.*'

At this point, the bell in reception rang with an impatient

'ting', and as Jefferson left to answer it, those in the kitchen considered that they had got off quite lightly. It was only first night nerves, and they had soon made up again, Mrs Ironmonger taking her 'precious' to her own room, where kitty was allowed out of the window. Her furry darling's way back was via the fire-escape, and she would just have to get used to the route.

Returning to the grand entrance hall, he found two couples waiting for him, both pointedly ignoring each other till they had heard a little more about the other, after check-in. The first couple was quite young – probably in the early thirties, and both were dressed in T-shirt and jeans, trainers adorning their feet. Jefferson coughed to draw attention away from the expression of horror that had appeared on his face, crossed his fingers out of sight, and hoped that they didn't intend to dress that way during their stay here. It would quite ruin the tone of the place. Anyone would think this was a holiday camp!

The man put out his hand, and introduced them as Bradley and Fiona Baddeley from Hove. ('Please call the wife "Fudge" – everyone else does.') Grammaticus briefly wondered if she was merely clumsy, or if this was a genuine pet name for her, while handing them the register to append their details.

'Ah, I see you're entering the legal profession,' commented Grammaticus, noting that the man had filled in his occupation as 'articled clerk'. 'And what do you do with your time, dear lady?' he chanced, flashing her one of his 'you can confide in me' smiles.

'I work for an AIDS charity,' she chirped back, totally unaware of how the couple behind them shrank away from them with a moue of disgust. Good grief, there was enough suppressed prejudice in this little gathering to spark a small war!

'I've put you in number seven,' he informed the Baddeleys. 'It's the mauve room. If you would care to put yourselves in the capable hands of the footmen, they will carry your bags and escort you to your room, but one moment, before you go. Here, he lifted the in-house telephone, and rang the kitchen, merely muttering, 'Tea, on the lawn, now,' before handing them their key. Addressing both couples, he announced that an *al fresco* afternoon tea would be served outside whenever they were ready, and moved on to the next couple.

As the last couple to arrive at check-in approached the counter, he was able to note that the woman was a noticeable number of years older than her partner, and was trying her best to beat the flapping wings of time. It was she who took the conversational reins, and introduced them as Madge (*she first!*) and Mark Berkeley-Lewis, flashing him an open-mouthed smile that revealed that her top four front teeth were patently false. After such work with cosmetics on the rest of her visage, it was like finding a boil on the Mona Lisa's nose on close inspection, and Grammaticus was not enchanted.

A quick glance at the register showed that Mark Berkeley-Lewis had declared himself as in 'banking'. 'Clerk!' was Jefferson's scathing thought, as he intoned, 'I've put you in number eight, the peach room,' and turned them over to the recently returned Freemans.

At this point, he left reception and made his way over to the office, from whence he returned a couple of minutes later bearing a lectern, with a programme for today's activities affixed to it, placing it next to the reception counter, in a position where it could be seen before a member of staff had been interrupted, to give out the same information that this offered. It read:

PROGRAMME FOR CHECK-IN DAY
MURDER/MYSTERY WEEKEND

Check-in onwards: Afternoon Tea, served on the lawn at the front of the Hotel.
6.00: Welcome Reception in the Library. Complimentary champagne and cocktails with canapés to be served.

6.45: Short explanatory talk in the Library to outline the details of the murder mystery planned for tomorrow night.

7.15: Inspection of costumes for the murder mystery drama, in the Billiards Room.

8.00: Dinner will be served in the Dining Room. Character booklets can be found by designated places, as per the seating plan displayed on the Dining Room buffet.

Post-prandial coffee and cognac will be offered in the Drawing Room, at your pleasure.

Dear Guest,

You will be afforded the opportunity to select a suitable costume to complement the character part you have been allotted for the murder mystery drama during the course of the evening.

These will be your responsibility until after the entertainment is over. This will 6.30 pm tomorrow, after Afternoon Tea, which will be available again on the front lawn, and also in the Summer House to the rear of the hotel, overlooking the sublime view of the river and the surrounding countryside.

Please try to take time, during the day tomorrow, to familiarise yourself with the part you will be playing during the evening, as this will ensure that everyone has as fine a time as it is possible to have.

Good luck, and have fun!

Jefferson Grammaticus

With all guests now accounted for, he took the opportunity to make his way outside to see if anyone had emerged to take tea. He was surprised and pleased to see that the staff had already covered the allotted pair of trestle tables with the snowy white damask cloths he had specified, and that on the cloths, there rested three silver (plated) tea services, along with a plethora of fine china, from which to imbibe the refreshing liquid.

Large plates of assorted sandwiches also adorned the

surface of the cloths, along with several stands with assorted cakes and tarts. That ought to keep the punters busy until it was time for more chow, and a bit of the old free boozy-woozy! Hands clasped in satisfaction behind his back, Jefferson turned back to the hotel and went back inside to have a last-minute inspection of preparations for their first dinner of trading.

Had Jefferson headed upstairs on his tour of inspection, instead of into the bowels of the ground floor rooms, he would have heard some very interesting comments on not only his person, but on his décor and establishment as well, but he didn't, so he entirely missed these few gems, unfortunately, unattributed, unless one happened to be a fly on the landing wall.

'Pompous fat prig. He's so condescending, he ought to stand on a chair to talk to us.'

'He's just like an old-fashioned Dickensian character, isn't he? And I think the décor's just yummy.'

'I hope this is worth all the dosh I've shelled out. I don't fancy being shafted by an over-dressed dandy and a couple of Uncle Toms.'

'Oh, those gorgeous uniforms! If I were here on my own, I'd be after those two like a ferret up a trouserleg.'

'I hope this place isn't staffed by a bunch of poofs. I don't fancy having my jollies fondled during the murder!'

'He'll have to go. I need to do something about this. But what?'

'I've got to find some time for us to be alone together.'

'He must be on his own. It won't work unless he's on his own, and it has to work.'

'I'm right out of my depth here. How do I always end up being made to feel so uncomfortable?'

'Nobody will ever find out, if I'm really careful and stick to my story.'

'It's like a tart's boudoir in here. Who the hell did the interior decorating, Danny la Rue?'

'God, I can't wait to be alone with my little bunsy-wunsy again.'

There were enough seething thoughts and emotions within the walls of The Manse to fuel any number of real murder mystery weekends, although at this stage, fortunately for him, Jefferson Grammaticus was totally unaware of how Fate would play games with his carefully laid plans and ambitions, and leave them in ruins about him.

Chapter Five

Outside, the guests had taken advantage of the weather and the inclusive afternoon tea, and there were now figures dotted here and there, in various individual styles of clothing. Fruity Newberry, it seemed, had now adopted a brightly coloured, flowing cravat and discarded his faux-squire suiting for something a little more suitable for the prevailing weather, his outfit mainly composed of a pair of light-coloured flannel trousers and a cream linen shirt, to offset the brightness of his neck attire. His wife, Teddy, was in some sort of ankle-length afternoon dress in a dazzling red and green print, and both of them sat at the tea table with self-satisfied expressions on their faces.

Fruity was simultaneously admiring the quality of the silver and porcelain, while mentally examining his possible chances of rekindling old flames on the quiet. His heart beat with a slightly greater speed than was usual for him, as he contemplated anticipated pleasures, blending with fond memories of past passion.

Teddy was just relaxing: glad to be away from the hustle and bustle of the casino and their rather claustrophobic apartment. It was all very well for Fruity to indulge himself in life by being a professional gambler, but it had never offered her any stability. They had never been able to buy a property, because his winnings were mostly wiped out by his losses, and she had never had the luxury of the choice of whether or not to have children. Their somewhat precarious existence simply couldn't support the risk, and so she had ceased to raise the subject years ago.

It had always been a definite 'not' with Fruity, and she could never have been certain of enough income to feed and clothe a child, let alone leave herself with enough emotional energy to nurture one. She had spent just about all of her time with her husband worried about how they were going to pay the rent at the end of the month, without adding the repayments of a mortgage and the expense of child-rearing entering the equation.

She was a woman who had had to live in the moment, and for the moment, she was just content to sit here in these beautiful grounds and let the warm breeze ruffle her hair and make playful little waves with the material of her frock. She could stay here for ever: *would* stay here for ever, if she got the chance, and for one treacherous second, imagined working in this beautiful building; being part of the team that brought this gracious setting to life, having a room of her own, and no more financial nightmares. Well, as her mother would have said, she had made her bed, and now she must lie in it.

Jefferson Grammaticus stared over towards the summer-house, where he could just identify Enoch and Aylsa Arkwright, the former making dramatic gestures with his arms as he spoke, in what the part-owner assumed was a large part of his character; this semi-hectoring body language that would, eight or nine times out of ten, ensure him the upper hand in any conversation.

He could not imagine what Mrs Arkwright took from the marriage table, but supposed that such a self-important little man would absent himself a lot with work, and thus give her a free hand to do more or less what she liked for most of her time. If this were so, the formula must have worked, for they were neither of them in the springtime of their lives, and, he assumed, had weathered the storms of the years in an acceptably harmonious manner.

As he strolled around, enjoying the proprietorial air he had quite rightly assumed, he noticed that the Baddeleys were out on the river, lazily drifting with the movement of the water, neither conscious of the presence of the other. With regret, he identified an upraised knee in the body of the boat, as being still clad in denim, and recognised a need to specify a dress code for the establishment. He couldn't have jeans and trainers on his property – it smacked too much of jellied eels, bingo, and kiss-me-quick hats. This was no venue for a works outing; this was *class*, and he'd not have his projected standards of behaviour and dress eroded by any hoi polloi from some solicitor's office.

Remembering that they came from Hove, he wasted a second or two wondering whether they knew the Newberrys, who came from Brighton, dismissed the subject from his mind as unworthy of his high-brow consideration, and strolled on to see where his other guests were, and that no one was actually having a bread-and-butter fight.

It appeared that the Berkeley-Lewises had joined the Arkwrights at the prettily clothed trestles, and they seemed to be involved in animated but pleasant conversation, Madge Berkeley-Lewis raising her hand to cover a small tinkle of laughter that floated over to him on the bright June air. It boded well for the weekend that the couples were already beginning to socialise, and he moved on, mentally awarding himself a house point.

The weather, as if in congratulation, had provided a perfect June day, little candy floss clouds floating across the vast blue expanse of the sky, and intensifying the colours of the flowers planted out in the beds. The light sparkled on the water, and a few ducks and a pair of swans glided gently downstream, as if on cue. Trees moved gently in the soft, warm breeze blowing from the south, and appeared to be dancing, very slowly, to the inaudible music of a benign mother nature. All it needed, he thought, was a couple of peacocks, to add the finishing touch, and it would be perfect. He'd have to look into the cost of a couple, and see if he couldn't arrange for them to be delivered before he welcomed the next batch of guests.

As he made his way back to the hotel, he caught sight of the Veedes at the riverbank, obviously engaged in conversation with the Baddeleys, and he congratulated himself again. From what he had seen, the Newberrys would get on with everybody (with the exception of himself), and here was everybody else, busily getting on with each other, instead of warily pacing round each other trying to get the upper hand. He looked on his work, and he found it good.

Pulling himself out of this self-congratulatory mist, he stiffened his determination and made his way, somewhat more briskly, to the hotel. It was time to corner Percy Boyd-Carpenter, and make sure she hadn't been physically consumed by the computing and printing machinery in the office. It was time all the character booklets were printed and ready to be placed, with appropriate name cards, upon the dining room table for later use. It was all about to happen, and it was all down to *him*. He would, actually, later deny this, in the light of what was to happen, but for now, he was more than pleased to be credited for his endeavours thus far.

'Twas good that he had returned thus, for Persephone Boyd-Carpenter was, at that very moment, printing sheet two of each character booklet upside down. Some of the sheet ones had, somehow or other, overprinted themselves on top of the scene-setting notes, and she was in a dangerously bad mood, swearing like a trooper – which one would never have guessed at, given her appearance – and ripping sheets of paper to shreds as if to line the cages of a thousand hamsters.

'Let me take over, Percy,' he advised, pushing her to one side and placing himself before the printer. 'There's no need to get your knickers in a twist. It's only a few characters, and in a few months, you'll be able to do this standing on your head,' he soothed.

'Well, you can just shut your bloody mouth, you slimy fucking fiend. If I want bleeding advice on how to buggeringly do someth …'

'Percy! I will NOT have language like that used under my

roof. You come from a very privileged background, and have had a screamingly expensive education. You have access to a wide vocabulary, and I can never understand it when you descend into the gutter like that. Now, pull yourself together, tootle off and get yourself changed for tonight, and I'll do this.'

'I'm sorry, Jefferson. I picked up "the fouls" when I was doing some charity work after university, and it sometimes rises, like scum, to the surface – especially when I'm frustrated at not being able to do something that should be perfectly simple, like this printing.'

'Go and get Steve to mix you a martini so dry it's never even heard of vermouth, then go up to your room and get ready. I'll see you later, when you've re-joined civilised society.'

It was the work of just a few minutes to sort out the mess that the author had made of the character booklets, and it wasn't long before Jefferson found himself standing before the enormous antique bowl-shaped gong under the staircase.

With enormous satisfaction, he brought the leather-muffled head of the hammer into contact with the beaten metal surface of the gong, and the *boom!* it emitted echoed and reverberated around the grand entrance hall, calling the attention even of those who were still in the garden. It was the dressing bell for dinner, and he announced as much as they wandered inside to see what all the noise was about. He wasn't about to let his finely tuned timetable be overturned by an insignificant factor like a small gaggle of tardy guests.

'The dressing bell,' he intoned, projecting his voice so that it reached beyond the limits of the doors. 'Please feel free to change for dinner, and assemble, as instructed, on tonight's schedule of events, to commence our first evening together.

'Costumes will be available to view, after an explanation of the setting for our special event, and cocktails will be flowing in The Manse's welcome to you, our very first guests, in this new establishment. Please adjourn to your rooms, and I shall see you anon.' On which cheesy final remark, he gave a little chuckle, just loud enough to reach all ears, and disappeared in the direction of the billiards room, where the sound of some movement was just discernible.

As he had suspected, it was the back door arrival of the ladies from DisguiserGuys with their combs, hairspray and make-up, setting up in readiness for the influx of customers later. Although they would not be actually 'making over' any of the guests tonight, they needed to consult their pallets and plan masks and wigs, making notes in preparation for the morrow, so that it would run as smoothly as possible, in the limited time that would be available to them.

As he entered the room, Alison Meercroft was ticking off costumes already on the rails from a list on a clipboard she carried, and her new assistant Céline was wondering out loud what they themselves would do for food, if they needed to be constantly on hand for queries and physical help, but Jefferson had his answer off pat.

'I shall have the same food as is served to our guests served to you in the staff room while dinner is actually in progress. I wouldn't want you to feel that an association with The Manse is bad for your blood sugar levels, and staff should always be treated well, in my opinion.' He thought he'd blown it with that last remark, so pompous was it, but, to his relief, it seemed to pass unnoticed.

'You 'ave a good chef?' enquired Mlle Treny, who had been combing out wigs, and now stood, the handle of a comb just removed from her mouth, where she had been giving it a good chew. It would seem that she was going to be starving later, as she already seemed hungry.

'Antoine de la Robe; direct from Paris,' he informed her, with a small smile of satisfaction, and was then slightly thrown by her returning expression of smug confirmation. 'Have you ever come across him before? I mean, I know France is a huge country, but I …'

'France 'as many Antoine de la Robes,' was her enigmatic reply, and he didn't push his luck with further enquiry, as he had yet to drop in on the kitchen for a final inspection, and get Steve Grieve up to speed with the way he wanted cocktails mixed and distributed.

It was already gone five-thirty, but Steve was on the ball, having set himself up a temporary bar in the library, and arrayed himself in the appropriate uniform for the occasion.

A quick check of the dining room showed that other staff members had been just as conscientious, the table being beautifully laid, fresh flowers scenting the air and, most importantly of all, character leaflets (for character booklets would not be distributed until tomorrow night, to avoid any surreptitious cheating) were laid enticingly beside place settings, with their name-cards. Linen, cutlery, and glassware all looked immaculate, and he whistled quietly under his breath, as he continued on to the rear of the hotel, where the kitchen was situated.

For the first time today, there was no sound of raised voices penetrating the barrier of what was a not-quite-kosher baize door. Inside, he found Chef and Dwayne Mortte working in apparent harmony, Chastity Chamberlain on hand for any stray jobs that were necessary, and no sign of Beatrix Ironmonger or her blasted cat. He could hardly believe his good fortune. Things could not have been going more smoothly.

After his first view of the guests, his mood had darkened and left him feeling that he was chasing rainbows, but his walk in the grounds had done much to lighten his mood, and now an unexpected peace had descended on The Manse, and he began to feel that what he intended to do here was actually possible; really within his grasp for the very first time.

Time had proved to be extremely elastic since he had first found the property. At the beginning of the venture it seemed to stretch out like rubber, everything taking an inordinate amount of time. As the opening had approached, it had speeded up again, and he felt like he was running just to stand still. Today, however – well, at least since he had settled himself behind the reception counter – it had returned to the turgid passage it had pursued at the outset, and he felt as if the afternoon had been at least a week long.

He was eager, now, to get on with this first performance of his actors in the drama, and wished it into a higher gear; willed the hands on the clocks to move, so that he could step out on to his very own stage, and act his bursting heart out. Percy may be a pain in the arse where technology was concerned, but she could write her little socks off, and if he got everything right from the word 'go', he could find the entertainments at The Manse appearing in the gossip columns within the year, and that way lay huge success.

Returning to the entrance hall, he was delighted to see Jocelyn and Jerome already on duty in their set places, one either side of the staircase, and once more admired his own superb taste in the choice of their livery style and colours. By Jove, they looked damned attractive. He ought to get a medal for providing the ladies staying here with two great objects of sexual fantasy. Why, if he were batting for the opposition, he'd probably fancy them himself.

With a sudden jolt of pure glee, he realised how even more beguiling they would look, with the added sinister attraction of their fancy dress costumes tomorrow evening, and even he could hardly wait to see them wearing them.

Trotting smartly up to his room, he contemplated his own costume with pleasurable anticipation. Maybe the ladies wouldn't stop with fantasy, and he might even get in on the old flirtatious stuff himself. Silly to think like that, of course, but his abrupt swoop into optimism left him defenceless to the thought.

His departure left the hall empty, with the exception of the two completely immobile figures that stood there in their eye-catching livery, silent and still as statues. No sound now penetrated from any other quarter of the hotel, and the ticking of the clock could be easily distinguished from behind the reception counter.

The silence lay like a blanket, thick and heavy, over the hall, and the rhythmic tick-tock took on a sinister quality, like the regular beating of a renegade heart, intent on mischief and mayhem. The twins neither sensed nor heard this, but the Fates did, and chuckled gleefully to themselves, as they planned their version of the evening.

The only movement was the dancing of myriad dust motes like minute particles of dark magic waiting to coagulate, and caught in the spears of sunlight shining through the gloom of the space, the doors now shut against the blinding sunlight and the outside world at large. The hotel was a cocoon, suspended in space and time. Across the elasticity of the latter, slunk a silver-grey shape in feline form, eyes shining with mischief. Whether this was Perfect Cadence or the shade of the original Manse cat will never be known, for the Freemans noticed nothing.

Chapter Six

Friday 18th June, – the first evening

The guests, who almost floated down the staircase, were quite different to the motley crew that had checked in earlier. Everyone had taken the opportunity to dress for dinner, had chosen their finest outfits, knowing that the following night they would be in costume, and, therefore, only able to show off their personal preferences in sartorial elegance on this first night.

As instructed by the itinerary, they foregathered in the library, where Steve Grieve was on duty behind a fine library table, a tray of Bellinis already mixed and set out on a silver tray for self-service, his array of shakers at the ready for any un-Bellini type orders. He was, personally of the opinion that the Bellinis would go down a treat, and anyone ordering anything else wasn't really playing the game, but there was no accounting for taste, let alone idiosyncrasy and good old-fashioned bloody-mindedness.

Fudge and Bradley Baddeley – they of the earlier denim attire – were the first into the room, dressed unashamedly in finest Marks and Sparks, and accepted the proffered peachy nectar almost with relief that they did not have to name a desired pre-prandial cocktail themselves. Their daily round was the simplest: Bradley would normally have ordered a pint of bitter, Fiona a gin or vodka with tonic. The pre-mixed drinks gave them a chance to conceal the lack of sophistication in their tastes, and gave them a warm feeling inside for the consideration of the host. They had realised their sartorial blunder on arrival (although it had not moved them sufficiently at the time to change for afternoon tea), and were anxious to dispel the notion that they may be of the plebeian order, such is ego and self-image.

The second couple, joining them shortly afterwards, were the Arkwrights, Enoch in full evening fig, Aylsa in a full-length floaty number, with an overtunic of batwing sleeves trimmed with satin, the whole in an off-white colour that enhanced the dark tan of her skin, and went well with the beige curls of her hair. If not exactly top-drawer, they did at least make a handsome couple, provided they did not speak.

Unfortunately they did speak, or at least Enoch did. 'A side-car for me, my man, and a white lady for my, um, white lady, if you would be so kind.' His imperious and condescending attitude did nothing to buoy up Steve's spirits, and the strong Yorkshire accent merely made his hackles rise.

How dare this pompous old pseud treat him like a ... like a ... His mind raced as he searched for a suitable word. Like a serf – that was the best that he could come up with, but it felt more or less right. The evening had only started, and already he had been talked down to. If he had the chance, he'd spit in their drinks, and see how they liked the flavour of that!

Lew and Sue Veede entered together physically, but were not at all in tune mentally. Lew looked around the library in admiration. He had been pleased by the white and gold décor of their room, considering it quite French in his humble opinion, and the library appeared to him to be exactly what a library in a country house should be – full of books and solid, heavy furniture.

Sue, on the other hand, clearly had her mind on other things and, although she too scanned the room, she appeared not to be giving it the once over, but more like she was scouting about for a person, and was quite happy to accept whatever she was offered to drink without demur.

The rest of the party arrived together, having met either on the landing or the stairs, and the only incident of note was the mischievous twinkle in Fruity Newberry's eyes, when they met the eyes of a lady other than his wife.

The Berkeley-Lewises headed straight for the Arkwrights, Mark having instinctively smelled money coming off the couple in waves, and insisted on champagne cocktails, rather than the themed drink of the weekend.

Jefferson Grammaticus finally joined his cocktail-party, trailing Lloyd and Percy Boyd-Carpenter in his wake. Percy was still in muttered consultation with her husband, still unable to believe that all the character booklets were printed and assembled ready for use. She had not tackled anything like this before, being more of a short-story writer, and was on tenterhooks about whether the whole thing would work, or be shot down in flames by an inadvertent mistake, on her part, in the plotting.

Jefferson had OKed it, but had he really read it properly, or had he just accepted it as watertight, because he knew her and trusted her? Would that she would not let him down, or this whole opening weekend might be the most almighty flop, and it would all be her fault. They had such plans, Grammaticus having asked her if she would write more of the same, until they had a good repertoire going which could be repeated at suitable intervals. He had also asked her to conduct residential creative writing courses, and had offered good money as well as board and lodging for both her and her husband. Life was quite tough financially at the moment, and they could really do with the boost, the economic climate being what it was.

Jefferson stood by the doors of the room, surveying the little kingdom in which he owned thirty-three and a third per cent, and pondered his plans for prosperity. The physical nearness of Percy had reminded him of his hopes for an alliance between them, stretching well into the future, and of course he had a fabulous chef, to whom he had also proposed in-house cookery courses, with an additional bonus in salary to accompany this extra work.

Of course, the extra remuneration could not be too generous, as he might lose him to a rival establishment, but if he kept his wings clipped sufficiently, he could hang on to him for a long time to come, and thus enhance the culinary success of his own establishment. This was an 'I'll scratch your back ...' agreement, and he would remind Chef of that, should it become necessary and he became a little too big for his boots.

With his best Edwardian country house squire smile spread across his face, he surveyed with pleasure the sight of Steve mixing drinks and clearing away as he worked, the Freeman brothers circulating in their best upper-servant manner, each with a silver tray, to keep the guests happily oiling themselves. It was time to call the proceedings to a halt and make his announcement about the setting for their little dramatic exercise.

Clearing his throat loudly, he called for their attention. 'Ladies and gentlemen, may I have the pleasure of your ears? I know you are probably eager to hear when and where our murder mystery is set, so let me apprise you of the details.

'Imagine you are in Venice. It is the pre-war era,' (sneaky, avoiding an exact date like that, so no one could challenge with the legitimacy of Bellinis being served), 'and it is the time of the Carnevale. You are all moneyed people, staying in one of the grander hotels, and tomorrow evening, you will be attending a grand ball.

'During the evening, you will all retire to a private dining room for the finest of Italian cuisine. During the meal, you will have the opportunity to get to know your companions – a necessity, as at the commencement of the meal, it is announced that there has been a murder.

'The meal is your opportunity to uncover that murderer, with the aid of your character booklets for your own personality, and your investigative and interview skills to uncover the villain. Between courses the narrator, I, in suitable Carnevale costume, will relate to you additional information, and you will be allowed to turn a page of your character booklet to learn more about the person you are playing.

'At this moment in time, I beg you not to look forward in

your character booklets ahead of any given signal. It may not ruin the game, but it will mar its playing out, and I want everyone to get maximum enjoyment from our play-acting time together.

'I have decided that tonight, only character leaflets will be issued.' At this point Percy looked at her husband with fear in her eyes, but Lloyd merely nodded and smiled at her, letting her know that this had all been sorted out when she was having her fit of heebie-jeebies, earlier.

'Quite quick and simple, my dear. Don't worry your little head about it.'

'Tomorrow night the full booklets will be available to you, to embellish your characterisation. And now, if you would be so good, please adjourn to the billiards room where my 'ladies of the wardrobe' are waiting to provide you with your ball costumes, wigs, and masks. Let us be gone!'

He was rather pleased with his 'ladies of the wardrobe' and his 'let us be gone', and trotted on ahead of them, leading the way, his mouth almost watering with the taste of success, sweet and nourishing as it was for both the bank balance and the soul.

While cocktails were commencing in the library, the ladies from DisguiserGuys were making last-minute checks on their stock and display, both in a state of twittering nerves about the success of the venture, Alison Meercroft in particular, as it was her business, Céline Treny on a little side-road, as she had business of a rather different sort to conduct during their time at The Manse.

In the kitchen, Antoine de la Robe, amidst the clatter and chatter of his working environment, whirled round in surprise as he was tapped on the shoulder. 'Sacre bleu!' he ejaculated. 'My 'eart, it have nearly ceased to beat!' he cried but, on whirling round, he became silent as the grave, and stared at the figure behind him with wide and frightened eyes.

''ow deed you fahnd me?' he asked, in a voice hoarse with

apprehension. "'ow in ze name of ze *bon Dieu* did you know Ah was 'ere? You devil! Weel you dog me to mah grave?'

The figure merely nodded. It stood stock still in absolute silence for what was, in fact only about twenty seconds, but what seemed to Antoine like hours, then smiled and nodded, still without speaking, and disappeared out through the kitchen door as suddenly as it had appeared behind him.

'Deed you see zat?' shouted Antoine, thoroughly rattled.

'See what, Chef?' asked Dwayne Mortte.

Chastity Chamberlain looked up from her vegetable preparation, as if emerging from underwater. 'What was that, Chef?'

'Don't know what you're talking about. What were we supposed to have seen?' asked Beatrix Ironmonger, who was stirring the contents of a large saucepan.

'Never mahnd!' said Antoine. 'Ah theenk Ah am seein' theengs. Eet eez ze fahnly tuned artistic temperament of mah culinary calling. Eet is nossing!'

With a little more mental effort, he would be able to convince himself that he had just experienced a crisis of nerves, a hallucinatory return to his past, and that nothing of moment had happened.

The guests thronged into the billiards room like a flock of excited starlings, eagerly anticipating the next part of their 'out of time' adventure in this beautiful building, but as they crossed the threshold, they were effectively silenced by the bright rainbow colours and fine, rich fabrics of the garments that hung before their eyes, before falling on them as if to devour them in their richness.

As Jefferson departed, he was aware of Fruity Newberry arguing furiously against wearing a wig, no doubt worried that he would be far too hot under a double helping of hirsute assistance. And he had noted for the first time that some of his guests wore glasses – an absolute no-no where full-face masks were concerned.

Whether they had arrived in contact lenses and changed to

something a little more brain-friendly where drinking was concerned, he did not know, but concluding that they would all have to remove their facial coverings to eat, he let it drop from his concerns, and just wondered at the choice of frames by some of those foregathered in the billiards room.

It was the spectacles worn by Teddy Newberry that had first caught his attention. Her nose was adorned with a ghastly concoction in bright red plastic, with winged corners and inset diamante. *Zut alors!* – as Chef would no doubt have remarked.

It took a lot longer than he thought to recapture his birds, and he stroked his beard meditatively as he surveyed the squiffy crowd that assembled at the dining table, a full half hour after he had planned. Bonhomie and alcohol rolled off them in waves, and he could only imagine the state of hysteria that his chef was no doubt currently enjoying, at the thought of his beautiful creation spoiling, his reputation curdling before his very eyes.

He really would have to speak to Steve about the strength of in-house cocktails, He could see how inhibitions had been shed, and a fair amount of twinkling and furtive eye contact was going on between guests who had not arrived together. In fact, he was left in no doubt that, had the table been made of glass, he would have been able to see rather a lot of hand-stroking and footsie being played.

The drinks needed to be more carefully monitored, if he didn't want this weekend to end up resembling a teenagers' school trip. He had no personal objections to people forming extra-marital alliances, so long as it did not interfere with the smooth running of the business, nor include any unpleasant, embarrassing scenes of the '*coitus interruptus*' sort. There must be nothing of that sort to mar this launch, as word would get out, and he would be lampooned in the business.

Food, however, seemed to calm everyone down, as bodies accepted fuel to mop up the alcohol and, although the first course was bolted with greedy enthusiasm, as the meal progressed, a slightly less rowdy atmosphere prevailed for a while. The Freemans served with their normal gravitas, and Chastity cleared away in silence, but with a quiet servility (even if feigned) that won her his silent praise.

Table talk was all of the evening to come tomorrow, and of the fabulous creations they would be wearing, and it was not until everyone retired to the drawing room for coffee, allowing the staff to clear away the detritus of the meal, that things hotted up again. An indiscriminate amount of cognac was ordered, to ease the coffee down their throats, and the mischief in people's faces began, once again, to assert itself.

Fruity Newberry cast frequent longing looks, charged with middle-aged fire, in the direction of Sue Veede. His wife Teddy, however, noticed nothing, as she had her eye firmly on Mark Berkeley-Lewis who responded with little lowerings of his eye lashes, making what Jefferson had always referred to as 'come-to-bed' eyes at her.

His wife Madge had sat herself down on a sofa beside Enoch Arkwright (*why?*), and was clearly flirting, although it was difficult to say what could have been in the least attractive about the man. She must have been wearing her Bellini-goggles, and Jefferson had to admit that, if the man kept his mouth shut, it was vaguely possible that someone could have taken a shine to him, but it was still difficult to swallow. Perhaps Madge took a genuine interest in the intricacies of the scrap-metal trade?

Thank goodness Aylsa was ignoring the whole thing, probably glad to get out of the man's company for a short while, during which she didn't have to listen to his constant carping. It was only Lew Veede who seemed at all put out, and he eyed his wife with slitted eyes, which carried a look that said that he would mark her card before the night was out.

'May I get you a refill for your cognac, sir?' Jefferson asked, swooping over to the frowning form that was Lew with the motive of distraction, and it worked. As the host congratulated himself on his speedy interjection, Mark Berkeley-Lewis strolled over and began to quiz Jefferson about the price of the hotel venture, going into great detail about the purchase price – a steal – and the cost of the refitting. Even if not in a senior position within his branch of banking, Mark knew his stuff, and Jefferson was soon bored enough that he resorted to the old 'freshen your drinks?' trick again.

By this time, Lew Veede had been supplied with yet another immoderately generous cognac, and was sitting back in his chair, thoroughly relaxed and with a silly smile on his face, seemingly completely recovered from his earlier fit of the sulks.

Only a short while later, and after consulting his watch to assess the lateness of the hour, Jefferson's ascension to an upright position was like a cue, and some of the guests began to gather their things together and announce their intentions of turning in for the night. After all, tomorrow was the highlight of their stay, and they didn't want it to pass while they were still in the throes of gargantuan hangovers.

It was gone two o'clock before he had managed to shepherd the last of them up the stairs, and he sent Jocelyn and Jerome up with the final two stragglers, conscious that he had no wish whatsoever to have to summon an ambulance at this hour of the morning, because a drunken guest had taken a tumble down the stairs.

After a final check of the premises, a large brandy (not cognac) for Chef, who had seemed more distracted than furious at the delay of the meal, and the locking down procedure, Jefferson sat down on his bed in the green bedroom, utterly exhausted, both mentally and physically. This was all much harder than he had thought it would be, and the wearing of his squire's uniform had proved an uncomfortable and restricting practice, after his usual casual attire of jeans, T-shirt, and trainers, which he had lived in for the duration of the refurbishment.

If he had arrived at his own hotel in the gear he normally wore, he would not have allowed himself admission, and was overcome by a sudden wave of sympathy for the squires of the past. They knew no different in the clothing department, to what he had worn tonight, and must have spent their entire lives in a sort of sartorial prison. The corseting of the women he didn't dare envisage, as it was far too horrible to even contemplate, but he understood just a tiny bit more why they had wanted emancipation, if only to earn the right to let it all hang out!

Chapter Seven

Saturday 19th June – morning

The first full day of the hotel's business started on a quiet note. A few guests requested breakfast in their rooms – continental, not full English – others asked for only tea or coffee and juice to be delivered. The dining room, therefore, held only Percy and Lloyd, who were not great imbibers of spirituous liquors, and who had retired first the evening before, refusing any other after dinner drinks, and sneaking off to the kitchen where they knew they could make themselves a nice cup of cocoa to send them off to sleep.

Percy was in a strange mood, which consisted of a storm of self-doubt that her story would work, and a belligerence that harked back to her more normal self. She constantly upbraided Lloyd for his table manners, his lack of conversation, and his general belief that he should be allowed to exist; but as far as food was concerned, she merely crumbled a slice of toast into small pieces, few of which were consumed.

In complete contrast, Lloyd seemed to have affected political deafness, no doubt used to his wife's attitude to the revelation of her creations, and ate like a trencherman, devouring cereal, a full plate of all that could be desired at that time of day, and several slices of toast and Oxford-cut marmalade with perfect enjoyment. All washed down with two glasses of orange juice and four cups of tea, he sat back replete, a happy man, who wanted nothing more than to digest his feast in peace, without any GBH of the earhole.

With this desire in mind, he left the table without a

backward glance at his wife, and headed for the library, where he could sit and contemplate the place where his navel was reputed to be without interruption. Percy, suddenly becoming aware of her solitude, went off in search of Jefferson, who represented another ear she could bend with her anxiety. He'd know just what to say to sooth her frayed nerves, and if he didn't, she'd never write for him again: never!

The bright sunlight of morning was not welcomed in the five bedrooms that had been paid for, and curtains remained firmly shut against its intrusion.

In the white and gold room, Sue was the first awake. Her head was thumping, her mouth was like the bottom of a birdcage, so dry was it, and her first move was to the bathroom to gulp down some water and take a couple of paracetamol. It was only while she was swallowing these that she remembered her little flirtation of the night before.

She should have been more discreet – they both should have been. She knew Lew had noticed, for she had caught a glimpse of his face as she had accepted another – yet another – cognac. Oh, God! Whatever was he going to say when he woke up? He had been silent the night before, but then he had been extremely tiddly, not to say downright drunk, but she was probably 'for it' this morning when he remembered this unfinished business from the night before.

In the event, Lew said precisely nothing. Although he remembered the cocktails, the costumes, and the dinner, of post-prandial activities he had no memory whatsoever. Jefferson's personal attention, in serving him a lake of spirit, had completely done for any chance he had of remembering any event whatsoever, after he had laid his dessert spoon to rest, and he began to sweat slightly at the thought that he might have misbehaved himself while under the influence. He'd have to gauge Sue's mood before he could even guess at what had occurred in – where had they been again – was it the drawing room or the library? Even this detail proved elusive, through the post-alcoholic fug that enveloped his thought processes.

But Sue said nothing, giving him no real idea of whether he had made a fool of himself or not. She was very quiet and introverted, and kept glancing at him out of the corner of her eye, as if she expected him to say something, and for a while he wondered if she were waiting for an apology.

However, she was also a little shifty and embarrassed, and after some half an hour of mulling it over, he decided that 'least said, soonest mended' was probably the best policy, as they had paid what was in his opinion quite a lot of money for the short break, and he didn't want to spoil it with arguments and recriminations. If she said nothing, then neither would he, and maybe, whatever it was – if it was anything at all – would all be water under the bridge, eclipsed by tonight's grand performance.

It was reassuring to be handed some painkillers and a glass of water, as he hauled himself out of bed, and he decided that, with no obvious indicator to the negative, that his behaviour had at least stayed this side of respectable. What he was unable to observe was his wife's expression of relief, as she returned to the bathroom to scrape her copper-beech locks into a ponytail on the top of her head, something she only did when she was unsettled and ill-at-ease.

There was something about the way the waves stroked against her neck and tickled her face that irritated her beyond reason, when she had something on her mind, which at this moment was the fact that she seemed to have got way with her behaviour of the night before, as far as her husband was concerned, but she feared that someone else may comment on it to him. She would just have to hope that they were all as inebriated as he was, and would take no note of her flirtatious glances, or that sneaky little fumble behind the staircase, when she and the object of her current affections both left the drawing room to 'powder their noses' at the same time.

Seeing her emerge from the bathroom with her hair on top of her head caused Lew a temporary setback in his relief, and he worried anew that she had done this as a result of his behaviour, but she exhibited no overt signs of being angry with him, so he let it slide while he coped with the symptoms of his thundering hangover.

While the guests were waking up to their various demons of the night before, and Percy had gone in search of her husband, having given up on ever finding her host, Jefferson Grammaticus seized the opportunity to phone an employment agency in Market Darley, in the hope of securing extra members of staff for the coming evening, and was flabbergasted to hear that there was only one possible on their books. How could this be? The country was in the grips of a recession. Surely there must be someone out there who wanted to earn a crust by helping him earn his?

But the answer was a definite 'no'. They would contact the lone client currently resting on their books, and get back to him later in the day. Should she turn up of her own accord before they had phoned back, he should be sure to look out for a Melanie Saunders who would be coming from Carsfold, and actually had some experience in hospitality.

Well, he supposed, one pair of extra hands was better than none, and he would just have to be grateful for small mercies, and manage until he could apportion out the work better, and had a more realistic understanding of just how many people he needed to offer the service he had promised. With only another casual wage to pay out, he would have the opportunity to consult his little black book again, and trawl up some 'value for money' help. There were plenty of attic rooms where they could live in, and he had no qualms about what he was doing at all.

No sooner had he terminated the call, than he heard a high-pitched scream of despair from the kitchen, followed by a torrent of fast, loud, and probably quite demotic French. Jefferson may not be able to identify an individual by their scream, but he knew that Chef was involved, and he could not countenance a crisis on this day of all days, when the food was of paramount importance.

Rising from his leather captain's chair, he sped off across the hall towards the sound of what was now a quite vociferous argument. Beatrix Ironmonger was in there, and if his housekeeper and his Chef were at war, he might just as well send everybody home and bolt the doors.

As he entered the food preparation area, the tableau in front of him was not encouraging. Chef had a kitchen knife poised in a raised hand, and Beatrix Ironmonger stood with her fists clenched at her sides, her whole being bristling with fury.

'How dare you! How dare you, you despicable little ... *Frog*! How dare you kick ... how dare you hurt an innocent little cat. How you have the nerve to stoop to cruelty to animals – but then, that's the French all over isn't it? Especially you! If you can't eat it or seduce it, you have no conscience at all in inflicting physical pain!'

All the while she was spitting these vehement words in his face, Antoine was hissing and rumbling like a pressure cooker about to blow. 'You stupid woman! Deed you not see what your eenocent leetle pussy cat was doing? *Hein*? 'E was only leecking mah *viande* – oh, 'ow you say – mah meat, wheech Ah 'ave left out for tonight's *diner*. 'E is a thief! And you are an *espece de vache* ...' Again he struggled with the English language in his fury. 'You are a type of cow, you ugly old lady-fiend!'

'That's enough!' shouted Jefferson, from his position just inside the door. 'I don't know what has happened, but this is not acceptable behaviour for two members of my staff. Now, either sort it out amicably, or you can both pack your bags.' He didn't, of course, mean that, but he knew what the termination of their employment would mean to them both, and he had no doubts that this, above all else, would extinguish the flames of anger that had so violently broken out.

'I'm so sorry, Mr Grammaticus,' burst out Beatrix Ironmonger, 'but this foreign – this *deviant* has kicked my Perfect Cadence. He kicked her clean out of the back door, and I don't know where she's gone to ground. That's grounds for reporting him to the RSPCA, as far as I'm concerned.'

Chef cut across her sob story. 'Eet was leecking mah meat, the feelthy leetle beast!' he exclaimed loudly, took one look at his employer's face, and dropped his eyes to the floor. 'Ah am sorry, Meester Grammaticus, but 'ow do I do the *diner* now?'

'Do you have adequate meat in the freezer to replace it?' asked Jefferson with forced calm.

'Ah do, but eet iz frozen soleed.'

'Then defrost it in the microwaves I have so generously provided you with, and stop whinging. It's my loss, not yours. I shall be the one who ends up paying for it. If you start now, you will have lost no time. Now stop wasting *my* time with *trivialities*! If this venture fails, then out you go. In fact, if I find you behaving in this childish manner again, I shall turf you both out anyway. Do I make myself clear?'

'Yes.'

'*Oui.*'

'Right! Get on with your duties. Mrs Ironmonger, I must insist that, when your cat returns, you confine it to your living quarters. Chef, if you use your foot again in such a manner, I shall do the same to you, as you fly down the front steps with your bags following you. Now, get on with things in a civilised manner. I'm your employer, not your blasted nanny.'

After this little scrap, Mrs Ironmonger returned to her quarters at the top of the building. She felt much more at home here, than in the dove grey room, which she found cold and unwelcoming. She had lived, for a long period, without adequate colour in her life and, at least in her own quarters, she had all her little darlings around her, and her pretty things.

In fact, her room was a shrine to the cats she had owned throughout her lifetime. A long acquaintance with a taxidermist had given her the opportunity never to part from any of them and, scattered across the floor, was a series of tiny furry rugs, each bearing the head of a deceased feline.

Barnabas, her very first cat, looked up at her as she

approached her favourite chair, and Brian and Harry stared from the other side of the fireplace. Near her dining table were Marbles and Monkey, and Kelly Finn and Misty flanked her bed. She derived a great deal of comfort from her former precious furry companions, and returned to them this morning, to soften the blow of the way in which her Perfect Cadence had been treated.

After visually greeting her ex-cats, she raked the room with her eyes, taking in all the ornaments of which she was so fond, and which provided the room with a positive rainbow of colour. How fond she was of every piece, and how homely they made the room look. A sigh escaped her lips, as she settled back in her armchair for a little think.

Back in his office, Jefferson was subject to a sense of impending doom, and the first thing his mind alighted upon was the value of the collection of costumes, now left in his care. With a start, he leapt to his feet – calm! calm! calm! old boy – then moderated his steps, and decided just to take a short stroll to the billiards room to have a little check.

As he emerged into the foyer, he caught sight of the Newberrys making their way down the stairs, and the sight immediately lightened his mood with a sardonic amusement. Teddy didn't look too bad: a little shaky perhaps, but had managed a smudge of make-up and was tidily dressed. Fruity, however, was in a class of his own.

His tie was askew, a stretched leg down a step revealed unmatched socks, and his wig – oh, his wig! – was a magnificent creature today, struggling for freedom. Its join was askew, and, at the back of the man's head, stray wisps of his own hair fought the alien beast in their own bid for superiority. His complexion was a shade of pale grey, and his hand shook as he moved it down the banister. He was a broken man, indeed, who would have to look to the excesses he heaped upon his own body, if he wanted to make older bones.

Jefferson could only hope that his spirits might revive themselves sufficiently to allow him to play his part tonight.

He had been allotted the part of a loud and obnoxious fellow, the parts having been assigned only after the guests had arrived and sized-up, and it was to be hoped that he would be his normal unpleasant self after a few hairs of the old dog, and that the few hairs actually left on the old dog himself, would sleep peacefully under any powdered wig that he might assume at dinner tonight.

His confidence thus restored, he made only a short foray into the realms of fancy dress, just to put his mind at rest, then headed off to find the Freemans, to check that they were *au fait* with the parts they would play tonight – not that he had anything less than complete faith in them, but it was always as well to check, rather than leave anything to fate.

Harry Falconer lay staring into the darkness, his body and bedclothes soaked in the cold sweat that dripped and rolled from his body. His heart was thudding, his breathing fast and shallow, while his whole body shuddered. He hadn't had that dream since he was a major in the army, but the sheer horror of it still filled him with terror and shame. He could hear nothing, see nothing, except for the unfolding scene that he had just dreamt for the first time in years.

He could hear again the screams, the cries for Mother; the clash of metal on metal, and the harsh guttural syllables echoed in his ears. He could feel the agony he had experienced then, the sheer terror of the consequences of what was happening to him, and what that would bring down upon his world. Again and again, the screams of horror and sobs rent the air, in his memory, and he started to shiver, his teeth chattering with fear and disgust.

Nanny Vogel had been a real sadist, and the sheer brute force of her personality, forcing him to eat a whole plate of Brussels sprouts, had never left him: that and her threats to tell his father what a disobedient, stubborn, and downright rude little boy he had been.

The scene only ended when he threw up on his plate, when she admonished him for his ingratitude and wastefulness, promising him many more greens, if he didn't mend his horrible little boy ways, and start acting like a good, respectful young man.

Reluctantly, he remembered how her moustache had glittered in the sunlight, on particularly bright days, the bristling hairs on her chin positively winking at him in the light. But her lips were thin and cruel, her eyes pale and soul-piercing, and she had inspired terror in him for nearly twelve months of his early childhood.

She had held sway, for what had been an eternity for the young boy that had been Falconer, a prisoner under her baleful military influence. That she had inspired in him a greater fear than any danger military and police life had thrown at him, still failed to surprise him, however. She was the monster under the bed, and the beast that scratched at his bedroom door at night in an attempt to devour him.

After such an inauspicious start to the day, Detective Inspector Harry Falconer arrived at the office a little earlier than usual, to quell his clamouring thoughts. He had a lot of paperwork to clear away, and was anxious to get a head start on it, before Detective Sergeant Carmichael arrived. That was not to say that Carmichael was a distraction – well, he was, actually the DS was newly married with two stepsons, had appalling dress sense, and absolutely no inhibitions. Davey Carmichael was a one-off.

Built like a barn door, he still retained all the traits of a child in his behaviour. Falconer had thought, at first acquaintance, that the young man might be a bit simple, but nothing had proved further from the truth. He had not only preserved his 'inner-child', but had never, in fact, had to conceal its presence. He was totally without guile, and behaved exactly as he felt, never hiding behind the veneer that most of us wear to declare us adults. Carmichael was Carmichael, as he had always been and as Falconer hoped he would always remain. He might seem a bit weird to some people, but he had become a figure that the inspector knew he could trust and depend on; a very important aspect of their work together, as they were each responsible, not just for their own safety, but for that of their partner, as well.

Falconer's first instincts had been those of a man suddenly landed with the job of child-minding, his own background being so dissimilar, but his fears had proved unfounded, and he knew this was merely a difference in upbringing. He, himself, had been – well, we won't go into those early years, after the state in which he had awoken that morning.

He had gone to prep school at eight, boarding school at twelve, then straight on to university, and from there, into the army, from which he had emerged, only to join the police force. He definitely lacked Carmichael's *joie de vivre* and enjoyment in the simple things in life, but he liked to think that they each had something to teach the other, to the enrichment of both their lives, and, overall, he enjoyed working with him.

The paperwork soothed rather than irritated him today, and he was feeling more like his normal, in-control self, when the office door burst open, and Carmichael exploded into Falconer's morning, wearing a baseball cap, as he had been wearing when Falconer first met him, but this time, at a jaunty sideways angle, and what appeared to be a small white stick protruding from one corner of his mouth.

The DS shed his jacket, but sat at his desk, the cap still perched on his head, and enthusiastic slurping noises escaping his mouth, as he worked at whatever it was he had on the end of that white stick. 'Morning, sir. How's it going?' he asked, moving the stick from side to side, as he spoke around his oral obstruction.

This was more like it! Nanny Vogel could go to hell! She was probably in a nursing home by now, being treated like the helpless child he had been when under her dubious care. This was a confidence-restoring thought, and Falconer hoped, with a tiny frisson of embarrassment at his *Schadenfreude*, that she dribbled, was incontinent, and force-fed Brussels sprouts every Sunday, as he had been.

'What have you got in your mouth, Carmichael? And why

have you still got your hat on? Surely the sheer heat of this glorious day negates the necessity for headgear?' he asked, genuinely interested.

'Not for me, sir. I've got a real chilly head this morning.'

And with this cryptic statement, he removed the baseball cap with a 'Ta-da!' revealing a newly shaven scalp, pulled a lollipop from his mouth, and carolled 'Who loves ya, baby?' in an appalling imitation of an American accent.

Falconer's mouth fell open with surprised horror. What was the man up to now, but he didn't have to wait more than a couple of seconds for an explanation of this new phase in Carmichael's appearance. 'We've been getting repeats of an old American police series called *Kojak* on the telly. Boy, he's cool! And I got fed up with the bleached look. What with the hot weather and everything, I said to Kerry last night, let's have a go at that. It's got to be cooler than my mop, so she got out the clippers and – hey presto! But it felt a lot cooler outside than I thought it would, so I grabbed this cap while I got used to it.'

Daft as ever, thought the inspector, and advised him not to stand in full sunlight with his shiny pate. Not only would it burn easily (and Carmichael with a brain fever didn't bear thinking about), but he didn't want the police sued for any car accidents because the driver had been blinded by the glare. If his sergeant suffered sunburn of the scalp, he had no doubt that he would expect to go about his business with an ice-pack strapped to his head without giving it a second thought.

'Better keep the hat on when you go outside. Your scalp will be sensitive for a while, and you need to expose it slowly to the elements. Now, what have you got on for today?'

'I've got to write up my notes for that series of burglaries, and I'm in court this afternoon,' he informed his superior.

'Good grief! You're going to give evidence in court looking like a skinhead thug?'

'Sir! That's a bit harsh, isn't it?'

'Have you actually taken a look in the mirror since Kerry, ah, remodelled you?'

'Didn't see the point, sir. I never use one shaving: there was too much competition for the bathroom when I lived at home with Mum and the family, so I got used to doing it by feel. That aside, I know what I look like, so it didn't seem necessary to preen in front of a looking glass.'

'Take yourself off to the gents', then come back and tell me what you think,' Falconer advised, a small smile twitching at the right-hand side of his mouth.

Carmichael's journey of discovery took only two minutes and seventeen seconds. Falconer timed it. 'They're gonna marmalise me in court, sir. I look like a villain. No one's gonna listen to a word I say. They're either going to be terrified of me, or laugh their pants off. What am I gonna do, sir?'

'You're going to wear my Panama hat. That's what you're going to do, Carmichael,' soothed the inspector, rising to retrieve it from the stand, where he had carefully placed it on arrival. 'With that on, you'll look your normal everyday self.'

And then he winced. Carmichael's normal everyday self was not like that of other ordinary mortals, and although he had moderated his flamboyant taste in clothes of late, on Fridays, and at the weekends, he still looked like the victim of an explosion at a jumble sale, where all the most colourful items of clothing just happened to have landed on him.

'You'll be fine. I've got a spare tie in my drawer,' (*of course!*), 'and you can borrow that. The courtroom's always on the cool side, so you shouldn't get overheated, and the tie and hat will lend a certain air of respectability to your appearance,' he advised, but being careful to cross his fingers under the desk as he spoke this last.

'Thanks, sir. You're a real life saver. I don't know what I'd do without you.'

Falconer had a fair idea, and it wasn't a pretty thought. And, come to think of it, a 'life-saver' in the US was a small fruit sweet. Which he, most definitely, was not, and he hoped that his sergeant had not culled this expression from the elderly American television he had obviously been devouring with great enjoyment.

'If I want to look really different, I could go to that fancy dress shop in Carsfold and buy a false moustache,' Carmichael declared, breaking the inspector's reverie. Then I could really go undercover, with this new head of mine. It would give me an air of gravitas, I think.' (*Gravitas? Carmichael? Some hopes!*)

'It would give you an air of insanity, believe you me, Carmichael. If anyone spotted a bald-headed giant wearing a stick-on moustache, they wouldn't even consider calling the police. They'd dial straight through to the men in little white coats, and have you taken away to a place of safety.'

'Do you really think so?' asked the sergeant with a perfectly serious expression on his face.

'I know so. Now, get on with your work, and don't ever again contemplate the addition of false facial hair to your appearance.' He had no doubt that Carmichael's stepsons found him vastly entertaining and great fun, but if he kept no check on his thoughts, he could be as trying as a child himself.

He held up a hand as Carmichael's mouth began to work. 'No moustaches, no beards, no sideburns. I may let you wear sunglasses as it's so bright out, but that's the limit of my tolerance. Got it?'

'Got it!'

'Good!'

'Wig?' The hopeful interrogative barely stirred the air.

'Carmichael?'

'Yes, sir?'

'Shut up!'

'Yes, sir.'

Apart from the susurration of paper, a blissful silence descended on the office, and Falconer felt himself more at peace with the world than he had felt since before last night's blood-chilling dream. There was a second, at his firm squashing of Carmichael's am-dram ambitions, when Nanny Vogel's face had threatened to swim up at him out of the mists of time, wearing an approving smile, but he dispelled it with an imaginary bulls-eye in the chops with a wet sponge, and felt that he would sleep all the easier for this mental act of mutiny.

Chapter Eight

Saturday 19th June – afternoon merges into evening

Luncheon had had a few more takers than breakfast, but the guests were still recovering from their excited excesses of the night before, and ate little. It was afternoon that really revived them, and they arrived in a positive rush, when Jefferson rang the dressing bell as a cue for them to collect their costumes for the forthcoming evening.

At his word, the billiards room filled with eager figures, anxious that they should be the most peacock-bright character in the drama they were about to perform, and little squabbles broke out here and there, as to who had reserved which mask, whose was the powdered wig decorated with pearls, and to whom the fabulous embroidered waistcoat belonged. There was a small tussle over the ownership of a rich purple velvet creation with a plunging neckline and some exquisite lace, but no actual punches were thrown, and Teddy Newberry emerged triumphant, Aylsa Arkwright retiring from the squabble with an ill grace and a slightly scratched hand.

Grammaticus could hardly believe his eyes. Although their enthusiasm for the event was unquestionable, their behaviour was not of the refined sort he had imagined. This smacked more of the playground than a grand ball in a fine hotel in Venice, and he hoped they would moderate their moods for the dinner itself. The last thing he wanted was a food fight in his beautiful dining room. The silk wall-hangings alone had cost a small fortune, and he feared that it might prove impossible to remove the bright colour of an Italian tomato sauce, if flung indiscriminately by an over-excited diner.

There was no way he could afford to replace that on a regular basis, and he didn't relish the thought of having to corner a miscreant and insisting that they paid for it, as his insurance company expected his guests to behave like grown-ups.

But after the first few hectic, almost hysterical minutes, the babble died down, and people began to wait, not without a certain amount of impatience, for their wigs to be combed, powdered, and dressed, and for last minute brushings to remove microscopic particles of dust from the fabrics of the costumes. The exodus was begun after about twenty minutes, by the Arkwrights, as Enoch had been the most reserved in his choice of garments, and Aylsa was still sulking a bit from having lost her bid for the purple, but not too upset to be compensated by the offer of a rich lamé gown that, in reality, suited her colouring better, and enriched the tint of her dull, beige curls.

A slight hiatus occurred during dressing, when Dwayne Mortte reported that Chef had eaten all the Parma ham, and there was none left for the meal, but Mrs Ironmonger swiftly cut his off at the knees, with the information that she had feared that the beastly little foreigner would not be able to resist the temptation, and had removed a sufficient amount to the small refrigerator in her room on the top floor for safe-keeping.

'The man is a glutton, Mr Grammaticus. I've seen him in there, stuffing choice mouthfuls down his throat and hoping that no one will notice. Anything toothsome and not nailed down finds its way down that revolting character's gullet, and he'll cost you a fortune if you don't curb his appetite somehow, or organise an adequate system of stock-taking for the comestibles.'

Jefferson heard the good sense of her suggestion, but was slightly miffed that she should criticise any aspect of his running of the hotel. His nod of agreement was, therefore, somewhat cold, as he departed for the library to see that Steve Grieve had set up the bar, and had sufficient Bellinis made in advance, for what he optimistically expected to be an onrush of takers.

Sneakily, on his part he believed, the peachy potions were the only 'inclusive' cocktail for today, as today was the main event, as far as participation was concerned, and any other concoctions – side-cars and white ladies came to mind – would be added to the guests' bills at the end of their stay. This lot didn't appear to have any loyalty to what they threw down their necks, and he confidently expected them all to opt for the freebie.

On the dot of the cocktail hour, a babbling stream of rainbow hues began its descent of the grand staircase, the chattering heads oblivious of their surroundings, as they flaunted their silken and velveteen grandeur to each other, and Jefferson took advantage of their lack of attention to anything other than themselves and each other, to snap a few photographs on his mobile phone, from his position, unnoticed in the office doorway.

For this first weekend, he had only been able to use shots of the staff, posed in their glad-rags, for publicity. A few discreet shots of his guests in Carnevale costume would do much to enhance his brochures and advertisements, and he was aware of an opportunity, almost passed over in its obviousness.

A posed shot of boating on the river, or the taking of afternoon tea on the lawn was perfectly acceptable, but to capture this crew in their masks and wigs, in full fig, was a licence to print money, so long as he made sure that his camera did not dwell on any excesses that the evening might produce. As individuals they were as anonymous as shop window mannequins, due to the full-face masks, and even the most commercially sharp of them could not hope to profit from the exercise.

A quick trip up to his room saw him arrayed in his outrageous red and white outfit, a mask over his face showing only his eyes. Glancing in a mirror, he realised that even his own mother would not have recognised him, and that he looked positively terrifying. That should get them talking, and then when they caught sight of the Freemans in their costumes … That should give them a real turn: something unforgettable to pass on to their friends and colleagues. Free publicity was worth every penny he never spent on it.

Standing around in the library, the dozen or so souls gathered made sufficient noise for four times that number, and he noticed, from his place of concealment just outside the library door, that the consumption of Bellinis was slower than on the evening before. That was as expected, as he was sure that they had learnt that dulling the senses too early in the proceedings would blunt their enjoyment of the entertainment to come, and were thus moderating the flow of alcohol to their brains.

And that was all to the good, for with a little relaxation, they should give of their utmost in the acting of their characters, and then catch up with after-dinner dinks when they felt they could relax. This was also a plus point, as he realised that if the hotel offered enough inclusive drinks – the components of which he got at a steal of a discount – then the real, local costs in food for breakfast and lunch, would be diminished, showing a concrete saving on outgoings.

Making a sudden entrance with a booming 'Good evening, ladies and gentlemen', there was an initial second or two of silence, as the stunned guests looked on what had appeared in their midst. Then a couple of the ladies shrieked in surprise, and a nervous laugh arose from the men, to cover up the shock they had felt when the figure had appeared amongst them. It had seemed, to one or two of them, at least, that the Devil himself had joined the feast, and their nerves, already heightened with excitement, were now taut as wire.

Taking a quick, gratified look round at the surprise and consternation his outfit had caused, then rubbing his hands together in a moment of almost Dickensian glee, he ushered his guests through to the dining room, checking a handy unnoticeable pocket for the little spiel he needed to deliver, before he could launch the good ship 'Murder/Mystery

Weekend' on the high seas of his commercial ambitions. Percy, at the very least, would be glad to get things underway, as she had been squawking like a demented chicken since they had assembled, her nerves, as the author of the drama, clearly getting the better of her. When everyone was settled into their places, and a certain amount of leeway had been allowed for them to get used to the sheer bulk of some of the costumes, he cleared his throat noisily, pulled his pre-prandial script from the aforesaid concealed pocket, and began to read in his best courtroom voice.

'Ladies and gentleman, I beg your attention please, for tonight's inaugural event. Allow me to set the scene for the forthcoming entertainment. As I informed you yesterday, you are at a grand ball in Venice during Carnevale. You are all moneyed figures, known to European society, and have been allotted a private dining room at this function, so that you may eat without interruption from the hoi polloi.'

Smug grins from several of the diners appeared at the thought of being a VIP, and he knew that soon he would have them eating out of his hand. 'During the meal, a member of staff goes unaccountably missing, and a search for him will discover him dead. That, ladies and gentlemen, is my unpleasant task for the evening.' A chorus of 'Aaah!' went round the table in mock sympathy, as he went on, 'He is, in fact, a career criminal of mongrel origins called Willie Nickett.' A small titter of laughter greeted the name, and he continued with enthusiasm.

'Beside your plates you will find details of your own characters, pages only to be turned at a given written or spoken instruction. Through this, you will learn more about your own back story, with details you can reveal at will, and others, that you may conceal, unless directly asked about.

'As an efficient tool for opening the curtains on our performance, I shall now read a list of names and nationalities for the benefit of you all, but at this point, only you know who you are.' And he read:

'Gathered in the private dining room at the fateful dinner

are Albert de Pub Boer, a South African gem dealer, and his wife, Zelda.' A small nod of appreciation was exchanged between Enoch and Aylsa Arkwright, and Jefferson realised that it would not be long before everyone had, probably unconsciously, given away who they were.

'Also present are Herr Doktor Klaus Heraus, a well-renowned German psychiatrist who denigrates marriage, and his rather racy girlfriend, Fraulein Inge Gefinger-Flex.' At this second announcement, Lew and Sue Veede both smiled, confirming his opinion of their lack of guile.

'Also in attendance are Jean-Luc Plume de Ma-Tante, a French aristocratic amateur sleuth, and his wife Emmanuelle.' Fruity Newberry's head came up with a self-important jerk, and the sexual undertones of his wife's name caused Teddy to indulge in a very small blush.

There were a couple of wolf-whistles at the announcement of the latter name from the no-longer-young gentlemen present, who remembered a film from their past that, perhaps, they should not have indicated that they had seen, but it was all grist to the mill for the success of the diners' acting, if there were already character traits established.

'Also seated at the table are a Dutch couple, Peter van der Skiddink and his wife Yolande, about whose activities a curtain shall be drawn.' This was, actually, a red herring, as these were padding parts designed for Percy and Lloyd, so that they could remain in the thick of things, and assess how the off-the-cuff drama worked, but even they could not suppress a little movement of the body, to indicate that they had been allotted these parts.

Bradley and Fudge Baddeley's ears now pricked up as Jefferson smiled, and intoned. 'The private dining also admits to the pleasure of the company, all the way from the US of A, of Mr Seymour Skinflicks, and his luscious actress wife, Miss Miracle Belledame.

'And finally, tonight we are also graced with the company of the famous Italian crime writer, Gianni al Forno, and his beautiful, dark-eyed wife, Florentine. I give you, ladies and gentleman, the cast for tonight's performance of *Death of a Footman*.' This appeared to be right up Mark and Madge Berkeley-Lewis' street, and brought forth approving little smiles.

'Between courses you will have full access to the ground floor of the hotel to conduct your investigations, and when you are re-seated, I shall apprise you of any updates on the situation, or new pieces of information that you might like to take into account. For this evening – for one evening only, ladies and gentlemen – I am your host; the American manager of your Venetian hotel, Willard Hamilton-Goldfish III, and my only *raison d'etre* is the comfort of the esteemed guests in my establishment. Please feel free to avail yourself of my services throughout the course of the evening.'

There was an enthusiastic round of applause as he finished his little pep talk, and Jefferson realised that he had landed them, hook, line, and sinker. They already believed in their characters and, the mood being thus propitiously set, he announced the service of the first course. A gasp rose from the assembled company as the Freeman brothers entered with the food, the sinister masks of their jester's outfits leering ominously in the soft light from the chandelier. They really did look intimidating, when costume was coupled with height, thought Jefferson, as he surveyed the shocked faces of the ladies present. That one of them should be the victim, and not the murderer, was obviously a great relief, and their appearance had made the stage set seem even more real. These were alien creatures from a foreign land, and had been adroitly presented as such to the players, and gave every appearance of being allied to the brooding red devil who had announced himself as the fictional hotel's manager.

The only negative comment came from Enoch Arkwright, who hissed a little too loudly for comfort in his wife's ear, 'Glad to see they've got rid of that darkie couple and got in a couple of good old English lads. You know how I feel about darkies.' Aylsa did, and she knew why he felt as he did, but she ignored him; in fact she snubbed him, thoroughly

97

embarrassed that he could utter such words in front of relative strangers, and turning to the diner on her right, commented on the general impression made by the entrance of the two, impressively tall, disguised figures.

As for the masks of the diners, although fantastic in their air of the surreal, these had been removed to imbibe when they had gathered in the library, and at the moment were discarded beside their place settings, to be ignored until the prowling around, and the interrogations to be carried out, after the murder had been committed.

In the kitchen, Chef shooed Dwayne Mortte outside for a cigarette, so that he could gather his wits for the next offering to the dining room, and let his eyes roam around his little kingdom. Everything was as it should be, with the exception of an unidentified object on the kitchen table which proved, on closer examination, to be just over half of a small, uneaten quiche, and if Chef wasn't mistaken, there were chanterelle mushrooms just under its golden surface.

Ah, yes, someone must have put it down here unfinished, rather than eating it in the staff room. And he did adore chanterelles so much. Surely, he thought, the natural gluttony that had dictated his adult bulk asserting itself in the form of undeniable temptation, they would not miss it. He could tell them that he had thrown it in the 'poobell' (*rubbish bin*), as its origin was unknown. His hand stretched out. His fingers grasped. His mouth opened in greedy anticipation. No one would ever know. With an almost sexual pleasure, and the phrase, 'Oh, Ah cannot reseest you, mah leetle treasure,' his teeth bit into the soft, yielding surface of the enticing morsel.

DI Falconer had had a longer day at the office than he had anticipated, and was home much later than anticipated. He had planned to go to a little bistro he knew that served excellent French food, but if he didn't get a move on, he would not arrive in time to order, and he had nothing in particular in the house for his supper, having planned to pick up a few groceries on the morrow. After a day drowning in paper, he looked forward to nothing more than a well-cooked morsel or two, and an early night with his book, in the hope that the scenario enacted in the novel he was currently reading would oust all thoughts of Nanny Vogel, and give him a less hectic night than he had enjoyed (*not!*) the night before.

He turned the key in the lock of his front door, and was surprised when no furry little form arrived to greet him. At least one of his three cats, Mycroft, Ruby, and Tar Baby, usually made the effort, but this evening there was a disquieting silence and lack of movement that stirred him uneasily. There was something afoot, if his detective instincts were not at fault.

Slowly, he entered the house, his first thoughts being that the cats had fled because of intruders, but one slightly nervous peek round the sitting room door soon dispelled this myth. No human form had defiled his castle, but nonetheless, his desk and the carpet surrounding it were strewn with what appeared to be the aftermath of a snow storm; a positive haunting of more pieces of paper, this time in minute form.

Three guilty figures had been startled into immobility by his cautious approach to the room, and three feline faces looked alarm at him, at this unexpected discovery, and his small cry of surprise suddenly galvanised them into life, as they fled, a trio caught red-pawed, to try to utilise the cat-flap all at the same time, in a squawking bunch of guilt and panic.

The camel's back snapped with this final straw – first 'Kojak' Carmichael, then the endless reports and figures that had delayed him so unexpectedly. He'd never get out now, if he had to clear all this mess up, and what was it the little sods had shredded? He was distracted enough by this unexpected turn of events, to have forgotten exactly what he had left out on his desk the night before, and approached it now cautiously, bending down to retrieve a few scraps of whatever it was, and hoping it was not something irreplaceable.

It was, more or less. 'You little feline buggers!' he yelled at the top of his voice, as he identified a translation into

English that he had struggled with for hours the night before, in his eagerness to discover some sense the mysteries of the plot of a book called 'I Fonnissa', available only in its original language of Greek. He'd sweated buckets as he had ploughed through its turgid prose, wrestling with the untrustworthy and unreliable timeline that had allowed young characters to go out for something, only to return shortly thereafter, many years older, and others to be asked to fetch a loaf of bread from the bakery, never to be seen again, their presence un-noted in the text.

He had devoted hours with his dictionaries and verb books, to unlock a particularly knotty few pages of almost incomprehensible plot, and now his work lay in ruins, and he had not had time to commit it to his computer translation, so involved had he become, and now it had all been for nothing. Little of the actual events in the story were in his memory, because the use of language had been so difficult, the errors in chronology so mystifying, and now he'd have to go back and do it all over again. He was absolutely incandescent with rage.

It was nearly an hour before the detritus of his blood and sweat, if not actual tears, had been cleared away to his own fastidious satisfaction, and he knew that his fridge, like Old Mother Hubbard's cupboard, was bare. It was definitely too late to dine out not, and he'd have to scrabble around in his small freezer to see if there was anything he could throw together, for his evening sustenance.

He didn't even, at the moment, possess a can of his guilty secret, baked beans, and he knew that his bottle of brown sauce had been jettisoned the previous week, to land in tinkling obscurity in his recycling bin. So hungry was he now, that he would even have considered retrieving this receptacle and swilling its inside with a little water to extract the last scrapings of sauce from it, had he at least had haricots in tomato sauce. How shameful!

His freezer was almost as empty as his fridge, its contents consisting mostly of tiny spicules of ice where he had not defrosted it for so long. At the bottom, however, nestling under a pile of snow-like particles, a small bag of oven chips and a lone packet of fish fingers stared balefully up at him, and he remembered now when and why he had purchased them.

In the not-too-distant past, he had been horrified to espy Carmichael, *en famille*, arrive outside his property, on what looked to be a jolly little jaunt to 'cheer up' the boss, who had no one around him to call his own. Falconer, not in the least unhappy in his own company, and being thrown into a blind panic, at the thought of all the uninhibited company intent on descending upon his peaceful tidy home, had taken refuge under the baby grand piano, then felt a little shamefaced at his inhospitality, when the coast was clear. On his next shopping expedition, he had picked up these items of supposed food, should the event recur, and had vowed to welcome them in, and offer the boys something to eat that they wouldn't find too far removed from what was considered child-friendly food.

And here he was, hoist by his own petard, and with no option but to eat the damned things himself. Hastily mixing a little tomato paste with some red wine vinegar to serve as a sauce to disguise the lack of taste, he put his oven on to heat, and chewed moodily on an out-of-date cereal bar he had discovered in a wall cupboard, while in search of his beloved, but previously consumed, baked beans.

At The Manse, the meal was just getting into full swing, as Alison Meercroft finished the tidying and gathering of discarded items that had resulted from the scrum for costumes, before cocktails. There had been wigs to re-comb, dresses to pick up from the floor and pack away, and various other accoutrements of fancy dress to return to their packing boxes.

Although she would not collect anything from tonight until the next day, she needed to return to her shop and make a formal inventory of all that had been borrowed, to ascertain that everything was accounted for in the morning, when she would return to collect what was currently in use. This was a first for her, as well as for the hotel, and she wanted nothing left to chance, that may lead to disagreement between her and the management.

Snapping the last box closed, she looked up to see her assistant Céline re-enter the room, and rounded upon her in displeasure. 'Where the hell have you been for the last half an hour? You know damned well that I took you on to help with this extra business, and on the very first full night, you swan off somewhere without a word to me, and then don't come back until I've done all the work myself. If you want to keep this job, my lady, you'd better be a bit more use than you've been, this evening. There are plenty of other people out there who would give their eye teeth to have regular employment, and it's not exactly a dirty or arduous job, either.'

'Ah 'ave not been gone that long,' stated Céline with an arrogant curl of her lip. 'Ah just neeped out for a leetle ceegarette and – 'ow you say? – to make *pipi*.'

'You *have* been gone that long, my lady, and there's no use denying it, because I looked at my watch just after you left. I don't mind you slipping off to the ladies' for a couple of minutes, but you must smoke your cigarettes in your own time in future, and not mine. You took enough time to smoke a whole packet of cigarettes, and never mind the pee-pee, you could have fitted in a *caca* as well. There's no point in me keeping a dog and barking myself, now is there?'

'What eez zees dog you talk of? Ah 'ave no dog. Where eez dog?'

What an impenetrable, buggeringly infuriating barrier language was, and how exasperating it was, not to be able to express one's anger and disapproval in an effective way. With a sigh, Alison shook her head in despair, and briefly envisaged advertising and interviewing for another assistant. No, definitely not something she wanted to contemplate right at this moment. She'd have to let it go this time, and consider that, if anything like this happened in future, then the girl would be on a final warning, and then it would be a case of 'three strikes and you're out'. She had seemed so sensible and practical when she had started working in the shop, but her performance here, had been very lack lustre and slapdash, and she simply wouldn't tolerate it. The girl's brain seemed to be on another planet, and that was no use to man nor beast,

'Ah am desolated, Madame Aleeson. Ah theenk Ah am much surprised by ze elegance of zis place. Eet is lahk a leetle Versailles, and mah eyes were dazzled.' Céline had always been good at flannel, and she employed it shamelessly now to get her out of her boss' bad books.

'Never mind, Céline,' Alison replied, comprehending that there really was no point in being cross after the event. She should have gone to look for her after five minutes, but what was done was done. And then suddenly realising that, fingers crossed, she could be on to a nice little earner here, if her costumes went down well. 'Come on, let's get this stuff packed up and back to the shop, before it gets too late. Mind, I want you here at ten o'clock on the dot tomorrow, and no shirking off for a crafty puff. Understood?'

'*Oui*, Madame Aleeson.'

The first course was nearly finished, and, apart from a rather dodgy moment when Enoch Arkwright, aka Albert de Pub Boer, had asked dear old Jean-Luc Plume de Ma-Tante if he would pass the 'syrup', conversation was becoming lively. While keeping an eye on his guests gastronomic and vinous needs, Jefferson caught brief phrases of conversation.

'... haven't a clue what a South African accent sounds like. I don't want anything to do with being a foreigner, and that's that.'

''Ow are you, mah leetle cabbage? Wah don' you 'ave anozzer leetle dreenk?'

'... I'm going to settle this matter once and for all.'

'I don't see why I have to be a mucky filmmaker. How does that work? Old Wiggy would have been more suited to the part.'

'... and now I'm marking your c ...'

'... and at least someone has cast me as a dark-eyed beauty, whereas you ...'

'I don't understand why you've got a down on foreigners. What have they ever done to you?'

'... so what exactly do you do, Mr van der Skidding?'

'You know why. It was the new site. Bloody little upstart and his sodding ecology.'

'I don't want to see any more of these silly games. I will not be taunted.'

'Oh, Monsieur Plume de Ma-Tante, how naughty you are!'

'I used to sing in a night club, where I met my aristocratic husband. Sorry I can't do an accent. It always lapses into Welsh, and I feel a right lemon.'

Attempts at foreign accents, with various levels of success, glided serenely in and out of the general conversation, like swans passing back and forth under a bridge, and Jefferson was incapable of sorting out the real life conversation, from that of the assumed characters, but for now, he wasn't really interested. The flow of wine and the atmosphere were his priorities.

Apart from the enthusiastic chatter, the guests bobbed in and out of the dining room, their bladders obviously excited by a combination of the alcohol, and anticipation of the fun of the charade. A surprising number of them also smoked, and had not been provided for inside the hotel, and throughout the course, there were usually one or two of the assembled absent on various missions. Jefferson was now viewing his guests with the fondness of an old uncle, and he noticed an air of excitement about Lloyd, Percy's husband. Now, why was that?

Of course: he and Percy were playing dud characters, and it had not been revealed that Peter van der Skiddink was, in fact, a drugs dealer, a fact that would remain concealed unless the hunt was in danger of catching its quarry with undue swiftness. He was looking forward to his minute in the limelight; that was all. They had decided to suppress this information for emergency use, for no red herring should smell suspiciously strong, and this information was only to be announced in the imminence of the failure of the enterprise to take its time, in wending its way to a satisfactory conclusion, over coffee and liqueurs.

Jefferson also became aware that Fruity and Teddy Newberry were not entirely at ease, as demonstrated by the beads of sweat that were rolling down Fruity's forehead, and a slight squirming by his wife. For a wild moment, he considered the thought that Perfect Cadence may have deposited a few 'little friends' on her trespassing trips through the rooms of the hotel, but enlightenment dawned when Fruity removed a handkerchief from his sleeve – good old-fashioned lad that he was – and mopped his brow.

Of course! The silly, vain old sod was still wearing his toupee – probably just in case he got lucky – and Teddy had that inward-looking expression on her face that declared that she would have to seek out the ladies' room to 'powder her nose'. She'd already excused herself once, but now looked like she had rather more serious business to conduct.

Jefferson's body stiffened with anxiety. Were there sufficient air fresheners in the powder room? A delicate subject, he realised, but a very necessary one, given the workings of some people's insides. Of course there were! He remembered putting them in himself just yesterday morning, and trying them to see that they all worked. What a worry-guts he was this evening, but it was only to be expected, so much hung on its success or failure.

Returning his attention to the table, he noticed that Fruity was first to his feet, claiming that he needed to fetch something from his room, but in reality to shed something that was causing him the greatest of discomfort, and threatening to destroy his enjoyment of this expensive little adventure.

Jerome Freeman had preceded him from the room, in plenty of time to arrange himself in comfort in the billiards room, in his role of victim, and the slight hiatus in the proceedings could easily be coped with by his twin. After the murder, he was to reappear in his usual livery, to represent a spare member of staff, summoned at the last minute to help out. At this leave taking, Beatrix Ironmonger also sought permission to leave the dining room for a short rest, before she was needed to be on her feet again, during the service of coffee.

As she was the senior member of staff, and had worked like a slave to prepare everything, Jefferson did not feel he could deprive her of this slender opportunity to put her feet up and refresh herself before fresh labours. And after all, he still had the comforting presence of Jocelyn – no, it was Jerome who had stayed. They really were so alike that, even after all these years of friendship, he rarely identified each from the other correctly. Well, one of them was here, and that was all that mattered. He could hardly ask him to show him his birthmark, here in the dining room, in front of all these people, could he?

He had a pair of hands at his disposal, and the other twin, whichever that was, would know exactly where and how the body should be presented, and if his watch did not deceived him, he would have to get a move on, with either the discovery of the body, or the service of the main course. Time was slipping by, and it may prove necessary to alter the ordering of the planned events. Really, smokers did so much to delay and distract, with their constant absences.

Teddy Newberry considered her husband's desertion of the table with satisfaction, and rose to her feet to acquaint everyone with the information that she needed to go fix her make-up, as good a euphemism as any to use, when she was really just busting for a wee, and didn't give diddly squat at the moment what condition her face was in, as long as she could relieve the pressure in her bladder.

As Jefferson surfaced from his fresh reverie and wondered what was holding up the main course – he'd have to nip through to the kitchen to see what the hold-up was – Sue

Veede, in the guise of the secret-drinking and enigmatic Fraulein Inge Gefinger-Flex, saw this as an opportunity and rose too, announcing her intention of checking her appearance, leading Jefferson to wonder why women always retired to mark their territory in pairs, but he didn't realise how on the button he was when he phrased this in his head.

The two women were, indeed, off to mark their territory – or not, as the case may be. At this unexpected company, Teddy was determined to prove that Fruity was hers to do with what she would, and was not laid out on a market counter for anyone else to poke and pry over. He was not only not for sale, he wasn't even for hire. Fruity was hers, and she was determined that he would stay that way. She'd noticed a few furtive little glances, and she knew her bird – silly, vain old goose that he was.

Sue Veede had exactly the same thing to impress upon the wife of someone who had unashamedly flirted with her, and whatever her intentions, she had to impress her lack of guile and complicity on her rival for Fruity's attractive old bones. In her eyes, he definitely had SA, and she would have been devastated to learn that Jefferson thought the man an unbearably pushy tit. She'd have to 'big up' Lew a bit, and play the disingenuous little innocent, if she wanted this particular blood-hound off her trail.

While all this feminine skulduggery was being formulated, completely unheard due to the sound of flushing cisterns and the thickness of the walls, a short but silent drama was being played out in the room next door.

The colourfully dressed figure whirled round at a sound that was barely a whisper, its face gradually taking on the look of a mask of disgust. What happened next was too foul for words, and the figure turned away to remove any traces of it. And that was the last conscious action of this player in the drama.

'N ...' The word died, unuttered, as the unnoticed implement glinted in the overhead light, then extinguished itself in a rich sunset red. There was a soft gurgle, a hiss of escaping breath, and the figure slowly drifted towards the ground, the terror on its face now replaced by disbelief, as sound and vision faded rapidly and darkness overwhelmed it. It lay prone and lifeless now, its blood puddling on the fine old Turkey carpet on which it had come to its final rest.

And we shall withdraw, lest we trespass on the territory of life's final visitor – Death. Coded message after coded message passed between the two women, as they washed their hands at the handsome Edwardian reproduction wash-hand basins, and warnings and assurances of complete lack of interest were conveyed and received, to the mutual satisfaction of both parties.

On leaving the ladies' cloakroom, which had been placed discreetly behind the staircase to the right, Teddy announced her intention to have just a peek at the facilities in the billiards room, in case they should finish early tonight, and there prove to be time for a game, while Sue was on form enough to state that she could see someone on reception, and would make enquiries about forthcoming events, as they were both having such a good time. Thus, each warned the other, once more, about territorial rights and future intentions, and they parted with claws partially unsheathed, but each feeling the undeclared winner.

Sue, in reality having no interest whatsoever in future events, disappeared back into the dining room, leaving her 'rival in lust' to go and look at a load of old balls, and was, therefore, quite unaware of the hubbub that was about to break out in the reception hall. Two internal telephones began to ring almost simultaneously, giving Chastity Chamberlain quite a start, as she was engrossed in a rollicking bodice-ripper of a novel, and then her world went completely mad, as a muted thudding was superseded by the appearance of a richly clad body at the foot of the stairs, and she was assaulted on both sides by two hysterical voices declaring that murder had been done in the hotel, and Chef had been poisoned.

Suddenly her newly minted little world and anticipated

future crumbled to dust, her face paled, and her eyes fixed on the thing that lay at the foot of the stairs, unmoving. She opened her mouth and screamed, her eyes screwed shut to banish out the sight of what lay before her and, unconsciously, she let go a stream of liquid that pattered and splashed between her legs to the floor, and gathering into a puddle of which she was completely unaware.

Troubles often came in three, like witches, and Jefferson had been caught with his pants down tonight, for Death had entered the hotel unannounced and uninvited, and stalked the building in search of his unfortunate prey, without knowledge or suspicion on the part of the ringmaster of this circus of an evening, his terrible presence escaping recognition thanks to the innocent entertainment that should have resulted in a highly successful venture.

Chapter Nine

Saturday 19th June – later that evening

The cats had crept cautiously into the house again, after their earlier fright, and it was with a sardonic smile that Harry Falconer viewed their slinking bodies. His food had tasted unusually good, so great had been his appetite, and the sudden realisation hit him that such victuals were not poison, but quite comforting, when one had had a bad day. And if it had not been for Carmichael's abortive visit in the recent past, he would never have found out what he had been missing. In fact, he thought he'd replace the items in his freezer for emergencies, get some of his baked beans for the stock cupboard, and add a bottle of tomato ketchup to his shopping list, too. After all, if a thing was worth doing, it was worth doing properly.

He was just mopping the last of his improvised tomato sauce from his plate when his phone rang. The cats gave a guilty start and fled to the kitchen, fearing that their master's attention might again be of the 'shouty' kind, and not wishing to experience the lack of dignity, for a second time that day, of being, metaphorically, in the dog house. For shame!

It was with a feeling of gratitude that he had already eaten, that Harry Falconer held the telephone to his ear, hearing unbelievable details of a double murder, and a third attempt on a life. Yes, they did get murders in banjo country, but not in such proliferation. It seemed that there were two people dead, and one awaiting the attentions of paramedics, apparently in a critical condition. And it had all gone off at that house that had been turned into a bijou snob hotel. What were they doing there? Entertaining or employing murderers?

Having made a quick call to his sergeant, merely informing him that they 'were on', he grabbed his car keys and headed for Castle Farthing. It would only take him a short distance out of his way, and he could bring Carmichael up to date with at least the bare bones as they drove.

Although it was well into the evening, the sun was only just slipping towards the horizon, and as he pulled up opposite the village green he was aware of the golden light bouncing from the lower levels of the now positively polished pate of his partner who, knowing him, had been engrossed in another abysmal episode of the elderly American cop show, and had decided to keep the look, at least for the time being. Suddenly he wished that they would screen re-runs of the Lord Peter Wimsey stories. Then, maybe, he'd get a super-sharply dressed sergeant that he would feel proud to be seen with, instead of keeping a furtive look-out for furtive mocks and sniggers.

'Get in and put your hat on, Carmichael. And I'd be grateful if you'd put that lollipop back in your pocket. We're not in the office now, and you need to make a good impression, and not give the idea that I'm part of Care in the Community, and you're my charge for the evening. You're an officer of the law – a detective – and I should be grateful if you reported for duty in that guise. Look on it as fancy dress if you will – ah, but not like your wedding, I must stress. Rather more in the role of being an undercover businessman or something similar.'

'What about that Belgian sleuth? He was always well-turned out.'

'I'll agree to that, if you promise only to do it from the neck down. I know how your mind works, and I told you earlier on about how I feel about false moustaches. That still stands!'

Carmichael sighed, as the highlight of his outfit had just been vetoed, and he sank, defeated, as far down in the seat as he could given his sheer length. 'Sherlock Holmes?' he suggested, with a note of hope in his voice.

'Without the hat,' came the answer. 'And absolutely no violin!'

'No, sir.'

Folding his arms like a teenager entering the realms of a grand sulk, the sergeant decided that he'd just have to give it some more thought.

During their journey the sun had disappeared with the suddenness that it did at this time of year, and the lights of the Boxster's headlights raked the bodies of two ambulances, parked in front of the hotel at angles that could only suggest they had been left in a hurry. Their front doors stood open to the wide, light streaming out onto the drive like golden pathways.

In silhouette, against this flood of light, stood a portly figure, wringing its hands and shaking its head in negation. This would presumably prove to be mine host, denying the explosion of circumstances that had been detonated in his establishment, and the resultant fallout that would inevitably occur in his personal bank balance.

As they exited the vehicle, Falconer was relieved to note that the crews had had the decency to switch off the red and blue flashing lights. A visual scream, he always found that they had the same effect on his eyes as did a wailing klaxon or siren on his ears. Although he had witnessed a lot in his life that was unpleasant, this particular sight always played a chilly minor key arpeggio down his spine.

In the event, it mattered little what he had witnessed in the past, in the realisation that he had some new disaster to deal with, that had great impact on those involved, either as witnesses or relatives. Carmichael also seemed similarly affected, as he ran a hand repeatedly across his uncovered head, and the glee with which he had treated their first case together had apparently mellowed as they had tackled other investigations.

Tragic events such as this must now be viewed as less of a

romp by the younger man now, and more of a catastrophe, the clearing up of which was their job, in which they were exposed to both physical and mental horrors. Blood and broken limbs may not be pretty, but neither were the thoughts of a diseased or deranged mind, and both had the quality to chill and haunt one's thoughts.

In approaching the entrance, they became aware that the figure silhouetted in the light was talking to itself, apparently unembarrassed by the fact that his voice was not moderated from that of a normal conversational volume.

'Good grief! What am I going to do? *How* did this happen? How *could* this happen? I had everything under control. Everything was planned down to the minute. If he dies in that kitchen, that'll be three of them – stone dead in my hotel. How, in the name of heaven, can there be three murderers on the loose in my first – my very first – weekend of business. What's going to happen now? I'll be ruined. I'll end up in some dreary little flat somewhere. How am I ever going to recover from this financially? Oh, help me, God. If I've never prayed to you before, I do it now. Please let this all be a nightmare. Let me wake up and find it hasn't really happened. What am I going to do? What am I going to do? What am I going to do?'

At the approach of the two policemen, he gave a physical jerk, in the act of pulling himself together, but nothing could expunge the expression of loss that he wore. He was a man, overtaken by events, and left trembling in their wake.

'Detective Inspector Falconer of Market Darley CID, and my partner Detective Sergeant Carmichael, sir. And you are?' Falconer effected the introductions and shook Jefferson Grammaticus by the hand, noting the sweaty palm and the dampness that had clotted the curls of his handsome head, the bizarre but dishevelled costume he wore, and a blood stain just above the place where the breast pocket would have been, had he been in everyday attire.. The man was clearly a mess. Whatever can have gone on here, to produce such a pathetic figure of a broken man?

Once inside the building, all three became aware of a violent retching sound, and screams of pain issuing from the kitchen door, which had been practically propped open with a fire extinguisher that had been grabbed from its wall bracket just outside the cooking area (situated there, in accordance with the recommendations of the local fire prevention officer). But disaster had struck from another quarter, in a way that could have been neither anticipated, nor provided for.

Shaking his head, as if surfacing from underwater, Jefferson pulled himself together, and took charge of the situation. 'Two dead, Inspector Falconer. One of my footmen was discovered in the billiards room, stabbed in the neck. Hell of a mess! Don't know how I'm ever going to get the stains out of that rug. Sorry! Inappropriate!

'One of my guests has, unfortunately, pitched down the stairs, and appears to have broken his neck, and it seems that Chef has been poisoned. As you can hear,' – here Jefferson winced, as he drew attention again to the unfortunate sounds emanating from the kitchen – 'he is currently holding his own, and we can only hope that he reaches the hospital in time for his stomach to be pumped, or whatever they do in cases like this. We don't even know what caused it, so I don't see how they're going to know how to treat him. But then, what do I know? I'm no medical man. And at the moment, I don't feel much like a hotelier, either.'

After a pause, he continued, mopping his forehead with a bright square of silk, which he had extracted from the sleeve of his costume with a somewhat abstracted air. 'Please forgive me. I think I must be suffering from shock. I've no idea whatsoever what I'm talking about. I'll just let you get on with your job. You'll find the bodies where I told you. I've collected the guests together in the drawing room, the staff in the library. The only people currently at large in the building are the paramedics. I hope that's all right.'

'Very responsible and forward-thinking, Mr Grammaticus. Thank you for making our task a little bit easier.' To

Carmichael, he said, 'I think we'll start with the kitchen, before moving on to the two beyond our help. Sometimes in this job, the victims take priority, simply because the living are still capable of waiting.'

In the kitchen, as they approached the tight little group of medics working furiously on the still-writhing body of Chef, inserting an intravenous line for fluids and pain relief, and administering gas and air to ease his agony while the drip-fed solution had time to take its effect, the smell hit them like a wall. Chef had evacuated from both ends of his body as the poison had taken its effect, and the fumes caused Carmichael to make a gagging noise in the back of his throat and step back a few paces.

Eventually, the now-inert form of Antoine de la Robe was loaded on to a trolley and wheeled from the room, leaving the two detectives free rein to work in the area without interruption. 'Use some evidence bags to scoop up some of that vomit from the draining board, will you, Carmichael? Oh, and mind out for that pool of liquid S-H-I-T in front of the sink. That must have happened after his first chuck-up, when he'd actually made it to the waste-disposal unit. Carmichael? Carmichael! What the hell are you doing?'

Carmichael had positioned himself at a remove from the aftermath of Chef's unfortunate experiences, and was standing with the back door open, his head completely hidden by a large plastic mixing bowl, his shoulders heaving, as if he were under the influence of an overpowering emotion. Which he was!

'Dicky   stom ... urg! ... stomach,   sir.   Can't   do vom ... yak! ... sick! ... huryagh! ... or poo. Remember our fir ... fir ... bleh! ... first case, sir?'

Falconer did have a memory of Carmichael's reaction when they had closed in on their first murderer, hunting down that person as partners for the first time – something to do with what he had eaten. He didn't wish to recall the exact details, but he did remember Carmichael demonstrating his stomach's lack of tolerance at the conclusion of the case.

'I seem to be allergic, sir. Graah! Sorry!'

'Get yourself out of here and cleaned up, and take yourself off to either the billiards room or the hall. I'll deal with things in here, and you can get a head start elsewhere. Oh, and chase up the SOCO team if you get the chance. The fresher the evidence, the better chance we have of getting the timing right. And give Dr Christmas a ring on his mobile, and make sure he's on his way with his handy little rectal thermometer. A lot's been going on here, and everything will be down to timing.'

With a final gulp and a puppy-like shake of his head, Carmichael made his exit with alacrity, pulling his mobile from his pocket as he left. Falconer, more experienced in the horrors that mankind could inflict on itself, prowled round the kitchen in solitary state, little moved by the fouls smells that pervaded it. Things would get a lot more crowded later, when the doctor and the SOCO team arrived, and he needed to make the most of what time he had before their intrusion on the scene.

In the library, the staff conferred in urgent whispers, not even noticing the restful effect that the green of the walls was supposed to induce, or the tooled green leather of many of the books, the colour-scheme enlivened, here and there, with red, green, and brown tooled spines, and all of them displayed in exquisite mahogany bookcases with leaded glass doors that softly reflected the light from the central chandelier.

All they could think of was their own skins, and they wouldn't have noticed if they had been gathered in the cellar, instead of this elegant room with its dark oak partners' desk acting as a library table, and its grand, studded leather porter's chair.

'Of course they're going to think it's one of us, even if one of us got clobbered. I can't see that pompous ass keeping his mouth shut with all this going on.'

'He wouldn't dare spill his guts.'

'Think how that would look in the tabloids.'

'He'll be desperate to keep everything he can under wraps.'

'If he talks, they'll crucify him.'

'And if he doesn't, he'll be charged with withholding information.'

'Well, if anyone can get away with that, he can.'

'Even he can't work miracles.'

'What do you mean? We're here, aren't we? That's nothing short of a miracle.'

'And now it's all over.'

'Not necessarily. I bet the smarmy old bugger could turn even this into something positive.'

'He's hardly a bleedin' magician.'

'Not a magician? He's a bleedin' wizard to have got this far.'

'But he's definitely got us by the short and curlies, hasn't he? We've just got to hope he goes for damage limitation, that's all.'

'Ooh, look who swallowed a dictionary and woke up as a professor!'

'Well, I've got nothing to hide.'

'None of us ever has, dearie. None of us ever has.'

'We've just got to stick together and cover for each other, and no one can prove any different.'

'You're right! Now, let's get our heads together and see if we can't weather this storm.'

'You mean lie?'

'If it so happens that any of us was alone at the time of the actual events, then yes, we lie.'

'Suits me.'

'Me too.'

'Where's that other Freeman brother? I thought they'd sent us all in here. Cunning bastard's probably, at this very moment, squirming to get himself off the hook, leaving us to take the fall.'

'Well, he was never one of us, was he? He only went on the staff for a laugh. Catch him having to earn an honest living, like what we're all doing.'

'Best get on with things, then. Who's going to vouch for who?'

'That should be 'whom'.'

'Yeah? And I should be the Prince of bleedin' Wales. Now, let's get plotting.'

A general murmur of agreement disturbed the dusty sleep of the books, as they began the concoction of false alibis.

As Carmichael picked his way round the body of Fruity Newberry at the foot of the stairs, Jefferson Grammaticus seized the moment to try to explain what had supposed to have happened this evening.

'It was just a game, Sergeant – a charade. My partner in business, Jerome Freeman – the body in the billiards room – good grief! That sounds like a Golden Age crime novel – was to have been the victim for our murder mystery dinner. He was supposed to go and drape himself over one of those spindly French sofas, and make out he had been knifed by one of the people at the ball. No, this is getting too complicated. I can't possibly go into Venice at a time like this!'

Carmichael was fascinated by the workings of the self-important man's mind, but was left completely in the dark about where a ball came into it. As for going to Venice at the commencement of a murder investigation, he could whistle for that. He wouldn't be allowed to leave the hotel, let alone the country, until he'd been cleared of any complicity in the matters under investigation.

'I'm sorry, Sergeant. I can't seem to take in the enormity of what has happened. It's probably simplest to say that we were playing a game of detectives, and would have to find the pretend murderer during the course of the evening.

'When I heard that the wife of the unfortunate gentleman at the foot of the stairs had taken a peek into the billiards room, and telephoned reception in a state of hysteria, I hoped at first that she was just playing her part – even though discovery of the body was to have been *my* task. I thought she was just stealing my thunder, in her eagerness to get on with the fictitious investigation.

'It was only the voice on the other telephone, and Mr Newberry lying at the bottom of the staircase, that made me realise that events had progressed far beyond my control. Even old Fruity having fallen could have been explained, considering his age, and the amount of alcohol he could put away. But that other telephone call from the kitchen, and the noise that accompanied that, finally banished all hope. At the very best, we had a well-posed fake murder victim, but on the down side, we had a yodelling Chef – I beg your pardon: that sounds very unfeeling – and a dead guest. And things didn't get any better: they just went from bad to worse.'

'So who discovered the bodies?'

Carmichael may still be in the dark as to Jefferson Grammaticus' future travel plans, but he could at least get that information straight in his head.

'It was the wife – oh, I suppose she's now a widow – of that chap that fell down the stairs who went into the billiards room. That was the body of one of my business partners, Jerome Freeman. This is a three-way venture between myself and Jocelyn and Jerome Freeman; they're twins, you know, and we've been friends since our university days.

'My housekeeper, Beatrix Ironmonger, found Chef. We were running a bit behind schedule, and I suppose she must have come down from her rest, noticed that things were a bit behind, and gone to the kitchen to hurry things along. Mr Newberry just tumbled down the staircase, frightening the living daylights out of my poor receptionist. Thank God there are tiles on the floor down here, for I doubt I'd ever get the urine stains out of a wool carpet without a great deal of trouble and expense.'

Carmichael's face was still a deathly pale from his unpleasant misadventure in the kitchen, and this fresh mention of bodily fluids turned his stomach anew. 'Excuse me. Got work to do,' he chirped in a somewhat desperate manner, and hurried off in search of his first actual corpse of the evening, determining to visit the gents before he actually had to gaze on a dead body. He didn't want another conversation on the big white telephone; not in public, anyway.

The drawing room in which the guests were confined was decorated in a somewhat unsuitable fashion, given the circumstances. The walls were a country house red, too reminiscent of blood to be comfortable, and a glass-topped display table between two of the sofas contained a collection of mourning jewellery, yet another reminder that they were in the midst of death, and violent death at that. There was at least one murderer on the loose, and no one knew when, where, or even if, he would strike again. There would be a lot of chairs wedged under the handles of locked doors tonight on the guest floor, and not much restful sleep being enjoyed.

But even with paramedics and police scuttering around the ground floor, and the play-acting that had turned to reality, some of the guests were getting restive at their unexpected incarceration. Granted, Teddy Newberry still wept, Aylsa Arkwright sitting with an arm round her, and trying to offer comfort by a steady stream of platitudes that murmured on the air like the hum of insects.

Other members of the party were in recovery from the initial shock, and beginning to realise that this was the end of their posh weekend – over before it had really begun – and wondering about the possibilities of a refund. Selfishness was several leagues ahead of fellow feeling for their host.

'Well, I hope we all get our money back.' Enoch Arkwright could not contain his anxiety at the fate of his hard-earned money disappearing like that, without full benefit to himself.

'You heartless old git!' Aylsa's quiet flow of comfort momentarily stalled, as she reacted to this display of lack of feeling on the part of her husband. 'How you can, with a grieving widow in our midst … Where's your respect for the dead?'

'Sorry, m'dear,' he muttered, looking a little embarrassed, but bristling at the criticism.

From inside the right-hand cupboard of a large and elaborate sideboard floated the voice of Percy Boyd-Carpenter. 'As the writer, I am well aware of who should have played the part of the victim, but I'm still a bit puzzled as to who exactly is dead, or whatever – with the exception of your dear, departed husband, my dear.' Her head emerged to nod in Teddy Newberry's direction, and the rest of her followed, litre bottles of spring water in each hand.

'Will someone come and give me a hand with these bottles, and put out some glasses? There are decanters too, but I rather think we should all keep as clear a head as possible. The police are going to want to interview us, and it doesn't really matter whether that happens tonight or tomorrow morning. We shall all need our wits about us if we are to help them find whoever is responsible for these outrages. Do you know, Lloyd, I quite fancy myself as an amateur sleuth, unravelling the fiendish plots that even the best brains of the police could not fathom.'

'Shouldn't do that, m'dear. Might get yourself biffed on the head for your pains, what?' advised Lloyd, taking a rather more realistic view of the situation. 'This isn't one of your stories, Percy, and it won't necessarily have a neat and tidy ending, with everyone living happily ever after. This is real life, and you'd better keep your nose out of it, if you know what's good for you.'

'Spoilsport!' retorted his wife, with a toss of her elderly head. 'Now do something useful, and help me get these drinks distributed, or we'll all die of thirst, and then the inspector really will have a sensational case on his hands. Anyway, who's dead? I never really got that straight in my mind before we were hustled in here and told to wait.'

As the elderly couple poured glasses of water and handed them around, Fiona Baddeley furnished her with the details she required. 'Apparently they found that footman who was to have played the corpse, actually dead in the billiards room, – oh, my dear, I nearly forgot. It was you, wasn't it, who found him? Teddy's dear husband, Fruity, took a most catastrophic fall down the stairs, and it seems that Chef has been poisoned.'

At the word catastrophic, Sue Veede pricked up her ears, thought for a second or two, then added her two-penn'orth. Not having paid attention to the sense of what was being discussed around her, she had caught only one syllable, and now seized on this with sudden enlightenment.

'There *was* a cat, wasn't there? When poor old Fruity tumbled down the staircase, I mean. Just before that terrible thudding noise that must have been him falling, there was a loud yowl, like you get when you tread on a cat's paw, or trip over it. I remember it distinctly, because I've been admiring that spotty grey cat that seems to live here – very pretty little animal. I wouldn't mind one of those, myself. Maybe he did tread on it, or trip over it, or something. That would explain why he fell, wouldn't it?

'And maybe the chef ate something that had gone really off, and become toxic. Or maybe he was even trying to do away with himself. I've heard him in there, you know. I'm sure we all have, and he certainly seemed to be hysterical to me.'

'And what unlikely accident is your fluffy little mind lining up for the unfortunate footman? Crossed in love? Tripped and fell on a knife on the way to open a new bottle of whisky?' asked her husband, sarcastically.

'Oh, shut up, Lew. You're always so horrid if I have an opinion.'

'I'm only being realistic. There's no use relying on false hope.'

'No, I've noticed that over the years, even if you didn't realise it.' With this cutting remark, fully understood by its recipient, a gloomy silence descended again, and Aylsa's low voice resumed its maternal hum.

The clock in the entrance hall showed twelve minutes past one before Falconer and Carmichael had taken care of what they could for the evening. 'I'm not going to keep us or the staff and guests up all night,' Falconer explained. 'I'm going to leave a few uniforms here for the duration, just to see that's there no monkey business during the night, and I've asked for the main gates to be locked as soon as we have vacated the property.

'The first should ensure that no one leaves the grounds in our absence, and the second should keep any press out tomorrow. I'll do my best to ensure that nothing is leaked tonight, to give us a freer rein tomorrow, but better safe than sorry.

'I want this place sealed up tight as a drum. I have no idea what happened tonight, but it looks like a right nest of spaghetti to me, and I want us to be the ones that have first pick at it in the morning. We'll do interviews as soon as we get out here, and compare notes at lunchtime. There should be plenty to keep us here until at least then, and probably a good deal more. Make sure your get as good a night's sleep as you can, and we'll meet here at eight-thirty.'

On the drive home, only three words were uttered in Falconer's car.

'McCloud?'

'No cowboys!'

Chapter Ten

Sunday 20th June – morning

When the two detectives arrived at the Manse the following morning, Falconer noticed what had failed to attract his attention the night before. At the bottom of the flight of stone steps to the entrance doors stood two stone lions, life-sized and magnificent, and all along the front of the house were old lichen-covered and weather-beaten marble urns and troughs, overflowing with the bright colours of summer annuals. The effect was enchanting, and for a moment he felt a stab of envy. This wasn't 'banjo country' this was definitely 'string quartet' territory. But he had things to do, and people to interview, and this sort of thinking wouldn't get him any further forward.

Inside the hotel, a hue and cry was in the process of setting its sails to the wind. (*Author's note: I do like a picturesque mixed metaphor now and again, don't you?*) In the shock and confusion of the night before, no one had noticed the absence of the remaining Freeman twin. The staff had assumed that he would be with management and the police; Jefferson, that he would be with the staff in the library, and it was only when he had not made an appearance at breakfast that Beatrix Ironmonger had been sent to rouse him from his supposed slumbers.

Getting no reply to her knocks and discreet calls, she fetched Grammaticus, who used his pass key to enter, only to find the room empty, the bed un-slept in. A quick check of the other twin's bedroom – one never knew – confirmed that neither of them had made it to their rooms the previous evening, Jerome because he had been lying dead in the billiards room, Jocelyn, for no known reason whatsoever.

A few brief enquiries revealed that he had said nothing to any of the other members of staff, and Jefferson summoned Henry Buckle the gardener to check the outbuildings specifically, and then do a rough visual search of the grounds before the police were informed. A head count of the guests would reveal whether he could possibly have made an assignation the night before, and had spent the night otherwise engaged, but it was a slim chance, and could only involve a few snatched hours in an out-of-bounds attic bedroom, due to the presence of husbands. How the mind threw out explanations and solutions when one didn't want to think the worst!

There being no call for spirituous liquors at this time of the morning, Steve Grieve was dispatched to the unused floor of the hotel, so that it could be stated, quite honestly, that every possible place of concealment had been searched.

By eight-twenty-five, there had still been no sign of the second missing footman, when a call sounded from the kitchen. 'I've got 'im 'ere with me, Mr Grammaticus. 'E were in the summerhouse, with a couple of empty wine bottles, clutching a picture of 'im with some woman or other.'

In the kitchen, a completely dishevelled figure had been propped on a kitchen chair, which was lodged against the side of the large pine table, so that it did not topple over on to the floor. 'Freeman, what the hell do you think you're playing at? Last night was our opening night, and you just ran out on me – on all of us – without a word of warning. What the hell did you think you were doing?' This last was asked as Jefferson took charge of the photograph that Henry the gardener held out to him.

'But this is his late sister-in-law, not his ex-wife.' Jefferson stared hard at the pathetic figure, whose head now drooped drunkenly towards the table top. 'What's going on, Jocelyn? Why did you go? And why were you looking at a picture of your brother's late wife?'

'Not,' was the only reply.

'Don't be daft, Jocelyn. You were caught red-handed.'

'Not,' came the reply again.

With a sigh of exasperation, Jefferson shook him by the shoulders, and asked, 'What do you mean by 'not'? What are you trying to tell us? Jocelyn! Jocelyn! Try to wake up and talk to us. This is vitally important.'

With what appeared a good deal of effort, the figure lifted its head a little and murmured, 'Not Jocelyn.'

'And what the hell is that supposed to mean? If you don't already know it, Jerome was murdered last night, and I need you to tell me anything you can remember, about anything unusual you saw or heard before …'

'Not Jocelyn,' was intoned again, but this time in a raised voice. 'Not Jocelyn,' it continued, rising in volume. 'I'm Jerome, and I'd know if I'd been murdered. What the hell are you playing at? It was only a game.'

'Jerome? But you were supposed to be the body in the billiards room. One of the guests found you, dead from a knife wound in the neck. You were carted off in an ambulance, with your death certificate all signed and sealed …'

'I don't know what in the hell you're talking about. I'm Jerome, if somebody'd only please listen to me. I felt a bender coming on, and Joss said he'd cover for me. We knew it'd be all right, because we're too alike to be caught out, even by you, without us both mooning at you.

'Joss, well he knew I sometimes got like this, and he said he could cover my serving duties and play both parts. Of course, he wasn't happy about it, but I'd already poured a quarter of a bottle of whisky straight down my throat, before he even got wind of how I was feeling. I can't go on without my wife,' he declared in a voice full of tears and self-pity, nodding towards the photograph that now sat, face up, on the table.

'I had to half-carry him back from the summerhouse. He couldn't stand up by himself. I don't think he's fit for anything, at the moment, Mr Grammaticus, except a good long sleep, get all that booze out of his system,' was Henry Buckle's opinion, at this juncture, and Jefferson could not help but agree with him.

Lifting the receiver of the internal telephone, he rang the housekeeper's room, and was fortunate enough to catch her before she came down to supervise the guests' breakfast, if that occasion were attended at all in person, by any of those staying here. Somehow, after last night, he doubted it.

'Can you come down to the kitchen and give me a hand? First, I need to tell you that it was not Jerome who was killed last night, but Jocelyn.' An audible gasp came down the phone line.

'How on earth did that happen?'

'It doesn't matter for the moment, Mrs Ironmonger. Our first priority is to get Jerome up to his room. It would seem that he has been absent all night, and is rather tired and out of sorts this morning. If you can keep an eye out for anyone leaving their room, Henry can take one arm while I take the other, and then perhaps you could find something that might take the sting out of his condition. I'm sure you understand what I mean. One of your prairie oysters usually does the trick.'

'One prairie oyster, coming right up. I'll be on guard momentarily.'

Falconer and Carmichael had rather let the search and discovery of the missing footman carry on around them, as they formed the strategy for who would interview whom that morning, only really showing an interest when it was announced that a body had been misidentified the night before, and that the death certificate had been issued to a man who had been drunk to the wide in the summerhouse when Dr Christmas had been appending his signature to the bottom of it..

'Well, I'll be darned!' exclaimed Carmichael in his best American cowboy.

'Me too,' agreed Falconer, not noticing the phraseology. 'I've never known that happen in such a straightforward case of identification before. This is a first for me, and I just hope they don't have reams of forms relating to it. I think I might have a quick word with Dr Christmas; see if we can't get this sorted without the usual half a mile of red tape that everything else seems to be tied up in.'

'Well, be careful, sir. You know what a stickler old 'Jelly' Chivers is, if he even finds a box un-ticked on a form.'

'I know, Carmichael. I'm a condemned man, but at least I've got a chance to get my humble pie in the oven before he even knows I need to bake it. Anyway, there didn't seem to be any question that it was the wrong man last night, and that can't be laid at my door. In fact, the more I examine it, the more I realise that this can't in any way be brought back to me. I was only acting on information received, as was Dr Christmas. Carmichael, you had me going there for a minute. I must learn to be less gullible. Did you do that on purpose?'

'Only a bit, sir. I knew I was wrong as soon as I spoke, but I wanted to see how worked up you'd get before you twigged.'

'Blast you, Carmichael! I used to think you had hidden shallows, but of late, I'm not so sure.'

'Is that a compliment, sir?'

'By crikey, it is! Now, if you can take statements from the staff, I'll start with our squire, and move on to the guests. Anyone left after lunch we'll divide up between us, if that's agreeable?'

'Durned right, sir.' This time Falconer did notice!

As the inspector and Jefferson Grammaticus disappeared into the hotel's office, Carmichael went in search of Steve Grieve who, not being in the bar, he finally bearded in the cellars, where he was sorting out bottles with which to restock after the run on certain drinks over the weekend.

'Bit spooky down here, don't you think?' was the sergeant's unexpected opening gambit.

'Nah! There's nothing to be feared from the dead. My grandma always told me to keep an eye on the living, and to let the dead rest in peace.'

'Good advice, but did she have anything to say about the restless spirits of the murdered?'

'You're an odd sort of chap for a detective, aren't you? What's this all about? I don't believe in any of that paranormal stuff.'

'Nor do I, really. I was just making conversation. This is a pretty grand place to find work, though, isn't it?'

'Not bad. Although I'm not too happy about all that stuff last night. Have you got anywhere, finding out who done it?'

'Not so far,' admitted Carmichael, feeling that he was establishing a definite rapport with the young man in charge of all the fancy cocktails served on the premises. As far as Carmichael was concerned, a rum and black was as far as he could see himself enjoying a cocktail, and he knew that this didn't really count. 'I'm kind of hoping that I can string bits and pieces that people remember together, to work that out. Can you remember what you were doing during, say, the first course of dinner?'

'I was in the bar, like I'm supposed to be. Mr Grammaticus said he'd call me if he needed me to do anything else, but that I'd better save myself for the after dinner rush and the clearing up. Me, I wasn't going to argue with that, now was I?'

'Suppose not. So you didn't leave the bar at all?'

'Well, yeah. 'Course I did. I wanted a smoke when I was on a break, and there's no smoking anywhere in this place.'

'So where did you go?'

'Just outside on the terrace, so I could hear if I was wanted.'

'Did anyone see you there?'

''Course not. I didn't want to be seen smoking. They might've thought I was skiving.'

'They?'

'Anyone who saw me.'

130

'But nobody did?'

'No. That's what I just said, isn't it?'

'I'm not sure. Look, can we start again? You were in the bar, then you went out for a smoke on the terrace, and nobody saw you.'

'That's dead on, so I don't think I can really help you.'

'No, I don't suppose you can. Well, thanks anyway. I'd better be getting on.'

'Before you go, Chastity – that's Chastity Chamberlain, the chambermaid – she told me that just as that bloke took a header down the stairs, she heard a cat howl, maybe like it had been tripped over. Well, the housekeeper's got a posh little grey cat that she dotes on. I wondered if maybe he could've caught his foot on the cat, and that caused his tumble.'

'Thanks for that,' said Carmichael, scribbling in his notebook. That would be a feather in his cap, if he could definitely prove that Newberry had died by misadventure, and not been helped on his way. They had taken it more or less for granted that it had been an accident, but this sounded like proof positive.

'You're welcome. Oh, and good luck!'

'Thanks again.' Carmichael realised that his questioning technique was rubbish, even if that last piece of information had been very useful. He just hadn't felt comfortable. The barman was only a few years younger than him, and he'd seemed straight enough. There'd been no guilty looks or evasions, so he thought he'd stick with what he'd got, and go back to him later on if anything came up that might implicate him. It was just that he just didn't feel comfortable having to think up the questions himself. With having to take notes as well, he'd felt like a third-rate actor asked to improvise, and the result had not been a great success.

He really had been spooked down in the 'dungeon' level of the hotel, and the grandness of the first floor had already intimidated him. He wasn't used to posh and moneyed places, and they always made him feel, somehow, inadequate, as if he should be tugging his forelock in deference, and minding his p's and q's, in case he got put in the village stocks by the gentry.

Making a conscious decision to re-establish his right to be here, he removed a small machine from his pocket – his new toy. An inkless electronic fingerprint machine – and did a lightning tour of the hotel, meeting little resistance, as each new person was fascinated with this advance in technology (with the exception, unsurprisingly, of Enoch Arkwright, who felt it breached his human rights), and delighted at not having to spend ages washing ink off their fingers afterwards.

Assuring them that someone would interview them in due course, he then headed for the kitchen. He knew there was a sous chef, because he'd seen the job title in the list of employees, and he always felt comfortable in a kitchen, whatever its size or contents. Food was food, and everyone had to eat, even film stars and the Queen. In the simple need for fuel, everyone was equal, no matter what their station in life. Even cowboys, he added, as he doffed an imaginary ten gallon hat at the bust of a lady, sitting on a pedestal just inside the entrance hall near the kitchen doors, and mouthed, 'Howdy ma'am,' as he replaced said invisible hat on his head.

In the office, Harry Falconer was still getting the lowdown on what was supposed to have happened the night before, and wondering at the ingenuity of a mind that could turn a game to its own advantage in such a way, and that's exactly what this looked like, when one examined the demise of Jocelyn Freeman. It might have been the wrong footman that paid the price, but was this by accident or design?

Had the murderer realised that Jocelyn had taken his brother's place at the last minute, or had he or she killed Jocelyn in the sure and certain knowledge, now proved to be flawed, that it was Jerome? Which of them had been the actual intended victim? And had he been chosen as the victim before or after Jerome had started pouring booze down his neck?

As for the departure from this vale of tears by Freddy Newberry, the jury was still out on whether that was an accident or by design. There had been some talk of hearing a cat, as the man had fallen to his death, but he'd have to follow up on that piece of information. If he was lucky, it would prove to be a case of an inebriated man losing his footing when a domestic animal cut across his path.

Chef's misadventure would also have to wait. On telephoning the hospital this morning, he had learned that swift intervention medically and the man's copious vomiting had left him alive, but desperately ill. He was still in the ICU and under sedation to allow his body an opportunity to recover, but there was a fair chance he would not be allowed to recover consciousness for some time, and anything he could offer them about how he might have ingested poison or who might have administered said toxin would greatly advance the investigation.

All other considerations aside, there was something he dearly wanted to know about those employed here. 'I'm puzzled Mr Grammaticus, and I wonder if you'd enlighten me. How did you manage to get staff to come out here to work? I mean, Carsfold's the nearest town, but it doesn't have any noticeable night life or entertainment. The nearest cinema's in Market Darley, and we aren't exactly blessed with good bus services in these parts. Oh, I know it's nothing to do with the investigation. I just wondered, that's all. Don't give it another thought.'

After an initial sharp glance from under his eyelashes, Grammaticus summoned up his genial 'mine host' expression and said, 'It's no secret. Each member of my staff was in need of employment when I was setting up this enterprise, and they were all existing on benefits in some quite unpleasant little bedsits and flats.

'All I did was to identify their various talents, and give them a chance to get on their feet and get on in life. Living-in would give them an ideal opportunity to build up some savings, and work towards a really good reference from a first-class establishment. I don't see that a little help along the road to those we pass on life's journey can do any harm, do you, Inspector?'

'Not at all, Mr Grammaticus. Not at all.' answered Falconer, while getting just the hint of a suspicion that there was more to this staff business than met the eye. That one sly little glance had told a totally different tale, and if he or Carmichael couldn't winkle it out of the one or other of the members of staff, he'd eat his straw hat – and without brown sauce too.

'Tell me about last night. Did you see or hear anything that may have any bearing on our investigations,' asked Falconer. 'As an hotelier, you need to have eyes and ears everywhere. Is there anything at all that you can tell me that might point me in the right direction? Let's start with your late business partner. Is there anyone here who might have wished him harm?'

'I wouldn't have thought so, but on the other hand, we all thought it was Jerome who was dead, didn't we, so are we looking for someone who had an axe to grind with Jerome, or with Jocelyn? I certainly didn't know about the change of roles, but that's not to say that someone else didn't.'

Damn! The man was perfectly correct. Was Jocelyn killed as Jocelyn, or was he killed as Jerome? He'd have to ask the man when he recovered from his night on the tiles and the shock where they were when they agreed to the switch. That was the only way they could establish whether they had been overheard or not.

'Very astute of you, Mr Grammaticus. Now, moving on to another member of your staff: was Chef well liked? Was he a popular character? Or was he temperamental, as so many of these culinary gentlemen seem to be these days?'

'Antoine was a handful, make no mistake about that, but he cooked like an angel. His food was, literally, heavenly, and we had great plans to hold residential cookery courses. I have to admit that he and Persephone Boyd-Carpenter were my two greatest assets for the future. A hotel is, no matter how

134

sumptuous, just a hotel, and excellent service is something that any discerning establishment may offer. But to have a tame author on hand to write original plots for in-house dramas and present creative writing courses, and a chef who loves food so much that he would die for it, and be willing to pass some of his secrets on to punters, was just a dream for me. I didn't see how this place could fail.

'If we added wedding packages into the mix – and I have been having talks with a wedding planner on the sly – we could just about mop up the market in this county, and possibly draw in people from all over it. I've just got to hope to get an angle on what's happened, find a way to turn it to my advantage, and make sure I'm not left dead in the water.'

Cold-hearted bugger! thought Falconer, then steered the man back to Chef. 'Is there anyone here that had fallen out with Chef? We've identified, from what he brought up, that he was poisoned by a toxic fungus – I can't remember its Latin name, but it's commonly known as the Death Cap and is very similar to a type of perfectly edible mushroom – and a search of the kitchen last night produced a small morsel of quiche that contained the same – er – ingredient. Basically, did Chef have any enemies?'

'Anyone who didn't praise his cooking to the heights, I suppose,' was the answer, then Jefferson's face clouded over, and he paused, as if in thought. 'He did say something odd. Oh, I don't think it was last night. It was probably the night before, because of all the excitement with the arrival of the costumes. Yes, it was Friday night. Someone – I can't remember who – mentioned the name of the costume company I've employed to dress the guests, and Chef said something about the name.'

'That's "DisguiserGuys", isn't it, sir?'

'That's right. Now, let me think. I've got it! He said something like, he was the one who should be in disguise, not the guests.'

'Did he say why?'

'I left just about then. I can see him, but I can't … Hang

on. He said … he said … it was something about a woman, or someone chasing him. I had no idea what he was talking about. I suppose I put it down to his usual over-dramatization of every little thing that happened, or a jilted girlfriend. I certainly didn't take it seriously. Should I have done? Is that what you're implying? Someone got at him? Someone real, and in my hotel?'

'It's too early to confirm that, sir, but I'm grateful for the information. Now, just a quick word about Mr Newberry. At the moment, we're treating his unfortunate demise as an accident, pure and simple, but I need to ask you, just for the record, whether you noticed anything about him that could have caused resentment; or maybe any signs of him knowing any of those already present here?'

'I don't think … Actually, I don't know. He was definitely a ladies' man. Yes, a terrible old flirt, and I did notice him making eyes at one of the other guests, and she returned the interest. I did think that he was just a fast worker, and how alcohol was a great breaker down of social barriers, but … I don't know what it was, about the way they behaved towards each other. I mean, I could be mistaken, but it wouldn't surprise the hell out of me if I discovered that they had already made each other's acquaintance before.

'I don't want to cast aspersions, Inspector. I'll not blacken someone's character – especially a lady's – without some proof. I probably shouldn't have said anything.'

'Don't worry, sir. Anything you say to me will be treated in the strictest confidence. If it proves to have no bearing on events, it will not be mentioned again. If, on the other hand, these signals that you seem to have picked up have a direct bearing on what happened, I should be very grateful if you would confide in me.'

And, of course, he did. There was no way he wanted to be tainted with the stain of withholding evidence. Not on top of everything else.

At this point, there was a discreet knock at the door, and Carmichael's naked head snaked round it, an apparition that caused Jefferson to visibly start. 'Good grief! Ringworm?' The words were out of his mouth before he could stop them.

'Could I have a word, sir?' asked the head, before glaring at the man behind the desk, and retorting, 'Kojak!' as if it were a curse, rather than an explanation.

Chapter Eleven

Sunday 20th June – late morning

In the various bedrooms of the hotel, conversations were taking place, and consciences were being searched, suspicions uttered.

Aylsa Arkwright was in full flow. 'Come on, Enoch; out with it. I know you've got something on your mind, and if I'm not mistaken, it's to do with that coloured gentleman who got himself killed. I know you're a bigoted old sod, but there's more to it than that, isn't there? You know something about it. Well, spit it out.'

'I don't know anything whatsoever about him getting himself killed. It was nothing to do with me.'

'That's as may be, but you know something I don't, and I want you to tell me what it is here and now, or I'll tell the police that you're hiding something.'

'I'm not hiding anything.' But he could not meet her eyes, and she suddenly declared, 'It's about that site you didn't get planning permission for, all those years ago, isn't it? It's that environmentalist chap who discovered some weird and wonderful toad, or flower, or whatever on that piece of land, isn't it?'

'Don't be silly, my dear. It's got nothing to do with that.'

'Oh yes it has! I can see it in your eyes. *That* was a coloured chap, wasn't it?'

'Look, shut up, Aylsa. It doesn't matter who it was that scuppered my plans. That's history. It's now I'm concerned about. I didn't know him. I've forgotten all about that. And so have you!'

So surprised was she by his vehemence that she stared at him in disbelief and held a handkerchief up to her mouth, as if to stop herself saying another word.

At the room diagonally opposite the pink room in which the foregoing conversation was taking place, another was underway in the white and gold room. 'I saw you with my own eyes, last night, fluttering your eyelashes at that revolting old lecher. No, don't deny it, because it's true.'

'I was only getting into character and playing along with things, Lew,' protested Sue Veede. 'I didn't mean anything by it.'

But her protests were in vain. 'So what exactly did you mean by being such a caring, loving wife when I woke up with the hangover from hell yesterday morning?'

'I was just concerned. You know you don't usually drink, and you had been going it a bit, hadn't you? You said you couldn't even remember having dinner.'

'I couldn't, then. And how convenient for you, that I should have had a bout of alcohol-induced amnesia. Know what, though?' he asked, his smile wolfish and cruel.

'What, Lew?'

'A couple of hairs of the dog last night, and the sight of you two practically drooling over each other – oh, you made me sick! – was enough to jolt a few of the old brain cells back into action. I remembered. Now, what have you got to say to that?'

'Lew, it was nothing. Nothing happened, I swear to you. I've never done anything like it before; it's just so long since I felt like a woman, and I didn't think a bit of harmless flirting was so awful. After all, we were all supposed to be acting a part, weren't we?'

'Maybe, but I've checked your mobile. Oh, only because I mistook it for my own, but it was very educational. You've got mail, my little darling. You should have checked it and deleted it, before I got the chance to look. *Now* what have you got to say for yourself, eh?'

In her staff bedroom on the top floor, Chastity Chamberlain hastily gathered together a number of small items that she had concealed in her chest of drawers and dressing table. They were not items of any high monetary value, but neither were they hers.

'You stupid cow!' she admonished herself, as she put them in a pile on the bed. 'Why do you have to go on doing it? It's not as if you needed any of this stuff, and it's not as if it'll be greatly missed. But you just have to go on doing it, don't you. Silly bitch!' This last, she whispered as she used the blade of a plundered kitchen knife to prise up a floorboard she had loosened during the first day of her stay here.

'You're going to have to stop this. You've got a real chance to get on here, and get good at something useful, and that'll be a first. A bit of time doing a really good job, and you can move away with a good reference in your pocket, and no more hassle.

'In a few years' time you might even be able to start up that little hospitality staff agency you've been thinking about – give yourself the opportunity to send other people off to do the hands-on work, and just take a cut for sitting on your bum and making a few phone calls.

'You might even get a little flat where you can live all on your own, and not have to be constantly looking over your shoulder, wondering if you've annoyed anyone enough to get yourself a clip round the ear. Come on, get in will you.' She shoved the last of her little collection into the hole, and trod on the board viciously, to make it flush with the others.

'Now, that's an end to that, my girl. And you just get rid, at the first opportunity, and keep your hands to yourself in future, otherwise you'll have no future to look forward to.' She was sure someone had seen her coming out of that last bedroom, but she'd done what she could to prevent any fallout. She just hoped that no one would discover her little peccadilloes.

In the cellar, Steve Grieve burrowed to the bottom of a pile of dust-covered empty bottles, making a small opening through several layers to the floor. As he set each bottle aside, he muttered to himself in anger at his own stupidity.

'What the hell am I going to do if one of those posh gits staying here smelled anything last night? They were in and out of that dining room like a fiddler's elbow, and I'd be willing to bet that any one of them could identify the smell of wacky baccy. God, how I had the stupid notion that it would just disappear if it were out of doors, I'll never know. It sticks around like shit to a blanket. Even going round the back, the wind seemed to be sending it round to the side terrace. It's bloody lucky that copper didn't come down here a few minutes later, or I'd be up to my eyes in 'possession of an illegal substance', and not a thing I could offer in my own defence.

'It was only the one joint. And I won't do it again, ever. I promise. How could I just forget about it the first night, then succumb the very next evening? I haven't touched the stuff since I got here weeks ago, and then I go and let myself down like that. Well, I've got to get the stuff hidden away. I don't say as I'll never do it again, but I've got to lay off, with the coppers around. I could be out on my ear. And I like doing all that stuff with the cocktail shaker. And I'm good at it. That's a first for me.

'Oh, God, give me another chance, please? I'll lay off the weed and work my socks off. I could be in a fancy cocktail bar in London, if only I play my cards right. No one will ever find it here, under this lot.'

From his waistcoat pocket he withdrew a small packet of herbal content, placed it in the hole he had burrowed for it, and started carefully to replace the bottles, trying to make as little noise as possible. You never knew who was listening, in a place like this. That copper, for instance. For a moment, Carmichael's mighty frame was conjured up in his mind's eye, and he shuddered. He'd frightened the life out of him when he turned up in the cellar. Lucky he wasn't burrowing through the empties then, or he'd really have been for it.

Up on the top floor in the room she had slept in during her settling-in and training period, Beatrix Ironmonger sat in her favourite armchair stroking Perfect Cadence, who condescended to make quiet purring noises in a bid to retain this comforting action. The housekeeper's chatelaine chain was hanging down at one side of her, slowly snaking its way down the side of the cushion, but she was unaware of this treachery on its part, and merely smiled around at all her little babies.

'Hello, my darlings. Mummy's come to talk to you again. I'm sorry I haven't been here with you much over the last couple of days, but Mummy does need a nice place to live, so she has to go and do things, so that we can all stay here in our own little world and dream together.' Her voice was soft and almost musical, not at all like her normal speaking voice.

'It's not like before, when I had to go away for a long time, or when you had to hide in cupboards and chests. We're free to do what we want to here, and I want you all to be happy. You're all so beautiful. How could anyone not love you like I do?'

At this thought, she began to scratch Perfect Cadence under the chin, an action which increased the purring to twice its previous volume. 'And you love me too, don't you?' she asked, focusing her attention on the still-living cat on her lap, the surrounding little ruglets forgotten as she enjoyed the weight and warmth of the plump little body, pressed close to hers.

In the yellow room, Lloyd Boyd-Carpenter was getting quite concerned about his wife. After her initial, fragile author's terror of her plot not 'cutting the mustard' with the guests and management, her mood had turned almost feverish with the news of actual murder being done. And then she'd had that ridiculous idea of turning detective – at her age, too!

On retiring to their room the night before, she had pulled

all the hotel note paper out of the writing rack, and commenced to scribble notes at a furious rate, ignoring her husband's pleas for an explanation. He had gone to sleep and left her still writing at about three o'clock, and here she was again, now muttering to herself as she wrote.

'You'll be pleased to know I've decided against detecting,' she informed Lloyd. 'But this could be the start of a whole new writing career for me. I could pull up my backlist, and go on to one of these electronic sites. The Crime Writer whose Creation was the Inspiration for a Real Murder. I can see the headlines now. And, oh the titles – Hotel of Death; Death Comes to Dinner; Sticky End at the Dessert Trolley; Cocktail for Death; A Canapé Too Far; A Trifling End ...'

'Whatever are you gabbling about, old girl?'

'Me! Us! A whole new career for my writing. This could be the beginning of a revival.'

'Slow down, m'dear. Best not to get too carried away, with your blood pressure.'

'Oh, damn my blood pressure. I must ring my agent.'

'But, Percy, your agent died five years ago.'

'Then I'll get another one.'

'But it's not that easy. You can't just order one on the internet. You know how long it took the first time. And it wouldn't have happened then if I hadn't put a word in for you with old Bingo.'

'Nonsense! He was just a senile old fool.'

'Who happened to work in publishing.'

'Talent shall override all obstacles.'

'More likely to be the other way round. Anyway, you're a has-been. You haven't written anything new in years; said it bored you to tears.'

'What rubbish you talk, Lloyd, dear. I feel positively charged with creative energy. What luck!'

'I say, old thing, that's a bit strong isn't it? If you crow any more, I shall almost feel that you had a hand in it somewhere.'

'Oh, you are a clever old dog! What a simply marvellous idea. I'll make a note of that before I forget it.'

With his head on one side, rather in the manner of a parrot, Lloyd began to think. 'She couldn't … She wouldn't … She hadn't … Not just for publicity? Although she had been acting a bit strangely, and been very forgetful. With an effort, he mentally pushed away the dreadful word Alzheimer's. She was just getting into one of her states. She always did when she'd cracked a plot in the olden days. He mustn't get carried away with the thought that she'd had anything whatsoever to do with what had happened last night.

Sighing in exasperation, he turned to his morning newspaper. She'd just have to blow herself out, like a storm, and then he'd be left to pick up the pieces. He'd been really pleased when she'd retired from writing, and now they were headed back there, he didn't know if he could face the endless insecurity, interspersed with the towering fits of ego that used to sweep over her. He should have put his foot down when Grammaticus approached her. Now he was on the highway to hell again, and there wasn't a single thing he could do about it until she paid her next visit to reality.

The final conversation worthy of note that morning took place, not in a bedroom, but outside the office in the entrance hall.

'Yes, Carmichael? What is it?'

'I can't do this, sir.'

'You can't do what?'

'These interviews.'

'Why ever not? You've done scores of interviews before. Why should these be any different?'

'Because I'm on my own, sir.'

'Well, you're a big grown-up boy now, Carmichael. What's the problem?'

'That I *am* on my own. We always do interviews together. You're good at the questions and catching them out, and I'm good at taking notes. I can't do both at the same time. I'm hopeless at knowing what to ask, and my notes aren't worth tuppence.'

'Notes?'

'The ones I try to do as discreetly as possible – out of eye-line – when you're asking the questions.'

'Notes!'

'Yes, sir – notes. What is it? You look kind of upset.'

'Notes, Carmichael!'

'Are you sure you're OK, sir?'

'Damn, blast, bugger, and bum! I forgot to take any blasted notes when I was in with Grammaticus. Well, just cast me as the village idiot, and you as the wise man, in this farce. You're quite right, Sergeant. I don't know where my mind was. We're a team, and we work together. I thought it didn't feel right in there, but I couldn't put my finger on it. I've had a few things on my mind the last couple of days, and I don't seem to be thinking straight.' (*Nightmares, Nanny Vogel, Mycroft, Ruby, Tar Baby, fish fingers, a most infuriatingly inaccurate book* ...)

'Oh, right, sir. Does that mean we can do things the way we usually do?'

'Darn right, cowboy. Now let's go and chase some outlaws.'

'Yes, sir!'

'But don't think I haven't noticed your bootlace tie, because I have. And this is where it stops, OK? No cowboy boots tomorrow, no shirt with metal collar ends, and definitely no – I repeat no – ride 'em cowboy hats. Do I make myself clear?'

'No ties, no collars, no hats, sir.'

'Correct!'

Good. He hadn't mentioned chunky leather belts with lots of metal studs and other manly things on them. He was in the clear, as far as that was concerned, thought Carmichael, as they headed, a partnership once more, towards the staff sitting room, to see what was afoot.

'Oh, by the way, sir, I've just been talking to that barman, and I know that this is only hearsay, but he said that the chambermaid said that she thinks Mr Newberry tripped over the housekeeper's cat, and that's why he fell downstairs.'

'That's good! We'll have to get that checked out; find out if anyone else heard it too. If we can turn hearsay into reality, then we can put that one down to an unfortunate accident – not that I didn't think it was anything else, but it is nice to be absolutely sure, isn't it?'

'Indubitably, sir,' confirmed Carmichael, forcing the inspector to do a double take of surprise at this multi-syllabic response.

Chapter Twelve

Sunday 20th June – afternoon

Jefferson, at the request of the police, had given permission for his guests to stay on at a disastrously reduced rate, to allow the investigation to proceed, and for them to be interviewed by the police. It was a request he could hardly refuse, for he was as anxious as they to discover the identity of whoever was responsible for stabbing Jocelyn Freeman and poisoning Chef. He had no idea whether this involved one or two people, and at the moment, he didn't really care. He just wanted things back to normal, whatever that was.

As he sat in his office with his head in his hands, he thought about what he had intended to do, after the guests had left at noon; the planning of the residential French cookery courses that Antoine would present; the creative writing courses that Percy would lead, inspiring with her past success and her impressive back list.

She had also promised to come up with at least five other murder mystery dinners so that he could rotate them and get full value for money out of each one, Percy only expecting a small fee for the repeat use, as long as she and Lloyd had free bed and board and their small parts to play in the dramas. As this would give him the added kudos of an author mingling with the paying guests, he had, at the moment, no objection to the idea. After all, everyone wanted to rub shoulders with someone of even minor celebrity.

But all that was out of the window for the moment, and suddenly it didn't seem to be in very good taste to be thinking of offering any more murder mystery weekends for a good while to come. Unless, of course, he could come up with an angle; a spin on what had happened to present it in a positive light. That was exactly what he needed – an angle.

For now, however, his whole world appeared to be in tatters. In fact, it had ceased to be. He could see no further than the next few hours, nor did he want to. If he couldn't find a way to treat these devastating events to his advantage, he could kiss goodbye to his investment here, and he hadn't enough capital left to provide him with the sort of genuine retirement that he had dreamed of. There had to be a loophole back to success, and if anyone could find it, he could. Lifting his head and shaking it, as if to loosen his thought processes, he set his mind to work on producing positive from negative.

Although the hotel could probably rustle up something for them to eat, the marketing had been done only to midday, and more supplies would need to be sent for to restock with fresh goods. There was also no chef, and bread and cheese would probably not be what was expected after what had come from the kitchen over the last two days, but it would just have to do, and Jefferson, deciding that action was better than moping around, steeped in self-pity, moved himself to action, no matter how mundane.

Making the decision to summon his reduced crew to set out everything they had available, picnic style, in the grounds, in an attempt to alleviate the air of desperation that sandwiches would represent in the dining room, he left the office and headed for the kitchen with a general call to arms. With the addition of fresh fruit and a couple of freshly baked sponge cakes, and the use of fine linen and china, a picnic might even suggest the air of adventure that the advent of the motor had given to *al fresco* meals in the past, and he suspected that the odd jug of Pimm's and lemonade (*not too strong, mind!*) might be well received, too.

Meanwhile, the two detectives had shut themselves in the drawing room with a 'Do not disturb' sign on the door, having refused the offer of the staff sitting room, so as not to deprive those running the place of their bolt-hole. Anyway, if they had the chance to gossip, all the better, as they might repeat it when interviewed. Someone might let something slip, and he doubted there was much loyalty between the various members of staff here. They had had little time to get to know each other, and would be looking out for their own skins first. The two men were just about to launch on an examination of what they had learnt so far when Falconer's mobile phone rang.

'When was that?' … 'Did it make sense?' … 'Did you make a note of it?' … 'Read it to me, word for word.' (*Longer pause this time*) 'And they're going to do that when?' … 'Ring me if he so much as stirs, and stay right by him. No sloping off for a cup of coffee, or a girly natter with the nurses, OK?' He hung up.

'That was PC Starr,' he informed Carmichael. 'She's been on duty by Chef's bedside, to make sure there isn't any monkey business while he's out cold, and to make a note of anything he says if he wakes up.'

'I gather that he must have said something.'

'He did, Sergeant. Give that man a cigar. He got a bit restless, about a quarter of an hour ago. Starr said it was just a jumble at first, but then he got a bit more lucid. Even though it didn't make sense to her, she had the nous to take it down, in case it made sense to anyone else.'

'So come on, sir. Shoot!'

'I said no cowboys, Carmichael.'

'Sorry, sir. Go on.'

The inspector lifted a small notepad from his lap, in which he had been scribbling, while on the phone, and read, in a surprisingly humorous French falsetto:

"No … no … not 'ere. Ah weel not do zat. Got to get 'way from Céline. She iz not 'oo she says she iz. Don' stalk me! No stalkairs! Een mah kitchen. No … no … not een mah kitchen. Must 'ide. Must 'ide."

Here, he resumed his normal speaking voice, noticing with amusement the expression on Carmichael's face. The younger man couldn't have looked more surprised if Falconer had produced a white rabbit from his jacket pocket.

'I say, sir! I didn't know you could do French.'

'It wasn't French, you doughnut,' – again, a look of disbelief at this expression from the prim and proper inspector – 'It was a French accent. And I learnt to do that at prep school. That was just how the French mistress spoke, and I got out of many a thumping by using it to amuse the bullies.'

'Not French?'

'Er, no, Sergeant.'

'But …' Carmichael still looked puzzled, and went as far to demonstrate this as to scratch his head. 'But if it wasn't …'

'What?'

'Dunno, sir. It's just that … Oh, never mind. It's gone now.'

'And good riddance to it, probably. Anyway, back to the phone call. That was all he actually said that made sense, and then, apparently, he slipped back into unconsciousness, and hasn't stirred since, although the doctors are going to withdraw the sedative this evening, so it shouldn't be too long before he can talk to us properly.'

'If he remembers anything.'

'Well, he was certainly frightened of someone, from what he said. It sounded to me as if he had a visitor to his kitchen that … What is that dreadful noise from the billiards room? It sounds like a hen party in full swing. I asked the guests to keep to the library and the dining room, if they didn't want to stay in their rooms, and heaven alone knows there are enough grounds here to satisfy a whole rambling club.

He rose from his seat as he spoke, and strode in the direction of raised female voices, drawing Carmichael in his wake in a wave of curiosity.

'Now look here, madam, I've had to literally drag you out of your flat this morning to bring you here, and the first thing you do is slope off again. Either you work for me or you don't. I'm not paying you a perfectly good wage to skive off, smoking and admiring the décor. I want those costumes collected from outside the guests' rooms as arranged, and I want them collected now. Now, are you going to do it or not?' Alison Meercroft had really lost her rag. Mademoiselle Treny seemed to have the greatest difficulty in lifting a finger to help, and she wasn't going to stand for it any more.

'*Non!*'

'What?'

'I go 'ome, so you must drive me.'

'Are you out of your mind?'

'I go 'ome now. I do not do thees job. It is not nice job.'

'You lazy little tripe-hound! How dare you put me to all the trouble I've had this morning actually getting you here and then say you're not going to do any work.'

'Good morning, ladies,' Falconer interjected, being averse to seeing a good quality carpet covered in torn out clumps of hair. 'I'm Detective Inspector Falconer of Market Darley CID, and this is my partner, Detective Sergeant Carmichael. And you are?'

It was the Englishwoman who spoke first, making it quite clear that she was the one in charge. 'I am Alison Meercroft, founder and owner of DisguiserGuys Costume Hire, and this ...' Here, she dismissed the Frenchwoman with a sneer and a flick of her wrist. 'This excuse for a human being you see before you, is my ex-employee, Céline Treny, who, I must say, is the laziest individual I have ever had the misfortune to come across.'

'Sir?'

'OK, Sergeant. Not now!'

'But, what you said ...'

With an effort to quell his sergeant's heavy hints, he raised his voice, addressing the young Frenchwoman, who stood sulkily before him, and announced, 'Céline Treny, I need you to go to police headquarters, to provide us with information on the attempted murder of Antoine de la Robe. I shall summon a car from Market Darley to take you there, where you will be asked to wait, until I am free to speak to you.'

'You are arresting me? Ah do nossing!'

'You are not being formally arrested, but failure to cooperate may result in my having to go through the formal arrest procedure. At the moment, I am merely asking you to do as I have requested.'

Even Alison Meercroft was shaken at this abrupt turn of events.

'Is that really necessary? We're not actually part of the hotel set-up. We're only here to provide the costumes and accessories, and Céline has only just started working for me – or *not*, as the case may be,' she added, with a flash of her previous ire.

'It is wholly necessary, Ms Meercroft. Something has occurred that we require Mademoiselle Treny to explain to us, and I think that would be better done at the station. I'll get a car organised now, and I want you two to stay in here together. I don't want you to leave the room without my say so, and I mean not even for the bathroom, or a sneaky cigarette. The doors opening on to the grounds were locked last night, and I have requested that they remain so. My sergeant and I will be in earshot, so stay put, and save us all a lot of unnecessary bother.'

With that, he shut his mouth with an almost audible snap, and bade Carmichael follow him back to the drawing room where, holding up his hand to keep the younger man at bay, he made a call requesting that PCs Green and Starr be sent straight to the hotel. It was necessary that he should have a female officer in attendance, and Starr had finished her spell of hospital visiting shortly after she had made her call to him, her relief being present, and just stuffing a doughnut and a coffee down his neck before he took his place beside Chef's bed.

As he replaced his mobile phone back in his inner jacket pocket, Carmichael seized his chance, and said, 'That was quick work, sir. Do you think we've got our poisoner?'

'Well, it seems a bit too much of a coincidence that her name is Céline, she's French, and she's only just started her job. Now, I don't know how common the name Céline is in France, but when we've got a Frenchman who's nearly gone to that great kitchen in the sky, muttering that same name from his hospital bed, and a Céline who was, presumably, in the building when he ingested the poison, it doesn't do to give that young lady the chance to make a bolt for it; especially in these days of unrecorded border crossings for EU residents. If it *was* her, she could have been back in *la belle France* by teatime, and us scratching our heads and looking like a right pair of idiots.'

'Way to go, sir! What's next?'

'Oh, I think we'll take a little stroll in the grounds, and join the guests for a bite of lunch. After all, we can hardly nip off to a little café or a pub from an out-of-the-way place like this, and I can see signs of a meal being set up out front. It would be a shame to waste the opportunity of a little mouthful, and we can do a bit of eavesdropping, and a bit of casual questioning while we're about it. It's a relatively small number of people, and they can hardly snub us, given the circumstances. Hungry, Carmichael?'

'Starving!'

'I just hope they've got enough,' murmured the inspector, surveying his partner's vast frame.

'What was that, sir?'

'Nothing, Sergeant.'

'Oh, I forgot to ask you earlier. Kerry says, would you like to come for your tea tonight? She doesn't like to think of you sitting down to eat with no one for company, and the boys would love to see you; and Fang and Mr Knuckles too, sir. They really took to you, the last time you visited.'

And if chewing holes in the bottoms of his trouser legs was a sign of affection, then who was Falconer to argue with him? Put that together with the facts that he still hadn't managed to get to the shops, and he wasn't particularly fond of the slacks he had grabbed this morning, and he supposed he'd better accept. It might even be fish fingers, if he was lucky!

They had eventually taken their food into the drawing room, their presence at the picnic being about as welcome as a fart in a lift, and it was while Carmichael was back outside, vacuuming up the leftovers before they could be taken back to the kitchen, that Falconer received a call from Dr Christmas.

'Here's a facer for you, old man. That dude that went a-tumbling down the stairs may have had a little help.'

'What?' Falconer's heart sank. Surely this had just been an unfortunate accident.

'We found a bit of a clue on the poor sod's right buttock.'

'Not a boot mark? Surely nobody here wears Doc Martens?'

'No, nothing that obvious. What we did find was a couple of little cuts; nothing more than puncture really, but they were fresh.'

'Somebody *bit* him on the bum?'

'Nice try, Harry! Then we could just take impressions of all the teeth, and get our man – or woman. No, I'm not quite sure what pierced the skin, but the two marks are small, clean-edged, and only about an inch apart – sorry, that was in old money – call that two to two-and-a-half centimetres. Single-edged blades, if they were blades. I've taken some photographs, so that we can look at them at a much higher magnification.'

'Oh joy! A close-up of old Mr Newberry's right buttock. I can hardly wait. But you think that someone may have used something to startle him?'

'It would certainly have done that. At the top of staircase, and caught off-balance, it would then have been the easiest thing in the world to give him a little shove, to send him on his way.'

'But I was told there was a cat's howl when he went down, and that he'd tripped over that cat the housekeeper treats like a baby. I was hoping to put it down to a simple accident.'

'You can hope as much as you like, old boy, but it won't

make it so, I'm afraid. You can put it down to Count Dracula himself fancying a nice piece of rump steak, if the fancy takes you, but the puncture wounds still stand, and that was no accident. I think you've got another murder on your hands, and that's what I shall put in my report.'

'Damn! Now I don't know whether I'm looking for one or two murderers.'

'And don't forget the jolly old poisoning. It could yet be three, and if it isn't, you've still got an 'attempted' on your hands. It looks like they hunt in packs at that place.'

'Thanks a bunch, Christmas. I curse thee. May thou suffer the indignity of haemorrhoids. And if that's not enough, may thou also have builders in.'

'Haemorrhoids I can deal with, but spare me that last. I promise to give you nothing but good news from this date forth.'

'Done!'

'You're welcome!'

As he ended the call, Carmichael returned, his mouth still full of sandwich, his jaws fighting to masticate the sheer volume contained within his mouth.

'Had enough?' asked Falconer.

The head nodded.

'Any left?'

The head shook from side to side.

'Right. Let's get back to business. That cat of yours on the stairs, when Newberry fell was, in fact, a red herring.'

With an enormous swallow and a slight bulging of the eyes as he suppressed a belch, Carmichael recovered the ability to speak, but didn't make full use of it, merely asking, 'What?' before wiping his mouth with the back of his hand.

'I'll explain later. Now, let's get off and have a little chat with the widow, see if the man had any enemies. I want to conduct the interviews in the rooms which will have become their comfort zones over the last couple of days, maybe even identify a murder weapon or two. I know it sounds like Fat Chance City, but we've got to make the effort.'

Teddy Newberry received them with dignity. Her eyes were swollen and puffy where she had wept, but overall she presented a solid front, and bade them sit down in the two armchairs which flanked a small table at the far end of the room, and after they had introduced themselves, she perched on the end of the bed, waiting to see what was expected of her.

'We're very sorry for your loss, Mrs Newberry. The suddenness of it must have been a tremendous shock.' Falconer was solicitude personified.

'That's very kind of you, but I'm not one to dwell on the negative.'

'No?'

'Not at all. I've had all night to think about what I'm going to do. Fortuitously, a friend of mine who works for a children's home offered me a job only a few days ago. Of course, I said nothing to old Fruity, because it was as a live-in house mother, and it would be tantamount to leaving the old boy, but I have been a bit browned off lately.

'Gambling is such an unreliable way of earning one's daily bread, and I'm getting a bit long in the tooth for working in a casino. I'd tried to get Fruity to understand that I wasn't getting any younger and, at my age, the possibility of not being able to pay the rent at the end of the month was a positive horror.

'I was going to speak to him this weekend. In fact, I rather think he booked the weekend because he could tell that there was something wrong, but he'd never do anything sensible, like ask me what was bothering me. He might not get the answer he wanted, then he might have to consider changing his lifestyle, and that wasn't what Fruity was about. He was a born gambler – loved the thrill of it; the adrenaline rush.

'Me, I couldn't bear it lately. I'd given up the idea of ever having children, because we led such a precarious life. One month we'd be drinking champagne and dining in the best restaurants, the next, I'd be scrabbling down the back of the sofa, just to find a few quid to buy basic foodstuffs.

158

'No, I'd definitely had enough. I wanted some stability. I wanted little ones to love and care for, and to know I wouldn't have to do a moonlight flit when the bills got too high. I've dodged many a bailiff in my time, and I can tell you, it's an overrated pastime.

'Fruity would just have gone on as he was. He was never the faithful type, and it never used to matter before, because he always came home to me, but lately I've just found his philandering boring and childish. I've always come second in our relationship, and I wasn't willing to do that any more.

'I'm sorry if this sounds harsh, with Fruity hardly cold, but I've rung my friend, and told her I'll be accepting the post. I'll move in at the end of the month, as soon as I've had the chance to clear the flat. It will be a relief to get something satisfying back into my life, and be able to call it my own for a change. I might not have had the chance to say anything to him, although, God knows, I've dropped enough hints, but I was about to give him the old heave-ho, and sail off into calmer waters for a change. Well, there! I'm glad to have got that off my chest.'

'I'll bet you are,' thought Falconer, but instead, said, 'I'm afraid we have some very grave news for you, about your husband's demise, Mrs Newberry. I'm sorry to have to tell you that he was, in all probability, murdered.'

That had shocked her. 'So, when I went into the billiards room and discovered that footman dead, someone was actually murdering my poor old Fruity? Oh, he didn't deserve that, whatever I thought of him!'

'Exactly so, Mrs Newberry. I'm afraid his death was no accident. Evidence from the post mortem shows that he received a small but startling injury, just before he lost his balance. He didn't fall by pure accident. We have reason to believe that he was helped on his way by person or persons unknown. Do you know if your husband had any enemies, or if anyone had a grudge against him?'

'Pass me some paper and I'll make a list. Oh, don't look so surprised, but don't expect it to be of any help to you either. When Fruity won, he usually won big, hence the champagne, and a lot of bookies in our area would like to have seen him move to the other end of the country. But here? In this out-of-the-way hotel?'

She paused momentarily as a thought struck her. 'Although I do believe there is someone staying here that had previously made his acquaintance. I can't be one hundred per cent sure, but I'd be willing to bet on it, and on the nose.'

They moved on, past the green and dove-grey rooms, towards the white and gold room that housed the Veedes. It seemed best to interview the guests first, as they would get restive in the very near future, and demand to be allowed to leave. The staff, provided they kept a discreet surveillance of the exits, could wait a while.

The reason they had decided on this direction, and not towards the front left hand corner of the building to the pink room, was because they could hear what sounded like an argument in full swing, between the occupants of room number six, and where there was an argument, there were bound to be things said in the heat of the moment that may have been best left unsaid and confined to silence.

'But I saw you with my own eyes. I know I couldn't remember anything yesterday morning, but as soon as I felt better, I could see what had happened. It was like a sleazy movie, right in front of my eyes, you faithless cow. And I checked your mobile.'

'How dare you interfere with my phone!'

'See! You wouldn't have reacted like that, if you were perfectly innocent.'

'I am perfectly innocent.'

'My big fat hairy arse, you are! What was all that about meeting someone in the summerhouse, when the old man was asleep then? I am supposing here that 'the old man' referred to me?'

'I don't know what you're talking about.'

'The hell you don't! There's no point in denying it. I've read your texts. Don't you understand, I've seen …'

A firm knock at the door interrupted this heated discussion, and there was a short interval of silence, before Lew slowly drew it open to greet the two detectives, his face red with anger, a vein beating a rapid tattoo in his left temple.

'What do you want?' he asked, his voice husky with suppressed emotion.

'Market Darley CID. We'd like a word with you and your wife, if that's all right with you, sir,' Falconer informed him, already pushing the door open wider, so that they could enter.

'If you mean about that footman who got murdered, you're wasting your time. We've never come into contact with any members of the staff here before in our lives, and if it's about whatever that ghastly noise from the kitchen was, you can discount that as well. Neither of us has ever set foot in that room. In fact, I'm beginning to wish neither of us had ever set foot in this bloody hotel.'

'Language, sir! Lady present!' interjected Carmichael, before he could help himself, but his remark hit home.

'I'm sorry. This weekend's been a total nightmare from start to finish, as far as I'm concerned. I never wanted to come here in the first place. It was all Sue's idea, and now here we are, mixed up in murder, and at each other's throats to boot.'

'You started it!' This was Sue Veede, who had risen from her seat at the dressing table, and seemed ready to give battle again.

'I rather think you did, my dear little trollop. I think you already knew that bewigged old lecher. In fact, if my memory serves me correctly, you were rather odd when I got back from that unleavened and sour-dough 'do'. You looked like the cat that'd got the cream, and you were all over me like a rash for the first couple of days afterwards. I think you'd been seeing that old bugger while I was away, and I, in my innocence, just thought you were glad to see me back.'

'But I was!'

'Tell that to the marines.'

Their voices had steadily risen again, and Falconer had to

161

shout to make himself heard. 'Will you two shut up and listen? I'm not here about the footman or the chef. I'm here to gather information in relation to the murder of Mr Frederick Newberry, aka Fruity, until last night, resident in this hotel.'

'Murder!' It was Lew who made this exclamation, his face draining of colour.

At exactly the same moment, Sue Veede gave a shriek and, screaming, 'You devil! You killed him! You murdering bastard!' She flew at him, kicking and punching and scratching like a she-devil.

It took both Falconer and Carmichael to pull her away from the cowering figure, now with long bloody scratches down both of his cheeks, his hair awry, and one of his eyes already beginning to swell where she had landed him a nice uppercut.

'Has that car arrived yet?' asked Falconer.

'No, sir, but I believe it's due in a very short time.'

'Where have we got that Frenchwoman stashed?'

'In the dining room now, under the eagle eye of that fearsome housekeeper, sir. Ms Meercroft had to get back to her shop to put the stock away.'

'Well, get this joker down here with them. They can both go off to the station, and they can kick their heels there until we're ready to question them.

'Get your jacket, Mr Veede.' This he addressed to Lew, who was examining his injuries in the cheval mirror. 'We want to have a little word with you about your movements last night, in relation to the fatal fall suffered by Mr Newberry.' Holding up a hand to stem the flow that threatened to pour from the injured man, he continued, 'No, sir, I'm not arresting you. I'd just like you to accompany a couple of my officers to the station to make a statement. At the moment, you're only helping us with our enquiries.'

'Mrs Veede,' he continued, 'I'd like you to remain in this room until we return to take your statement. Any refreshments you need may be ordered using the in-house telephone, and I understand every room has a bathroom or shower-room en-suite. Yes? Good. But I need you to wait here, and not communicate with anyone else before I return. Do you understand?'

'Yes.' Sue Veede now had a tiny voice, and seemed visibly to have shrunk. That she was in denial of what had just happened was evident from her face, and she looked child-like and bewildered, a mere shadow of the virago she had been just a couple of minutes before.

'I suggest you have a little lie-down, and get everything straight in your head. That way, it will be easier for us all when I question you later.'

Without a word, the woman turned and walked over to the bed, a waif-like creature with no fight left in her.

They learnt little from the Baddeleys, who were visibly upset at being present as such tragic events had unfolded, and next to nothing from the Berkeley-Lewises, except for corroboration that there had been a fair amount of flirting and inappropriately adolescent behaviour, mostly under the influence of alcohol. A bit of fortunate eavesdropping, however, and again at a fairly high volume, did add to their insight into some of the other guests.

Returning to room number one, where by logic they ought to have started, they were fortunate enough to find the door of the room very slightly ajar, and the buzz of voices issuing out on to the landing. It was the higher-pitched tones of Aylsa that first caught their attention. Stopping abruptly, and putting a finger up to his lips, Falconer effectively blocked any further movement from Carmichael and stilled his voice before it could give away their presence.

'But it wasn't him, Enoch. You might have thought it was, but it was the other one all along. You can hardly be glad he's dead if you never knew him. Don't be absurd!'

'Well, I couldn't tell them apart, and if they were twins – which they were – it doesn't really matter which one of them it was, because they were identical. Same bodies, same minds. It stands to reason that what one of them did, the other one would have done too.'

'Now you *are* being ridiculous. And you never lost anything by not getting the go-ahead. You actually found a better plot, and you went from success to success. If they had let you develop that other bit of land, you'd have been washed away in floodwater, time and again.'

'That's not the point. I will not be thwarted, and that young whatever you want to call him – seeing as you say I can't use the word 'darkie' – was an arrogant young whippersnapper who needed to be put in his place. I'd been in business for years before he came along, with his fancy degree, and his interest in lesser-spotted blue Martian toads, or whatever they were.'

'That doesn't make you right, and you know it. And it was nothing to do with his brother, and now his poor brother's dead.'

'Yes, a pity about that. Still, you can't always get it right, can you?'

'*Enoch*! You didn't, did you? You wouldn't risk everything for a petty act of revenge – not that there's anything petty about murder.'

'Of course I didn't, you silly cow. I was just saying that I'm not going to lose any sleep over it. If whoever it was got the wrong man, then the other one's suffering, and that's fine by me.'

'You spiteful old bigot. How you don't grow horns and a tail beats the hell out of me.'

'I think we'll leave them stewing a bit longer, and pounce when they're at the height of their temper. They're more likely to let something slip if they're at each other's throats. Come on. Let's have a word with our esteemed authoress before we tackle those two.' Falconer turned his gaze towards the sunshine yellow glow from room number two.

The door of this room now stood thrown back on its hinges, and a plaintive voice from inside it proclaimed its absolute intolerance of the heat of the day. A slightly deeper one suggested that she turn on the air-conditioning, and shut the window, as the insects were coming in at an alarming rate.

The first voice stated that it didn't know they even had such a facility, let alone how to use it, and this was followed by the rustle of a newspaper being set aside, and a thoroughly un-gracious offer to do it for her, then added, 'I say, Percy, old girl, you didn't have anything to do with that business last night, did you? I mean, I know you love publicity for your writing, but you wouldn't go as far as to push a man downstairs, would you?'

'Silly old Pooh! Ah, that's better. You may shut the window and door now. Lovely, lovely cold air.'

As Lloyd tottered over to pull the door closed, he found Falconer and Carmichael waiting just outside it, both desperately trying to look as if they'd just arrived there, but Lloyd was too much of an innocent for guile, and took their presence there at face value.

'Good afternoon, gentlemen. You must be the detectives who cast such a pall over the first part of luncheon.'

'Do come in,' trilled a voice from inside the room. 'You'll never guess what my silly old husband asked me earlier on? He thinks I've committed murder to publicise my triumphant re-launch into crime fiction. What a hoot, isn't it?'

'Good afternoon, Mrs Boyd-Carpenter. And did you? Commit murder, that is?' There was no point in beating around the bush when she had raised the subject herself.

'Of course I didn't, you silly young man. But if I'd thought about it a bit more, I could've staged a murder that even old Grammaticus didn't know about, just to add a degree of tension and verisimilitude. I could've talked to that nice woman whose husband went tumbling down the stairs. She looked like she might be up for a bit of jiggery-pokery. Still, it's something to consider for the next time, isn't it.'

'If there is a next time, madam.'

'I meant for another murder mystery weekend. Oh, there must be!' Suddenly Percy looked desperate. 'This is the start of a whole new career for me. There's a whole generation out there who know nothing of my books. I must have the opportunity to publicise myself. I've got a huge back catalogue, and with all of this, I could be a bestseller.'

'You'll no doubt make enough from what went on here this weekend to keep you in sales for the rest of your life, but I certainly couldn't guarantee there being another murder mystery weekend here,' Falconer said.

'Well, so long as my books are put back into print, I can probably find another venue if I want to continue. I've thought of turning this one into a dinner party game. There's money to be made out there, young man, and I intend to get in on the action.'

How selfish people were; how egotistical and self-centred. Two people lay dead, and another at death's door, and all she could think of was money. She spared no thought for those who had had their lives cut short, nor for those they had left behind. It was 'How does this affect *me*?' It was, however, an ideal opportunity to put the wind up the old bat, and it was with a suppressed feeling of glee that he issued his warning.

'I should keep to your room, if I were you, madam. We mustn't lose sight of the fact that there's someone dangerous out there, someone who is willing to resort to murder, and that a third victim's life is still hanging in the balance. Don't let anyone in unless you trust them absolutely, and keep your door locked at all times. We wouldn't want you to be the next corpse on our hands, would we, Carmichael?'

'No, sir. Indeed not!' Carmichael had taken the baton, and was now running with it. 'It could be anyone.' At this comment, Lloyd cast a sideways glance at his wife, then shook his head like a dog emerging from its bath, as the sergeant continued, 'It could be one murderer, or two, or even three guilty parties. Best keep your guard up, and stay where you're safe.'

Falconer was satisfied to note that as they left the couple in their room they both had worried expressions on their faces.

The shouting had diminished to an angry muttering in room one, and Falconer reckoned it was time that they made their presence known to its occupants.

A sharp rat-a-tat-tat on the door produced the empurpled face of Enoch Arkwright, with the charmless greeting, 'It's the pigs, Aylsa. No offence meant, I'm sure. Just a turn of phrase, like. You'd better come in, I suppose.'

'Thank you very much, sir,' replied Falconer, taking offence nevertheless, and clutching it close to his heart dearly. From what he had heard, this man was obnoxious. He was going to do his best to bring him down a peg or two, and he fancied that improvisation would be the way to get him rattled.

'I understand that this is not the first time that you have come across the intended victim of last night's tragedy in the billiards room.' Carmichael's mouth fell open at the inspector's blunt approach, but at a glower from the boss, he quickly turned it into a yawn, discreetly covering his mouth with one of his ham-like hands. So, it was going to be like that, was it?

'I have also learnt that you had a particular reason for disliking Mr Freeman, due to a business deal in the past that did not go exactly as you had planned it. Am I correct in my assumptions?'

Before Enoch could do anything to disabuse him, Aylsa had answered a rousing, 'Yes!' and added, 'Enoch doesn't like anyone who doesn't have white skin. He doesn't like any foreigners, if they weren't born here, and a lot of what he considers foreigners who were born here. He also doesn't like anyone who disagrees with him, and he can't stand Southerners. In fact, Enoch doesn't really like anybody except himself. And, of course, he's always right, aren't you, my little alligator?'

'Aylsa!' he bellowed, his face flushing an angry red. 'What on earth are you trying to do to me? You'll get me arrested if you're not careful.'

'Just the ticket, Enoch. You're an obnoxious old git, and I could do with a break from you.'

'But you're my wife!'

167

'Not for much longer, if you don't clean up your act and behave like a normal human being, instead of some sort of bad-tempered animal.'

'Mr Arkwright. Mrs Arkwright. Could you save all this till later? Enlightening though it is to witness your marital squabbles, may I point out that we have more important business to conduct. It may have escaped your notice, but we are now trying to apprehend the culprit or culprits for two murders, not to mention the attempt on Chef's life.'

'I do apologise, Inspector, for myself and for my husband, but it would seem that nobody's as good as he is, though I know for a fact that he was born practically in the gutter, and sometimes I get sick and tired of all his pathetic prejudices.'

'What are you talking about, woman?'

'Shut up, Mr Arkwright, before I arrest you for a breach of the peace. And I think you have something to tell us about one of the members of staff here. From what I overheard earlier – purely by chance, you understand – it would appear that you have had a run-in with one of the Freeman brothers sometime in the past.'

'Don't know what you're talking about,' blustered Enoch, beginning to pace around the room.

'And you suffer from an unusually acute prejudice against anyone who isn't of Anglo-Saxon origin.'

'It's not a crime yet to dislike coloured people, is it?'

'It is, if that prejudice is displayed publicly. And what about this business venture of yours that was blown out of the water?'

'A mere nothing, in the light of the success I achieved afterwards.'

'Would you say you are a man to harbour a grudge, Mr Arkwright?'

Here, Aylsa could not help herself, and burst in with, 'He can't let anything go. He always has to get even, even if it was something that happened when he was a child. He doesn't know the meaning of 'forgive and forget'.'

'Is that so, Mr Arkwright? And did this quality in you

surface yesterday evening? It sounds as if you recognised the man after all these years.'

This question, for some reason, seemed to raise a fire in him, and he began to puff up like a pigeon, before shouting, 'Damned right, I recognised the man. You don't forget something like that in a hurry. He hardly looked any different from the young man who trampled all over my dreams, and left me up Shit Creek without a paddle before I found another site. It was all set up for the planning permission ...'

'You mean you'd greased a few palms on the planning committee.' His wife was determined to reveal every detail about this blow to his ego.

'I mean it was set to go through without any objections, and then this darkie, barely out of short trousers, turns up at the meeting, bleating about it being a site of unusual interest because of some damned frog, or toad, or some such ridiculous creature that never did anybody any good.

'And he had the damned cheek to produce a report he had put together with some bloody wildlife organisation, and the next thing I knew, my application had been thrown out on its ear, and my plans were in tatters. A year and a half it took me to find somewhere else, and it cost me double what the original site would have cost.'

'So you did have a score to settle with him?'

'Of course I did, but you don't think I'd have been stupid enough to kill the wrong man, do you?'

'No, I don't, Mr Arkwright. But no one but the twins knew they had swapped roles, and they *were* absolutely identical.'

'And I'm sure he was as rotten as his brother. In fact, I hope something very nasty happens to his brother in the near future, then I can rest easy.'

'You can rest easy in the police station at Market Darley, Mr Arkwright. I think a little cooling-off period is called for before I can speak to you in a rational manner, because I'm sure you know more than you're telling us.'

'Damn your eyes! I'm English, and you can't treat me like this.'

'I'm going to call a car now and it would be in your best interests to go with the officers in that vehicle and just think about what you've said to me. As far as I'm concerned, you are the prime suspect for the murder of Jocelyn Freeman, and I suggest that you seek the advice of a solicitor. I'm not formally arresting you: merely asking for your cooperation in this matter. Do I make myself clear?'

'But you've no evidence …'

'Give me time, Mr Arkwright.'

The afternoon had worn itself away to a thin sliver of time when they finally went downstairs to take their leave of Jefferson Grammaticus. Things seemed to be progressing nicely as they made their farewells, and started off for 'Tea at Carmichael's'. They had three possible suspects awaiting questioning at the station, and Falconer was confident that at least one of them would let something slip. It was merely a case of building up a diagram for exactly where everyone was, starting with the interval in which Jocelyn Freeman had been stabbed in the neck, then progressing to who was out of the room and could have been upstairs when Fruity Newberry took his dive down to the hall.

He had every confidence that Lew Veede's jealousy and bad temper were sufficient triggers to have given the old boy a couple of pokes in the bottom. That would probably only result in a charge of manslaughter, but at least he'd have got his man. Chef's poisoning had a much wider window of opportunity, but he was fairly certain that he had the person responsible for that, in the shape of Céline Treny.

The last to be escorted to the station was a man who harboured an old grudge – granted, it was against Jerome Freeman, though the old switcheroony could easily explain that – but the old sod seemed perfectly capable of anything, provided he came out on top.

Jerome Freeman would not be sufficiently recovered to speak to them until tomorrow. In his hung-over state, he had hardly comprehended that his twin had been killed. After a few hours' sleep, he was sufficiently in charge of his wits to understand what had happened, and had collapsed with shock and grief.

A doctor from Carsfold had been summoned, checked the remaining alcohol level in his blood, and declared him unfit to make a statement. He then administered two sleeping tablets, and stated that he did not want his patient bothered until the next morning. But that hardly mattered. Falconer had three crimes on his hands, and three bodies in custody. That'd show that old bully Chivers what he was made of, and no mistake. A pat on the back would be definitely in order if he pulled this one off.

The sleeping tablets presented no real complication to the issue, as the inspector felt that he had a grip on the whole case now, and would have it neatly wrapped up by the time that Jocelyn awoke from his chemically induced sleep.

It was indeed, a quietly smug detective inspector, and an equally confident detective sergeant, that left the grounds of The Manse at shortly after six o'clock, and headed towards Castle Farthing for a welcome break from their investigations. Their evening was, by no means free, but at least they could switch off for a couple of hours before heading back into Market Darley to resume their questioning.

Chapter Thirteen

Sunday 20th June – later

On the drive to Castle Farthing Carmichael was unusually quiet and seemed to be lost in abstraction. This was unexpected, after such a successful and eventful day, and Falconer made an attempt to draw him into conversation, but with the cryptic comment, 'Talk to the face, because the hand's not listening,' being the only thing forthcoming, he gave up, and waited for the sergeant to think his way through whatever was on his mind. He'd speak when he was ready to, and the unaccustomed silence gave Falconer a chance to gloat on his unexpectedly swift solution of the case.

Castle Farthing presented itself as the perfect English village, as they made their way to Jasmine Cottage, with ducks paddling round the pond on the green, and residents, in twos and threes, stopped to exchange news and catch up with local happenings. The door stood wide open when they approached Carmichael's home, and the sound of children playing and a muffled 'wuff wuff' of dogs, issued forth from inside.

'In you go, sir,' said Carmichael in invitation, and Harry Falconer took his first steps into the living room, to be immediately set upon by two small figures in shorts and T-shirts, shouting, 'Uncle Harry! Uncle Harry! Look, Mum! Uncle Harry's come to see us.' With a child wrapped fondly around each leg, the inspector waded his way towards Kerry Carmichael, who stood just in front of the closed kitchen door, waiting to greet him.

'Come in, Inspector Falconer. We're all very pleased to

see you. Davey's always telling us about you, and now we've got the opportunity to spend the evening with you in our own home.'

Falconer looked very bemused. He felt he had received the greeting normally reserved for a favourite uncle, yet he had barely spent more than a few minutes here in past visits.

'Daddy Davey says you used to be a soldier,' shouted one of the boys, scrambling on to his lap, as he gave up the unequal struggle, and collapsed on to a sofa.

'A-a-a-a-a-a-a-a-a,' yelled the other boy, imitating a machine gun. 'Got you, Uncle Harry. Play dead!'

'No you didn't, you missed,' yelled the other, then clutched at his stomach and tumbled slowly to the floor. 'You got me instead, you dirty rat! Argh! You plugged me!'

'Did not!'

'Did! A thousand times did, and one more than you can ever say.'

'That's not fair!'

''Tis!'

''Tisn't. Mum, tell him that's not fair!'

'Come on you two, and let the poor man catch his breath. He's been at work all day. He wants to relax for a bit now, and not have you all over him like a load of ants.'

'Do you want to play cowboys and Indians, Uncle Harry? Look at me, I'm on my horse,' said the smaller of the two figures, raising his hands as if holding reins, and galloping round the room.

'Bang! Bang! You're shot now. You've got to fall off your horse, or it's not fair. Mum, Mum, it's not fair if he doesn't fall of his horse when I shoot him, is it?'

Their mother finally gathered them up and shooed them out into the garden to run off some of their energy, but in doing so, she let the dogs into the room, and Fang the Chihuahua, and his companion, Mr Knuckles the miniature Yorkshire terrier, came tearing across the carpet, their one aim to reacquaint themselves with the bottoms of Falconer's trouser legs. They had smelled enticingly of cat in the past, and did not disappoint on this occasion, and proving an open invitation to give them a good mauling. With little growling noises, they seized the material in their tiny jaws, and began to bite and chew with enthusiasm, dragging on the material for all they were worth.

'Oh, look, sir. They want to play, too,' offered Carmichael with a dopey smile on his face.

'Come here, you two little horrors. Out you go, too. I doubt the inspector wants to go home with shredded trousers,' admonished Kerry, grabbing each by the collar and depositing them on the other side of the back door to join her sons. 'There!' she commented with satisfaction, rubbing her hands together at her own efficiency. 'Davey's such a softie, he'd let them get away with murder – oh, I'm sorry. I forgot what you've been doing today. Now, what can I get you to drink?'

'What about a nice cup of tea?' suggested Falconer, half his mind on the fact that a Bombay Sapphire and tonic was out of the question, and when Carmichael had voiced his agreement, and she had gone into the kitchen to put on the kettle, the other half of his mind had a bone to pick with his sergeant.

'What's all this 'Uncle Harry' business? Since when have we been brothers? Did I go to sleep for a long time, and miss something important? Like being adopted by your mother, Carmichael?'

'No offence meant, sir. It's just that Kerry never had the boys baptised, and I've been thinking who I'd really like as their godfather. I mean, I know we only work together, but I wanted to choose someone absolutely straight and really good, who'd set them an example in life, and every time I asked myself who I wanted, I thought of you. I hope I haven't offended you?'

Slightly bewildered at this turn of events, but willing to go alone with it in theory, Falconer answered, 'Not at all. I'm really flattered. But what's the whole thing with Uncle Harry?'

'I've been telling them stories about you, so that they feel

175

they know you better. You remember that visit to my uncle's – the one with the dogs?'

'Only too well,' the inspector answered with a grimace[1].

'And that time in Stoney Cross when you dressed up like a parrot?'[2]

'I was *not* dressed like a parrot. I just ... developed a temporary blind spot in my sartorial selection,'

'Whatever you say, sir. But that's the sort of stuff that makes them laugh. And what your cats get up to, and how fussy you are about your appearance.'

'So you've turned me into some sort of comic caperer in their eyes?'

'No, sir. Nothing could be further from the truth. They think you're great!'

'Oh!' Falconer was surprised to find himself very flattered. 'That's very nice, Carmichael. In that light, do you think you ought to call me Harry while I'm here?'

'Absolutely not!'

'Why not?'

'Because I've told them that your other name is 'Sir', and I'm very privileged to be allowed to address you as such.'

Falconer decided that he'd never fathom the workings of the younger man's mind, and merely nodded in agreement.

'Does this mean you'll do it?'

'Do what?'

'Be their godfather?'

With no place to hide, Falconer gave in to the inevitable, and shook his partner's hand.

'I'd be honoured.'

Tea did, indeed, prove to be fish, but not in the form of fingers. Kerry had found some breaded fish-shapes that seemed to swim across the plate, with a waving sea of chips above them, and a seabed composed entirely of baked beans.

---

[1] See *Pascal Passion*
[2] See *Choked Off*

What was even better was the presence on the table of both a bottle of tomato sauce, and a bottle of brown.

Beans and brown sauce! And with the added delight of breadcrumbed fish! Falconer tucked in with as much enthusiasm as the boys, and even had a second helping when Kerry offered to fry another batch of crispy, golden chips. The icing on the cake, as far as he was concerned, was his instruction in the making of a 'chip butty' with rubbery bought sliced bread, ably demonstrated by Carmichael, and he retired from the table a contented man.

As Kerry herded the boys upstairs for their bath, the two men were left alone to talk, and the conversation was opened by Carmichael. 'I can't quite put my finger on it, sir, but that message from PC Starr ... Does she speak fluent French?'

'Why's that?' Falconer was digesting, and not much in the mood for small talk.

'Well, wouldn't Chef be a bit difficult to understand if he were mumbling, and not fully conscious?'

'He must've spoken in English. That seems blatantly obvious. Starr doesn't strike me as a linguist.'

'Me neither. I know she came up with that iffy question for Merv Green to ask that French barmaid, but it didn't sound like she knew much more than that. I may be wrong, but I don't think so. And so I got to thinking: why would a Frenchman speak English, if he wasn't fully awake? Surely he'd have spoken in French. I mean, he didn't even realise where he was, did he? He was just rambling. But you repeated what she said with a French accent. Does that mean anything?'

Carmichael did have a point, and Falconer put it down on his mental list, to check the next day. Maybe he had a point. Starr had used no other accent than the one that she used every day. He, it was, who had given it the comedy French flavour. Did it mean anything if Chef had spoken in English, or did it just confirm that he was so used to speaking it that it had crept out of his subconscious?

'Don't know, Carmichael, but there's no use in

speculating until I've had the chance to speak to Starr. I suppose it could mean something in the great scheme of things, but what, I don't know. What the hell's happening?'

As he had spoken, he had become aware of a curious warmth on both of his ankles, and as he asked the question, Carmichael leapt up from his chair and grabbed two furry balls by the scruffs of their necks, and held them up until they were right in front of his face.

'I know you love Uncle Harry,' he informed them, 'and I know you're just marking him as yours, but that really is very naughty. You know you're not allowed to mark anything in the house. Shame on you! You're going outside again, until you can remember your manners, decide to behave. Don't worry, sir, I'll get you a pair of my old jogging bottoms to see you home.'

With a look of horror, Falconer gazed down at the bottoms of his trouser legs, which were now wet, but cooling fast. The mutts had peed on him, one on each leg, and he wrinkled his nose in disgust, as his host deposited the miscreants outside the back door, and thundered upstairs, to return with the promised item of clothing in his hand. 'Here. Go into the kitchen and put these on, and I'll get you a carrier bag for the wet ones.'

Falconer accepted the proffered garment and did as he was told, saying nothing until he had returned to the sitting room, the legs of the trousers gathered round his ankles in concertinas of surplus material. 'I've only got one question, Sergeant.'

'What's that, sir?'

'Why are these – trousers – red?'

'Because it's a happy colour, sir. I like red.'

His re-appearance in the living room, and visibility through the back window, caused a positive volley of yaps to sound from just outside, and through the window pane, there appeared, first one furry head, then another, both with their tongues hanging out, and both intent on another session with Uncle Trousers, but Falconer turned away, still brooding on the colour that now enclosed his lower half.

'Because I like red! And orange, yellow, green, blue, indigo, and violet,' was his unvoiced thought. He didn't know if his partner could sing a rainbow, but he could certainly wear one when he put his mind to it. Carmichael's outrageous sense of colour had been a constant thorn in his side when they had first worked together, but his marriage to Kerry had resulted in him only dressing in anything 'unusual' on Fridays now, God be praised.

'Why don't you keep a pair of jeans in the car, then you can wear them when you come round here again. That should save your good trousers, and I do know how you like to look spiffy,' suggested Carmichael.

'Spiffy? What the hell does that mean?'

'Well, sort of freshly vacuumed and polished. You know; always perfectly turned out, with never a hair out of place.'

'You make me sound like some sort of waxwork.'

'Nothing like. You just seem to stay so clean and tidy. I don't know how you do it.'

'I patently fail to do it when I'm involved with your family. It doesn't seem to matter what I do, I always end up with egg on my face; or in this case, pee on my trousers, or, in the case of that visit to your uncle's, with my clothes covered in a variety of excreta.'

'Sorry about that too, sir. You'll just have to bring some old jeans, like I said,' reiterated his partner, not a whit embarrassed.

'Carmichael, I don't have any old jeans. In fact I don't even have any new, or even middle-aged, jeans. I've never worn them, because I've never owned a pair.'

'What, never, sir?' asked the younger man, scandalised that anyone could reach Falconer's age without benefit of denim.

'I tried on a pair when I was a teenager, but one look in the mirror, and I decided I looked like I was on my way to a barn dance, or a line-dancing class. Plus, I suspected that I must have a rather high waist, because they were uncomfortable in the, er, under-carriage region, if you get my drift.'

'Oo-er, very nasty, sir. Perhaps you'd better get some joggy bottoms.'

'I think I had a touch of that after I tried on those jeans, years ago. Anyway, thanks for a lovely meal, and I'll see you in the morning.'

As the two men moved towards the front door, Kerry could be heard clattering down the stairs to say goodbye. There was a slight squeal, as of unoiled hinges, as she grabbed at the back door, and then she joined them, explaining, 'I opened the door to let the poor things in. Why did you put them out?'

That was when she noticed that their guest had a furry attachment to each knee, both attachments busily growling away, as the twin bodies struggled to mate with Falconer's trousers, and adding a further embarrassing incident to the inspector's private collection of Carmichael-alia .

'That's why,' explained her husband, but Falconer was beyond caring, and waded the few more steps necessary to reach the exit from this madhouse, a dog on each leg, confident that Carmichael wouldn't allow them actually to leave with him. If not, he'd have to pull the little buggers off himself so that he could drive home.

'You're going to have to get these little chaps 'seen to' by a vet, in the very near future, he advised. 'They're a bit over-enthusiastic for my liking.' That was as controlled and polite as he could manage, given the circumstances.

'I agree completely, sir. They've never done *that* before, have they Kerry?'

'Never, Inspector Falconer.'

With a smile, Carmichael offered his opinion as solace to his superior. 'I guess it just shows how much they love you, sir.'

'Well, just see if you can persuade the vet to do something that convinces them that I'm not their type, will you?'

'I'll get on to it first thing in the morning, sir.'

But that was not to be his last humiliation. As Kerry gave him a little peck on the cheek, she stared at his face and said, 'Hold on! Sauce on your chin!' and proceeded to take a tissue from her pocket, spit on it, and rub vigorously at a spot just to the left of his bottom lip.

Driving off, all he could think of was the chaos that always seemed to ensue when he had anything to do with Carmichael that didn't directly involve work. He always felt afterwards that he had battled a whirlwind, and come off the worse for it. Take today, for example; he'd been wrestled on to the sofa, and had all the breath knocked out of him by two rumbustious boys, he'd had his trousers thoroughly chewed, as the puncture marks in the material testified to, he'd had his ankles peed on, and he'd been called, of all things, Uncle Harry. And then she gave me a spit wash. She actually gave me a spit wash, and I'm an inspector, he thought, grimacing in disgust.

It was the shower for him as soon as he got in, and although he had intended to put his trousers straight in the bin, he thought he might just have a look, to see if they had a 'machine-washable' label inside the waistband. He might not have any old jeans, but he did now have a pair of old 'Harry's' he could take with him, for the bizarre encounters he would have with his sergeant's family in the future.

'And what the hell did a godfather do these days?' he wondered. He knew it meant Christmas and birthday presents, but he fervently hoped it didn't mean taking the kids out to the cinema, or, heaven help him, the zoo. Or having them visit him unsupervised! Maybe for a whole day! He may have served abroad with the army, but he didn't feel up to the stress of having two boys running wild amongst his treasured porcelain and crystal. This whole thing could lead to many sessions of hiding under the piano, or even in the wardrobe, should it prove necessary. What had he got himself into?

Chapter Fourteen

Monday 21st June – the early hours and morning

It was half-past midnight when the telephone broke his slumbers, and Falconer awoke, bleary-eyed and numbed by tiredness. He had only been in bed half an hour, and he had been drowned in a deep sleep.

There was to be no more rest for him, though, as the telephone squawked in his ear the details of yet another 'happening' at The Manse. Struggling out of his bed, trying to shake off the feeling that he wanted to go back to bed and sleep for a month, he crawled into the clothes he had so recently discarded, wincing at the thought of wearing something that had already seen a day's work, then called Carmichael to be ready to be picked up in about twenty minutes.

He didn't see why his sergeant should sleep when he was prevented from doing so, and he needed another body with him. The call had not been specific, but had merely stated that there had been an accident of some sort, and that medics were in attendance. That could mean anything – even something quite trivial – and he sincerely hoped that it did, remembering the three bodies he had detained to help the police with their enquiries.

As he drove he began to feel the first twinges of guilt. He really should have gone back to the station after he left Carmichael's: but, what with one thing and another, he'd had enough for one day, and decided that questioning them in the morning, when he was rested and fresh, would bring forth better results. Bum! He hadn't even phoned Bob Bryant to let him know of his intentions.

If he had it all wrapped up with those three, then who was there left to cause mischief? It didn't bear thinking about, so he took the most sensible action he could and dismissed it from his mind until he had got there and saw for himself what exactly had occurred.

Carmichael was waiting for him just outside the front door of his cottage, yawning and vigorously rubbing a hand over his head. It would appear that both of them shared the same sense of having been aroused from the near-dead, and he anticipated a quiet drive to their destination.

The door of The Manse was slightly ajar, but Falconer knocked for the sake of good manners. From the other side, approaching across the hall, could be heard the gentle jingling of metal upon metal, announcing, before she reached the door, the presence of Beatrix Ironmonger, even at this hour wearing her chatelaine chain.

She bade them enter, her lips pressed tightly together, as if to demonstrate her disapproval of such goings on at this ungodly hour of the night. 'He's in his room,' she said without preamble. They didn't take him to hospital. He's just got to watch out for any signs that he might have a concussion.'

'Who, Mrs Ironmonger?'

'Why, Mr Grammaticus, of course. Didn't anyone tell you?'

'No. I was given no details whatsoever. I was just told there had been an 'incident' here.'

'I should say there has!' she almost spat. 'Mr Grammaticus has been the victim of a booby trap.'

'Where is he?'

'Upstairs, lying down.'

'So, what happened exactly?'

'Someone had been in his room, because the door was ajar. I know, because I saw it, and when he regained consciousness,' she continued, with a smug note of drama in her voice, 'he told me that he went up to bed deeply in

184

thought, and didn't notice that the door was open slightly, even though he usually locked it. You can't be too careful in a place like this,' she added, with a secret smile. 'And when he pushed it to go in, one of the hotel's stone hot water bottles fell on him, knocking him to the ground and rendering him unconscious for a short time.'

'It was balanced on the top of the door, you mean?'

'It must have been, otherwise it couldn't have fallen, could it?' In other words, 'thanks for stating the bleeding obvious'. She seemed a queer fish for Jefferson to have put in charge of housekeeping in this establishment; cold, aloof, and acerbic in her comments, and it must be assumed that she had qualities that Falconer did not, as yet, appreciate.

'Went down like a ton of bricks,' she murmured.

'You actually saw it?' asked Falconer, suddenly on the alert.

'No, no, but it's obvious he must've done; a man of that build. I was just expressing an opinion, that's all. Talking to myself, really.'

'Perhaps you would be so kind as to let us go up to speak to Mr Grammaticus himself – unless there were any witnesses to the incident.'

'Certainly not, at this time of night. I only found him because my Perfect Cadence was a little peckish, and I knew there were some leftovers that would only go to waste if they were left to the morning. I couldn't see my poor little kitty go hungry, now could I?'

I suppose not,' answered Falconer, the fact that she was a cat-lover being the only point in her favour, so far as he was concerned.

'Room number four – just opposite you, on the left, as you get to the top of the stairs,' she directed, then more or less floated off towards the staff sitting room. Her skirt was so long, and her steps so small and regular, that, in a dim light, Falconer thought he could almost mistake her for a ghost. There was no colour at all in her attire, and her suspiciously blonde hair lost its brassiness in a low light.

With a small shiver, he beckoned for Carmichael to follow him, and they made their way upstairs, to interview the latest victim of this now slightly sinister building.

They found the man tucked up in bed like an enormous sick child, several pillows behind his head, which sported a theatrically large bandage, and the counterpane neatly smoothed across the hilly bulk of his body. Against the right side of his head, right over the bandage, he held an ice-pack, and his face was paler than usual, as he glanced up at their arrival.

'Hello, there, Inspector, Sergeant,' he greeted them. 'I'm afraid I've been in the wars.'

'You certainly have. Much damage?'

'No, not with a skull as thick as mine.' He attempted a small laugh at this weak joke, but the effect on his head proved too much, and he gave up, and just shrugged his shoulders. 'Don't ask me what happened, because I can't really tell you.'

'You can't remember?'

'No, it's not that, so much as the speed at which it happened, and the fact that I was completely submerged in thought, about the future of this place. I knew I'd had quite a brilliant idea, and was mulling over the practicalities as I came upstairs, and the next thing I knew, I was lying on the floor with a thumping headache, and my housekeeper's face close to mine. God, that gave me a shock!'

'I should think it did. I don't think I'd fancy that myself,' agreed Falconer, with another shudder. 'Something she did mention, though, was that your door was open when you came upstairs. Is that correct?'

'Yes, I'd almost forgotten that. It was only open about five or six inches, or whatever that is in metric-speak, but you know what I mean. I should have registered it as unusual, because I always keep the door locked, but I was completely enthralled in my brilliant new idea, and by the time it registered consciously, it was too late. A split second later I was knocked to the ground.'

'Your housekeeper described the incident as a booby trap. Would you agree with that?'

'I think I'd have to. It can hardly have been a prank, or a practical joke with something that heavy, can it?'

'I don't think so, sir, and that means that we'll have to treat this as attempted murder. If it had hit you at a different angle, you could be dead, or in intensive care by now. Even though that's not so, we can't overlook the intentions of whoever balanced that thing up there.'

'But I thought you had three people in custody, and that everything was done and dusted.'

'So did I, sir; so did I, but it appears that I may have been somewhat hasty in my conclusions. By the way, what was your brilliant idea?'

'Haven't the faintest idea, Inspector. I can't recall a thing about it, apart from the fact that I was really excited, and thought I was on to a sure-fire winner this time. Oh, and by the way, something was removed from my inner jacket pocket while I was unconscious, and I should very much like it back.'

'What was that, Mr Grammaticus?'

'A small, black leather-bound notebook. I keep a lot of notes in it for ideas I have, and I'd be grateful for its return. I totally rely on your discretion not to pry into its contents, for some of the notes in there are very personal, and I should not like to think of them being read by anyone other myself, if you would be so kind.'

'We don't pry into anything that is not concerned with the case, sir. Are you sure you hadn't just mislaid it?'

'It's too valuable to me for that, Inspector, but I have every faith in your integrity, as both a policeman and a gentleman, if I may say so.'

'That's very kind of you, sir,' Falconer answered him, making a mental note that, if Grammaticus had been floored to obtain this notebook, it would no doubt be very pertinent to the case, and he hadn't actually agreed not to look inside, had

187

he?

Having taken the stone hot water bottle into custody, they stood at the bottom of the stone steps that led up to the hotel's entrance for a few minutes, to assimilate what this new attack could mean, and Falconer was convinced that it could only mean trouble – especially for him. Had he been somewhat precipitate in his decisions to send suspects to the station for further questioning? Did they really measure up as prime suspects? Did he have any evidence to back up his actions, other than circumstantial? Could he, in all honesty, defend what he had done?

Carmichael broke into his self-pitying reverie with the direct, but tactless question, 'Are you in the shit, sir?'

'I could be in more shit than I found myself in when we visited your uncle's. I think I might have some fast talking to do in the morning, along with a mort of grovelling, and an appetite for a large portion of humble pie.'

'Oo-'eck, sir. I wouldn't fancy being in your shoes.'

'Neither do I, Carmichael, but just one more thing before I take you home.'

'What's that, sir?'

'Why have you got stripy cuffs and anklets sticking out from under your clothes?'

Carmichael looked down at himself, and immediately inserted both his hands under his top, and gave an abrupt pull at each side of his body. He then moved his enormous hands to just below the waistband of his trousers, and performed a similar action, this time in an upwards direction.

'Sorry about that, sir. I just pulled something on over my 'jammies' when you called. They must have worked their way down since I left home.'

'Thank goodness for that. I thought it was Friday already.'

'Not yet, but I can promise you a beezer of an outfit for this week! I got some stuff at a boot sale a couple of weekends ago, and Kerry's got it all washed and ironed and ready for me to wear.'

'I shall look forward to that, provided I remember to bring

my sunglasses, and haven't been transferred in disgrace by then. If I'm on traffic duty, do feel free to visit me, won't you? I'll be in dire need of a good laugh.'

Back in his bed once more, if only for a few hours, Falconer found sleep elusive. Twice he managed to fall into a light doze, but awoke both times when bad dreams had come his way. The first time was a given, in that it represented Chivers' face about an inch from his own, shouting words like 'imbecile', 'incompetent', 'negligent', and 'stupid'.

The second dream, however, was a little more difficult to rationalise, involving as it did the ghostly figure of Beatrix Ironmonger floating before him, but instead of the small domestic items that usually hung from her chain, in addition there hung a bayonet and a pair of garden shears. In the end, he put it down to the disconcerting impression she had made in the wee small hours when she had let them in.

But, horror of horrors, the worst thing about the dream, or nightmare, call it what you will, was that she had Nanny Vogel's unforgettable face, and he awoke with a loud cry of 'Whaaa!', which he could still hear echoing in his ears as he sat up in bed with a start. He'd obviously let himself be spooked by his recent encounter with the slightly unearthly housekeeper, and his previous nightmare about that scary figure from his childhood.

He tried, once again, to capture sleep, tossing and turning, in search of the rest and repose that both his body and brain craved, but it was a state that he failed to achieve during the next hour and a half.

He had decided to give up his futile pursuit of sleep when he suddenly dropped off the edge of the cliff, and descended into the depths of a dreamless slumber, only to be awoken by the telephone's urgent summons at nine o'clock. Oh God! He'd turned his alarm clock off when he went out earlier in the night, not knowing when he would return, then had completely forgotten to set it again, amidst all his fears of having detained someone innocent.

'Falconer speaking. How can I help?'

'It's Carmichael, sir. I don't know why you're late, but Chivers is out for your blood. You'd better get here in double-quick time, before his head blows up, or that'll be your fault as well.'

'Cover for me, will you? Say I had a puncture or something. For God's sake don't tell him I just slept late, he pleaded, his bowels turning to water at the thought of what lay ahead of him at the station.

'Sure thing, sir. Leave it to me. I'll come up with something that'll melt his heart.'

'No, don't do that …' but it was no use, he was talking to a dead line. Great! Now he had something else to worry about. Carmichael's imagination was a place he didn't want to go, and he dreaded how the sergeant would explain his absence.

Falconer arrived at the station tired, pale, and apprehensive but, for once, his luck was in. Detective Superintendent 'Jelly' Chivers had only looked in briefly, and was now conspicuous by his absence. He had had to leave to attend a meeting to discuss current manpower and the use of community service officers on the beat. Perhaps everything would be solved by the time the man deigned to set foot in the station again, and there would be nothing for him to be dragged over the coals for.

No sooner had he sat down at his desk, however, than Bob Bryant rang from the desk. 'I've got a bone to pick with you, sunshine,' he announced without preamble. 'I've got three customers banged up down here, and a seething duty solicitor, and I'd be grateful if you'd come and clean up this mess you've landed me in.' This was strong stuff indeed from the usually cheerful and laid-back desk sergeant, and Falconer made his way downstairs as quickly as he could given the fact that he had had virtually no sleep the night before.

The duty solicitor awaited him in one of the interview rooms, and wasted no time in giving the inspector a verbal lambasting. 'I've got three clients detained here for further questioning, but I can't seem to locate any physical evidence that may back that up. Now, maybe there's something I don't know about, but I somehow doubt it. I've spoken to all three of them, and I don't believe you have anything to back up your decision to keep them here. Well, what have you got to say for yourself?'

'They weren't actually under arrest. None of them has been cautioned. It should have been made perfectly clear to them, that they were here in a voluntary capacity only, and that they were free to leave whenever they wanted to.'

'In that case, someone has signally failed in his or her duty, Inspector. From what my clients have told me, they were under the impression that they had to stay here until you got round to speaking to them. Would I be correct in my assumption?'

'They were prime suspects.'

'That is no defence. Who actually booked them into the custody suite?'

'PC Green and PC Starr brought them in.'

'Did you impress upon those officers that they were only helping the police with their enquiries?'

'I told them they weren't under arrest. I made that perfectly clear to each and every one of them when I detained them.'

'But did you actually tell them that they could leave whenever they liked?' This man was an absolute terrier, and Falconer felt a blush of shame wash over his features.

'I may not have done, but it's obvious, isn't it?'

'To someone in the job, maybe, but to an average law-abiding member of the public, I would think not. You have been slack in your duty to these three people, and I use very mild terms, for what I see as extremely cavalier behaviour. Do you have any solid physical evidence that would indicate a desire for their continued presence here?'

'No, I'm very much afraid I don't.'

'Oh, and just for the record, I don't know how much time

you spent questioning the woman representing herself as Céline Treny, but I have to inform you that the woman is an independent investigative journalist who was tracking the movements of a recently released guest at one of Her Majesty's prisons. She's no more French than I am. What have you got to say to that, Inspector?'

'She's a great little actress, isn't she?' What could he say? She'd given no indication that she wanted to confide in him. 'Are you absolutely sure of your facts?' he asked, grabbing at the last available straw.

'I spoke to the editor of a newspaper that she approached, to enquire as to whether they were interested in running her story, and, when I telephoned him first thing this morning, he confirmed that she had mooted the idea to him back in May, and she's even offered a perusal of her findings so far, if you still don't believe her.

I've taken a note of her temporary address in Carsfold, her permanent address in the outskirts of London, and I also took her mobile phone number, and that of her home address, but she's decided to stay on in Carsfold until you have reached a conclusion to this case, as she might be able to do a piece about that, instead. A sort of 'your reporter on the spot' type of thing, as her rent's paid till the end of the month, and she does have an inside angle from which to look at the various people involved.'

'I'll just get off and grovel then, shall I?'

'Oh, I shouldn't waste too much sleep over the two men. They demonstrated to me that they both possess foul tempers, and I had the rough end of their tongues about an hour ago. I should speak to the woman first – her real name's Penny Trussler – but take your time getting round to the other two. They seemed to have blown themselves out, by the time they'd finished having a damned good shout at me, but I'm so damned annoyed, they can stay incarcerated till Kingdom Come, for all I care.'

'Didn't you tell them either? That they were free to go, that is?'

'Having been roused from my bed on my day off – I never work on a Monday – at what I considered an ungodly hour, for a man who intends to spend the whole morning in bed, I thought I'd leave that pleasure to you. But they'll no doubt lodge a complaint, so if I were you, I'd have my story ready before they get the chance to say anything too damaging.'

It was nearly an hour later before he got round to pointing out that he had not, indeed, arrested the suspects, and that his sergeant's report would verify this. They both still had some fight left in them but, in all truth, they had each been so far gone in temper at the time that Falconer had asked them to allow themselves to be escorted to the station that neither of them had taken much notice of what he had actually said.

The suggestion that the incidents would probably be mentioned in a report finally scuppered them both, as neither of them wished what they had blurted out in anger the day before to be recorded anywhere official, and Falconer only hoped that Carmichael's notes would confirm the words he believed – he knew – he had spoken.

He was prevented from asking about this, thought as, on his return to the office, Carmichael was puffing and blowing with suppressed excitement. 'Sir, sir, you've got to hear this. I can't believe it. It's outrageous!'

'What is, Carmichael?' he asked, wondering whatever could have happened to fire up his sergeant to such a level.

'Well, first thing is, Chef's dead. And all the staff at The Manse are murderers.'

'What on earth are you blethering about? Is this some sort of joke to wind me up?'

'Of course not, sir. Antoine de la Robe,' – here, he gave a little snicker at what he considered a ridiculously la-di-da Froggified name, then recovered his serious face to continue – 'suffered a fatal heart attack at eight-thirty this morning, and all attempts to revive him were in vain. It seems that his system couldn't cope with the damage it had suffered. And what's more, *he's just as English as you and me*! The doctor from the hospital said that just before he pegged it, he had a few lucid moments, and he spoke with a real thick Cockney accent. I said it wasn't natural for him to speak English when he was barely conscious, didn't I?'

'You did,' admitted Falconer, wincing at his lack of insight and, remembering the fake accent he had applied to PC Starr's message from the hospital, his face coloured for the second time that morning. 'But what's all this, about every one of the staff at The Manse being a murderer?'

'I put those prints from that new electronic machine into the system, when you went downstairs to see Bob Bryant, and they've all come back as being on record. And what's more, they're all using false names.'

'That seems far too much of a coincidence, for them all to land up at the same place, and all with an alias.'

'Spot on, sir. I've printed out all the details for you to read, but I also checked up on who defended them at their trials, and guess what?'

'What?'

'It was that Grammaticus chap. He was a barrister before he retired. Not a famous one, or anything like that, but he must've made a fair few bob in his time – hence the posh hotel, and what that must have cost to refurbish.'

'I knew I'd heard that name before!' exclaimed Falconer, rubbing his hands with glee. 'Tell me all about it, Carmichael. This is all your own work, and I'm very pleased to hear some good news connected with this case at last.'

'You would've got the same result if you'd put the prints into the system, sir,' commented Carmichael generously, but he was beaming from ear to ear, like a child on Christmas morning.

'Don't be so modest, and before it slips my mind, have you spoken to the vet about your randy little dogs?'

It was Carmichael's turn to blush, as he found anything of a sexual nature highly embarrassing, and this seemed to apply to his pets as well. 'I made an appointment for next week.'

'Good!'

Carmichael knew that there would be an encounter with the two dogs and the inspector before the day was out, but decided to keep that to himself, until he couldn't avoid telling him. Kerry was going into the school this afternoon, to help out with the heats for next month's sports' day. As a consequence, he had been cajoled into picking up Fang and Mr Knuckles at lunchtime, to keep them from chewing everything within their reach, which was a favourite game of theirs when left unsupervised. After all, it would be cruel to leave them outside, wouldn't it?

'Out with it then. Who are these members of staff, what are they really called, and what did they do?'

'I'll start with Antoine de la Robe, as we know him. His real name was Nigel Cooper. He'd been to catering college all right, and come out top of his class, but he lost his rag one night when a drunken customer followed the waiter into the kitchen, to complain that his soup was cold – it was gazpacho, if that means anything to you, sir.'

'It's a chilled soup, and I don't blame the man for being angry. I would be too, if I'd made it, and had it returned for being cold,' Falconer informed his sergeant.

'Chef – I can't seem to see him as Nigel, even though I know it's his name – was boning meat at the time, and he says he slipped and lost his balance, accidentally plunging the knife into the customer's heart.

'The police charged him with manslaughter, as they could prove no premeditation, but Grammaticus went for accidental death, played his fairly respectable background, his clean record with the police, and the effect that all this would have on his career. He must have really poured out his heart on this one, and the jury found him not guilty on a split decision.

'Chastity Chamberlain was the alias of one Emma West, who was a cheating wife who suffered constant beatings at her husband's hands for her unfaithfulness. It says here that, after a particularly bad beating while the husband was very drunk, she waited for him to go to bed, and then took a hammer to his head. Medical evidence and the superb acting skills of our Mr Grammaticus got her off with 'justifiable homicide'.

'Next, we have Dwayne Mortte, the sous chef, aka Michael Little, who was done for giving a friend an Ecstasy tablet that led to the friend collapsing at a club and dying three days later, without recovering consciousness. Although Grammaticus did his best, his client went down for a couple of years for his reckless behaviour in supplying and possession of an illegal drug, but he only served fourteen months.

'Steve Grieve, the barman, otherwise known as Trevor Smith, had been in trouble for TWOC-ing since he was thirteen. He'd done some time in young offenders' units, but the last time he nicked a car he lost control of it and killed a pedestrian. He only did eighteen months inside, because Grammaticus produced a witness that said the woman had run out in front of the vehicle, and the driver could have done nothing to change the outcome of the situation.

'And finally,' Carmichael announced, still grinning at the thought of his own serendipitous success, 'We come to Beatrix Ironmonger. She used to be a tom, you know, sir, name of Ursula Freebody, if you can believe that. I don't, somehow, think that records got to the bottom of that one, but anyway, when she first started on the game, she was daft enough to give credit. Can you believe that, sir? And she had this punter who was her first regular, visited her for the best part of six weeks, three times a week, then buggered off without paying.'

'*Quelle surprise!*' muttered Falconer, shaking his head in disbelief at such naivety.

'Silly young woman lost her bedsit over it, and had to conduct business up alleyways and in cars after that, till she'd saved enough to get a new place. Anyway, one night she spotted that same character going off with one of the other toms, so she followed them across a building site to the shell of a garage for one of the properties being built, picking up a brick on the way, and lying in wait for him as he emerged.

'Once the other tom had scarpered in search of new business, she dotted him one, and he died from his injuries. Grammaticus did a good job with the medical evidence again, putting it to the court, that the man had an unusually thin skull, and that she'd only wanted to teach him a lesson, but they weren't having any of it, and she went down for manslaughter, and served seven years. That's the lot, sir, but it's plenty to be going on with it, don't you think?'

'An embarrassment of riches, in fact,' agreed Falconer. 'And they were all there, under the same roof: all cozied-up with their defence barrister. I tell you now, Carmichael, if there isn't something more to this, I'll not only eat my hat; I'll eat yours, too.

'I'm going straight off to get a search warrant for The Manse, and I'll not be satisfied until we've turned the whole place upside down. There must be something for us to find, even if it's only Grammaticus' little black book, and I've got a pretty fair idea what we'll find written in it, if this new information is anything to go by.'

Chapter Fifteen

Monday 21st June, – afternoon

I don't see why we have to go via Castle Farthing, Carmichael. Have you got to pick up something?'

'Sort of,' was the sergeant's cryptic and brief reply.

'What on earth does that mean, 'sort of'? You've either got to pick up something or you haven't. Which is it?'

'I've got to take the dogs for the afternoon,' replied Carmichael, his voice barely above a whisper, and his face a mask of apprehension. 'Kerry's usually at home for them, to let them in and out, and keep an eye on them, so that they don't escape. Today she's got to go to the school to help out with something, and I said I'd have the dogs. I didn't think we'd be leaving the office, as everything seemed so conclusive yesterday evening. I thought they might just have a snooze under a desk, or something.'

Fat chance of that happening with those two. 'Great! Well, you may have to take them, but I *don't*. I don't mind following you home, so that we arrive together at the hotel, but they're not – repeat *not* – getting into *my* car, and I expect you to keep them under complete control when we get there. Understand? And I hope that reference to yesterday evening wasn't a snide comment about my decision-making, either. I've had to eat enough humble pie to do me for months, and I haven't even seen Chivers yet.'

'I didn't mean anything when I mentioned about yesterday. I wasn't being snide, honestly, sir. I was only saying what we both thought,' which was perfectly truthful, for Carmichael didn't have a snide bone in his body, and

Falconer knew that, in his heart of hearts. He was just a little over-sensitive after what had occurred that morning. 'And I promise to keep the dogs fully under my control.'

Even fatter chance to this last! – in fact, it would have to be a morbidly obese chance, with pigs flying across a blue moon, the day that Carmichael demonstrated full control over those boisterous bundles of tumbleweed, but Falconer made no comment. He would believe it when he saw it, and he didn't think that would be today. There was certainly no sign of Carmichael's iron control, when he reappeared from the inside of his cottage with a water bowl and a blanket in his arms.

The dogs romped out in joyous disorder, and proved, once again, their magnificent ability to bounce as if on springs. As Falconer abruptly closed the driver's window of his car, two happy little faces appeared, one at a time, as if being juggled, into his field of vision, tongues once more lolling in their joy at making the acquaintance, once more, of Uncle Tasty-Trousers.

Flinging the blanket and bowl into the boot of his car, the sergeant caught each of them mid-bounce, and deposited them through the back door of his car, and onto the rear seat. The sheer energy of the little tykes didn't bode well, for when both men and dogs were out in the open, and Falconer could almost feel the cuffs of his trousers cringe as he followed Carmichael's battered old Skoda to The Manse.

His trepidation was, however, unfounded as once given their freedom, the dogs caught sight of Perfect Cadence and, boxing considerably over their weight, size for size, hared off in her direction, in the hopes of a good old-fashioned chase.

'Let them go, Carmichael,' advised Falconer. 'The cat will probably take refuge in a tree and, with any luck, they'll stay at the bottom, barking, until we've finished our business here.'

'But what if they get out on to the road and get lost?'

'Then you'll just have to take me to the gate and use my trousers as bait, won't you? Leave them. The grounds are huge, and they'd probably get exhausted just getting to the perimeter, given their size.'

'Kerry will kill me if anything happens to them.'

'And Chivers will kill *us* if anything else happens at this place. Quit worrying and let's get ourselves inside. The sooner we start searching the place, the sooner you'll be back to bath them and tuck them up in their little doggy beds for the night. We'll leave the door open for them, so that when they come back, they'll be able to get inside. I'm sure someone will field them for us, and let us know they're there.'

'If you say so, sir, but I'm not happy about it.'

'We can't be happy about everything we do in life, Sergeant. Sometimes we have to take something on faith, and I'd bet my shirt – or rather my trousers – that those two little tykes will come galloping in to investigate the place if they get bored.'

You're probably right, sir. They are very nosy.'

Once inside, they found Jefferson Grammaticus at his desk, the dramatically large bandage still wrapped round his head, and an accounts book open in front of him.

'Good morning, Inspector, Sergeant. Everyone's checked out, but I have got home addresses and telephone numbers for you. I'm just having a little tot up to see how much we've lost on this opening venture. I think I might have been a bit rash, including drinks in the price. It was a bit like having a shoal of fish to stay, with the amount they put away. But it could be worse. I didn't expect to make a fortune, and they say that no publicity is bad publicity, don't they?'

'I don't imagine that would extend to going away for the weekend and coming home in a coffin, do you, sir?'

'No, maybe you're right, but there must be a positive spin I can put on that. I just haven't thought of it yet, but give me time. What can I do for you?'

'I have a warrant to search the premises. We haven't yet located the knife, or the other sharp implement used to assist Mr Newberry down the stairs, and I have a feeling that they must still be here.'

'They could be in the river, for all any of us knows, but be my guest. I have nothing to hide.'

'Oh, I wouldn't say that was strictly accurate, Mr Grammaticus, but let's bide our time on that one until we've been through this place with a fine-toothed comb. Murderers, in my experience, usually overlook some trivial detail, and that's what we'll be looking for today – something that's inconsistent with its position, or difficult to explain away.

'I'd be grateful if you'd direct us to the staff bedrooms, and ask the staff to gather in their sitting room, so that I can speak to them later.'

'Their usual bedrooms are on the second floor, but our housekeeper has had a room on the guest floor for the last couple of nights. It was a way of vetting the rooms from an inside point of view, so you'll find that room to your right as you get to the top of the first staircase – it's number six, the dove grey room. The rest of them are up the other staircase, and turn to the right. That's the only side of the building that's been renovated, so far, for staff occupation. The left hand side is still in an uninhabitable state, being full of old furniture that may come in handy someday, pots of paint, and a load of old junk that was there when we bought the place, and that we haven't had the chance to sift through yet. Everything's covered in dust, and the whole place was hung with cobwebs the last time I went up there, so I'll probably have to give you a good brushing down if you spend any time up there.'

'Thank you for the warning, Mr Grammaticus. We'll get on with it then, if that's all right with you?'

'No problem.'

'We'll get the housekeeper's room on the first floor out of the way, first. That way we can concentrate on the upper floor,' declared Falconer, pointing, quite unnecessarily, at the door of number six, as they got to the top of the stairs. 'I really don't like that woman – I can't explain why – but she gives

202

me the creeps, and I don't fancy her coming across us riffling through her things.'

'She is a bit spooky, isn't she?' replied Carmichael. 'I think it's that old-fashioned dress she wears, with that weird old chain that hangs from her waist. It's got more stuff on it than a Christmas tree. It's like a great clanking old charm bracelet, but with none of the charm.'

'Damned good description,' Falconer agreed, briefly remembering how it had appeared in his dream the previous night. 'And as I just said, she gives me the willies, too.'

The bedroom was as tidy as one that had never known human habitation, and it took them a very short time to search it. All that the wardrobe contained was a spare black dress of the same rustling material as the one the woman wore for her duties, and the chest of drawers was the possessor of only a pair of knickers and a pair of stockings. There were no toiletries in the bathroom, and nothing under the bed, under the mattress, or behind any of the furniture. There were no rugs (not even some of the sinister little furry ones) under which to conceal incriminating letters, and no loose floorboards under which could have been hidden a weapon of any sort, and they soon mounted the smaller stairs to the second floor.

Having decided to start with Chastity Chamberlain's room, and work their way round to the housekeeper's normal abode, they entered the young woman's room without holding out too much hope, but as Carmichael crossed from the bed to the dressing table, Falconer bade him stop.

'What is it, sir?'

'That floorboard you just trod on. It made a slight clunk, as you put your foot on it. Reach down and see if it's loose, will you? Many a piece of incriminating evidence has been hidden under a floorboard, before now.'

'You're right, sir. And just look what a pretty little magpie's nest we've got here, then.'

Falconer joined him on his knees on the floor, and in the space now exposed to daylight were all sorts of little goodies.

'Just look at this: a brooch, a stick pin, a silver ring, a lipstick, a tiny bottle of perfume, a pair of earrings, a silver bookmark: all small, and likely to be overlooked by their owners when packing, and possibly not missed for quite some time. It's a clever little haul, and I think we'll need to have words with this young lady when we've finished.'

As they scrambled to their feet, a voice was discernible, calling for their attention. 'That sounds like Grammaticus, sir. I wonder if he wants to tell us anything.'

'It sounds more like he's in a bit of a temper, to me. Come on, we'd better go and see what he wants.'

Jefferson was indeed trying to attract their attention, and as they bustled down the stairs, it became obvious that he really was rather out of sorts about something.

'Does either of you know anything about a couple of little dogs?' he asked them, his brow creasing in disapproval.

'Why?' asked Carmichael, his manner a cross between defensive and apologetic.

'Why? A) because I don't allow dogs in my hotel, and b) because someone left the cellar door open, and they got in through the front door and shot straight down there. I don't know what they're doing as yet, but they're making a hell of a noise, whatever it is they're up to.'

All three of them cocked an ear, and could hear the tinkling sound of breaking and falling glass, coming from somewhere below.

'I'm afraid they may be mine, sir,' admitted Carmichael with a shame-faced look. 'We let them go for a run in the grounds while we took a look at things in here. I think they may have come inside in search of us. I do apologise. I'll go and fetch them.'

'I'll come with you,' volunteered Falconer unexpectedly. 'Well, you never know what you might find, tucked away down there out of sight,' he explained as they went through the cellar door, and down the ancient wooden steps.

The noise grew steadily louder the further they descended, and a short distance from the foot of the stairs they could see two little doggy behinds wagging in excitement as they burrowed down through a heap of empty bottles that had just been dumped there, after being emptied.

'What on earth are they after?' the inspector asked, noting that both little tails were wiggling around with canine glee.

'I haven't the faintest idea, but I'm going to find out,' answered their owner, grabbing the smallest body, and hauling it out of the cavity it had created. 'Here, hold this little devil. The other one's deeper in, and I'll have to move a few more bottles to get a grip on him.'

It took him a minute or two to create enough space to grab the other dog, which had made his way to the bottom of the heap by now, and was making muffled barks of excitement at whatever it had found.

'Here's another one for you, sir. I don't know what they were after, but I think I can see something under this lot. Just give me a minute.'

'I don't know if I can do that. It's like trying to juggle eels. Oh, you little buggers!' Falconer exclaimed, as they wriggled out of his grasp and landed four-square on the floor.

'Is everything all right up there?' asked a distorted voice from deep within the pile of discarded empties.'

'No worries, Sergeant. They're both present and correct, and using my trousers as a teething ring. But don't let that bother you. I'm made of trousers, I am!'

'I'm so sorry, sir. I'll pay for any damage,' the voice sounded once more, then Carmichael began to unwind himself from the interstices of the dump, and rose to his feet clutching a small plastic bag, and holding it up for inspection.

'Don't worry about the trousers, Carmichael. I think the dogs have had a find there. Let me take a sniff of that. Yes, just as I thought. You've got a couple of potential illegal substances sniffers there! You should enquire about them joining the drugs squad. Now, I wonder who this little lot belongs to?'

'I caught that barman down here, when I interviewed him the other day, sir. He was possibly looking for somewhere to stash his, er, stash. I've been careful with it, so we might get some prints off it.'

'Here, I've got an evidence bag in my pocket. I'll slip it in that, and we'll get it tested,' said Falconer, pleased with this second little hoard that they had uncovered, so that even if the rest of their time here was in vain, at least they had a couple of minor offences to justify their efforts. 'Come on, I fancy a crack at that Ironmonger woman's other room, while they're all bailed up in the staff sitting room. She reminds of me of someone I used to know, and I'd like to get it over with as soon as possible.'

'OK, sir,' agreed Carmichael, not noticing the hook of potential information that had been dangled in front of him, in his pleasure that the bad behaviour of his pets had produced something that they could use.

'I wonder if you could just disentangle them from my trouser legs, so that we can get on. They seem to be attempting to make puppies again, and I don't think I could cope with a litter of bottle-green corduroy doggies. The sooner you get them to that vet, the happier I'll be.'

'Sorry, sir!'

Beatrix Ironmonger's second floor bedroom was in complete contrast to her temporary lodgings on the first floor, and appeared stuffed to the gills with ornaments and little knickknacks. Falconer was sweeping the room with a collector's eye, and deciding that there was nothing here that he fancied, when Carmichael gave a shout of disgust, and covered his mouth with his hand.

'What is it, Sergeant? The overcrowding?'

'The floor, sir. Look at the floor. Look at what she keeps on the floor, and tell me that's normal.'

'They're just little rugs, aren't ... Oh, I see what you mean. How *very* distasteful.' A closer glance had revealed the presence on each 'little rug' of a feline head, and the rest of the thing, like a cat that has lost a fight with a steamroller. 'At least it shows she must have loved them, if she was prepared to go to the expense of preserving them like that. Just pick your way through them, and try not to think about it. We'll start with the bed, shall we?'

'Oh, my God, sir! Have you seen what's on the bedspread?' exclaimed Carmichael, covering his eyes this time.

'It's all right, sergeant. It's nothing more sinister than a nightie case in the shape of a cat. You can look now.'

When they had progressed to the wardrobe and chest of drawers, Falconer thought he heard the rustle of material out on the landing, and he put a finger to his lips to silence Carmichael, who was holding up a salmon-pink girdle with an expression of puzzlement. He'd never seen anything like it before.

Slipping off his shoes on the under-cat carpet, Falconer made his way silently to the slightly ajar door, and peered round it cautiously, in the hope of surprising an eavesdropper, but the only living thing visible was Perfect Cadence, sitting at the top of the stairs, washing herself in that position that cats adopt that suggests they are playing the cello.

'It's only the cat,' he called to Carmichael in disgust, but received no answer. 'Did you hear me?' he enquired, shutting the door firmly behind him, this time.

'Look at this, sir.' Carmichael was perched on the stool from the dressing table, and appeared to have been searching the top of the wardrobe. 'It was right at the back, almost out of sight. I could barely reach it and I don't think *you* could have. She probably poked it up here with a stick or something similar.'

'What have you got there?'

In the sergeant's hand was clutched a glass jar, which he handed down to the inspector, as he dismounted from his perch.

'This looks very interesting, and if I'm not mistaken,' Falconer said, twisting the top vigorously, 'this contains dried fungi. And why was it pushed to the back of a wardrobe, I wonder? Perhaps because it was used to poison Chef,' he declared, answering his own question.

'Do you really think so, sir?'

'I do. What other reason could there be for keeping a jar of dried fungus right at the back of the top of your wardrobe, if you didn't want to hide it from prying eyes? We'll get this off to the lab as soon as possible. Meanwhile, we've only got one more room to check out, then I think, for the sake of thoroughness, we ought to have a look in the other wing, and just take a peek in Mr Grammaticus' den on the first floor. Somewhere in this place there's a little black book, and I've a fair idea what's in it.'

'What?' Carmichael hadn't a clue, and didn't mind admitting it.

'Never you mind. We'll sort that out a bit later, but if we do come across it, I think our genial host is in trouble with a capital 'T'.

'You mean he's the murderer?'

'Oh, much worse than that. He's the three 'J's: judge, jury, and jailer.'

'I don't get it.'

'You will, and I think our Jefferson is going to have some fast talking to do when I confront him with what he's been up to, here. But first, I'm going to put a quick call in for Green and Starr, and get them to come out here in the van. I've a feeling, with what we've discovered this morning, there may be three people who are going on a little trip to Market Darley: one, for that stash we found in the cellar, one for the nest of petty pilfering we found under that floorboard, and that jingly-jangly, creepy housekeeper, for one murder, at least.'

'I've been thinking about her, sir.'

'Mind out; you'll get a headache, Carmichael. Anyway, out with it, and let it see the light of day.

'When we came here after Mr Grammaticus was injured, she definitely said something about the door being ajar, and yet she said she had been up in her room, and only came down because that cat of hers was hungry.'

'Correct!'

'So how could she have known the door was ajar, when she didn't actually see the accident happen?'

There was a short interlude of silence as Falconer took this in. 'By George, you're dead on the button, Carmichael. She'd only know that if she either actually saw it, or if she was the one who set the trap. She made a slip of the tongue, too, when she said Grammaticus went down like a ton of bricks, then tried to cover it up.'

'That's what I mean, sir. Nobody could've surmised that there was a trap. I mean, it could have been someone standing behind the door waiting to whack him.'

They were still standing in the housekeeper's second floor bedroom during this conversation, and Falconer came to a sudden decision. 'I think we ought to have a word with that woman before we search any more rooms. That's the second incident we can tie her to now. Come on, let's get down to the staff sitting room, and pull her out for a little chat. Well done, Sergeant! You've really been on form on this case.'

'Thank you, sir. It must be the heat. Hang on a minute! What's that in the grate? I didn't think to put my head in there earlier.'

What was in the grate was a pile of ashes, and what could be identified, without the application of too much imagination, were the remains of the outside covers of a notebook. 'That,' said Falconer, a faint chagrin in his voice, 'is the remains of Mr Grammaticus' little black book. We've got nothing to confront him with, now, but I'm certainly going to have a stern word with him before we leave here today. I can't have things like that happening on my patch, and he'll not get away with it twice, if I have anything to do with it.'

'Get away with what?'

'Hang on in there, Carmichael, and you'll find out.'

And with that answer, the sergeant had to be content, for now.

But they were to have no joy with Beatrix Ironmonger, who was not only absent from the staff sitting room, but had, apparently, never got there.

'I can't find her. I don't know where she's gone,' explained Grammaticus apologetically. We've searched inside the hotel, and I've just sent Henry Buckle – the gardener – to see if she's outside in the grounds, or possibly in one of the garden buildings. Sometimes she goes out for a sit in the summerhouse, and, although I made it plain it was off-limits when we had guests, we don't have any at the moment, so she probably didn't think it was a problem.'

'Well, let us know if he finds her. Meanwhile, we'll go back up to the second floor. We've still got to make sure that neither of the weapons is tucked away up there, it being the ideal hiding place, if it's not used, and houses a lot of lumber. Come on, Sergeant. We've got work to do.'

Two flights of stairs later – one elegant and shallow, one steep and uncarpeted – they arrived back on the top landing. Carmichael's first action was to check on his furry 'babies', who both proved to be happily asleep in a patch of sunlight on an old rug, and he left them there, dreaming their doggy dreams, paws bicycling in the air, the door slightly open so that he could hear when they woke up.

'Let's start with the two rooms opposite, then work our way through the wing. The rooms seem to be much smaller up here; typical of servants' quarters, and we'll take one each until we've finished them. Remember, we're looking for a knife with a fairly short blade, and something that could make two small puncture wounds; just enough to startle someone and make them lose their balance.'

'I'll call you if I find anything,' said Carmichael. 'If we don't close the doors right over, we'll be able to hear each other, without waking the dead.'

'Good idea! Good luck! And don't, for heaven's sake, wake the dogs.'

Falconer pushed open the door of the room next to the one Carmichael had entered, pushed it half-closed, and looked around him. By George, there was a fine collection of old tat and dust up here. The windows hadn't been cleaned in decades, possibly a century by the look of them, and what little light filtered through from outside formed shafts which looked like the beams of dozens of tiny torches, searching for something long-lost. In the shafts, motes of dust floated their lazy passage across the room, and cobwebs drooped from the ceiling, themselves ancient and dust decorated.

Dragging his mind away from the state of the room, Falconer focused his attention on the job in hand. As there seemed to be a lot of boxes and tea chests in this particular room, he began to scrabble around in the contents of the most conveniently placed, and found himself up to his elbows in old tennis racquets, their strings slack or broken, their presses still attached.

Delving a little deeper, he identified an old croquet set, its hoops determined to trap one of his wrists, but there was still yet another layer to excavate, and he dug further down, using his hands as his eyes, as he felt several tennis balls.

Bent over as he was, with his back to the door, he was aware of nothing other than his search, until he heard a material-like rustle and a muted jingle from the doorway, and then everything seemed to go into slow motion.

His intention of whirling round was more like the action of someone drowning in treacle, and seemed to take hours. His mouth fell open, and his eyes widened as he perceived what, at first, he thought was the figure of Nanny Vogel, standing in the doorway, then he shook his head – another task that seemed to take for ever – and recognised the housekeeper.

In her hand she held something that glinted in the slender beams of weak sunlight, and which, even with the reduced visibility produced by the filthy windows, he could identify as a short-bladed knife. As she brandished it, her chatelaine belt moved gently to and fro, and Falconer remembered the bayonet that had hung from it in his dream. There had also been an axe.

There were aeons of time to work this one out, given the

current elasticity that time had assumed, and he realised that his dream had given him a clue he neither reacted to, nor even recognised. His subconscious must have noticed what he could not identify as a small silver fruit knife, and enlarged it, in the hope that he would unravel the clue.

The shears also represented something, dangling from that sinister chain, and his eyes alighted on an attachment that he identified as a *necessaire*. In that, there would undoubtedly be a small pair of scissors: the perfect implement with which to inflict two small wounds on the unfortunate Fruity Newberry's unsuspecting behind. Everything that had happened was the doing of this ghastly woman, and he had been too blind to see it.

His ears suddenly became aware of a long drawn-out, 'Nooooo!' which seemed to be coming from his own mouth, but sounds from outside this trap of time in which he was caught, managed to break the spell, and several things seemed to happen almost simultaneously.

As time slipped back to its normal tempo, he heard a scratching at floor level, then saw two furry heads that bounced into view, each one grabbing a wrist of the woman with the knife. The shock of tiny sharp teeth digging into bare flesh, caused the housekeeper to drop her weapon, and as time now seemed to have undergone a process of acceleration, and was now running at double speed, it was the work of only a millisecond to grab the weapon from the floor.

As he arose, Beatrix Ironmonger wore a dog on each arm. Every time she managed to disengage one, it jumped anew, and her hands were now bloody from the small puncture wounds that had been inflicted on her.

Luckily for him, the two little dogs had woken up and gone exploring, and when they saw that forbidding figure standing there, they sensed that she was going to hurt Uncle Tasty-Trousers. And they weren't having any of that! They saw him as one of their family now, and nobody was going to lay a finger on him if they could do anything about it.

'Get them off me! For God's sake, get the little fiends off

me!' she cried, shaking her arms to try to dislodge the needle-sharp teeth.

At that moment, Carmichael, having heard the inspector's shout, came careering into the room, took the situation in at a glance, and grabbed the woman from behind, wrapping his long arms round her body to restrain her, and calling for the dogs to lie down.

As they dropped obediently to the floor, the housekeeper aimed a kick at one of them, but Carmichael, expecting some sort of retaliation, jerked her back and out of range. The dogs, now wary of the figure in the long clothes, rushed towards Falconer and scrambled up his legs with no more trouble than if he had been a piece of furniture, and he ended up with one crooked in each arm, two little faces turned up trustingly to look him in the face.

It was the work of a moment to place them safely on the seat of a mouldering armchair at the back of the room, and slip the lightweight handcuffs, which he always carried in his jacket pocket for just such emergencies, round the bloodied wrists of their now limp and compliant prisoner.

Falconer's next action was to take hold of the *necessaire* that dangled from her waist, and take a brief look inside. Yes, there was a very small pair of scissors nestling in there, with all the other little items it contained. Taking the scissors out, he opened them, and their span seemed a perfect match for the gap between the two puncture wounds that Dr Christmas had found on Fruity Newberry's nether regions. He'd got the woman bang to rights this time, and Chivers could go boil his head, if he had one word of criticism for the way he'd handled this case. Of course, Carmichael had helped too, but that fact wasn't at the forefront of his mind in this, his moment of triumph.

Without prompting, she offered them an explanation of sorts. 'It's been worse being here than in prison. He's used our pasts against all of us, you know. When he first contacted me, after such a long time, I was living in a bed and breakfast, and surviving on benefits.

'Then he came along, out of the blue, and offered me a job as a housekeeper, my own quarters – board and lodging and a wage. It seemed like a dream come true, but he made us all train, seven days a week, and get fitted for those awful uniforms – except for his precious partners, of course. No thank you, I'm perfectly all right standing, and here is as good as anywhere else,' she commented, when Falconer asked her if she would like to go somewhere else; somewhere where she could sit down.

'Then, when I saw my room,' she continued, 'it was just an unloved old attic room, and he said there would be no days off until we were open and in profit, and then it would only be two afternoons a week. And as for the wage! It was more like pocket money – an absolute pittance. It's no fun being at someone's beck and call all day every day, and after a while I just saw red.'

Falconer signalled for Carmichael to keep still, and not say a word, in case he interrupted the flow. The dogs had slumped into an exhausted heap, and were snoring gently, and not likely to be any further bother.

'It was seeing that man Newberry that really set me off. No doubt you've investigated my past, and know what I did, and why I did it. Well, he was a very near identical case. He picked me up at Goodwood Race Course, where I'd gone for a little flutter, worked out what I did, asked me back to his hotel room, and we came to an arrangement. I'd go back with him after each day's racing, for the duration of the week, and he'd settle up with me then, with a little bonus, if he'd had a bit of luck.

'What a stupid bitch I was! Once bitten, twice shy, didn't seem to be in my vocabulary. So there I was, on the last day of the races, scanning the faces of the crowd, and looking everywhere, but I couldn't find him. Right after the races were over, I went back to his hotel, thinking maybe he was waiting for me there. Of course he wasn't, the skunk. He'd checked out the night before, and there I was, with a whole week wasted, and not a penny piece to show for it. I decided there and then that, if I ever saw him again, I'd give him what for.'

'Are you sure you wouldn't like to tell your story down at the Station, with a solicitor present?'

'What's the point? I'm in the frame, and I can't see any way out of it, so I might as well come clean.'

'Beatrix Ironmonger, aka Ursula Freebody,' – that made her look up! – 'I am arresting you on suspicion of the murders of Jocelyn Freeman, Frederick Newberry, and Nigel Cooper.'

'Who the hell is Nigel Cooper?' she asked, clearly puzzled.

'That was Chef's real name,' Falconer informed her.

'But Chef was French,' she retorted, sounding quite sure of her ground on this one.

'Chef was no more French than you or I. He was just a damned good kidder. Now, let's get on with this. Anything you say will be taken down ...'

The official caution rolled on, followed its usual course, and she accompanied them downstairs without further resistance.

The police van had arrived, and they passed her gratefully into the custody of PC Green and PC Starr, returning to the hotel to complete their business there with relief. Both headed unerringly to the staff sitting room, where they arrested Chastity Chamberlain on suspicion of theft, and Steve Grieve with the possession of skunk cannabis, which had been of a sufficient quantity for them to suspect he was intending to deal. Both looked as shocked as Beatrix had done when their real names had been used, and, realising the gaff had been blown, Chastity came without a murmur.

Steve, however, claimed that he only had so much 'grass' because he was stuck out here in the middle of nowhere, and had no chance of getting his hands on any more for some considerable time. He'd had to stock up, he pleaded, as he was stuck here for God knows how long, and was only making sure that he didn't run out.

Falconer actually believed his story, and when all the

circumstances were explained to those with the real power, they would probably let him go with a caution. The laws on drug use and possession were somewhat less stringent than they had been in the past, and there was little else they could do with him, except, maybe, confiscate his stash, and he was glad he wouldn't be there when that happened. Steve would no doubt go 'mental'.

These other two bodies also now transferred to the van, Falconer banged on the side to send it on its way to Market Darley, where he would catch up with it later.

'Is that it, sir?'

'Not quite. Remember I said I wanted to have a word with that smug, supercilious, pompous old sod, Grammaticus? Well, I'm going to do it now, and if you want to learn the significance of the little black book, you'd better come with me.'

Chapter Sixteen

Monday 21st June, – a little later

Grammaticus was back in his office, and sitting at his desk with his head in his hands, not so much from the pain from his head wound, as at the thought that he had lost another three members of staff, and that left him with only a sous chef and a gardener and one partner. And without his handy reference guide to future staff, he was completely stumped. He was bemoaning the fact that he had never felt the need to make a copy, when Falconer knocked sharply on the door, and the two detectives entered, and sat without invitation.

Lifting his head, he immediately brightened up, asking, 'Have you found my little black book?'

'Not all of it, sir.'

'What do you mean, not all of it? Either you've found it or you haven't.'

'We have found the charred remains of what seems to have been a black-covered, pocket-sized book in the grate of the housekeeper's room on the second floor, and assume that this is the book to which you are referring.'

'The bitch! The absolute bitch! And after all I've done for her!'

'I think she's done you a favour,' Falconer stated baldly.

'Done me a favour? If you only knew what I had in that book …'

'Oh, I think I've worked that one out, sir, and finding it would have been more of a curse than anything else, especially if I'd been dishonest and devious enough to read it, don't you?'

Jefferson's genial smile slid from his face, as did the colour from his cheeks, and even the flesh under his beard paled to a chalky white. 'I don't know what you're talking about,' he blustered, but there was a catch in his voice, and a few buds of perspiration blossomed on his forehead.

'Correct me if I'm wrong, but I believe that book contained the names, addresses, and contact numbers of quite of few of your former clients who are finding life rather tough at the moment, due to their criminal records. Am I correct?'

Grammaticus sank down deeper in his chair as he listened, his eyes focused about three feet to the inspector's left, no attempt made at eye contact.

Falconer continued. 'I think you used some of these contacts, initially, to staff your hotel. They were, no doubt, living in dismal conditions and receiving benefits. I surmise that you offered them some basic training, followed by a job and accommodation. The only conditions were that they worked for an absolute pittance – I'd be willing to bet that there isn't a member of staff here who wouldn't have been overjoyed to receive the minimum wage, and consider it a considerable boost to their salaries – and that they changed their names.'

'You can't prove any of this!' challenged Jefferson, now slightly bolder and not quite so much on the defensive. 'This is just speculation on your part. You've got no evidence to back that up.'

'I have not, Mr Grammaticus, but I do have the opportunity to interview three members of your staff about a number of incidents that occurred in this hotel, and no doubt they will be extremely anxious to provide me with any information they can to defend their own positions. No doubt they will explain your little naming game to me with no coercion whatsoever.'

'Oh, what the hell! I'll tell you. You've obviously checked the records to see what their original crimes were. Steve Grieve and Dwayne Mortte I named to remind them of what they had done, every time their surnames were used – I just took a bit of a liberty with the spelling of that last one. Chastity Chamberlain's husband beat her because she was sleeping around, so Chastity seemed a particularly apt moniker, especially as she did away with her old man actually in their bedroom. And I got a bit Dickensian with Beatrix. I made her 'wear the chain she forged in life', as did Marley's ghost, and that lady is more guilty than any police records show. When I met her for the first time, I insisted that she shouldn't keep any secrets from me, and she was younger then, and more trusting than she is now. She confided in me that she had pushed her father under the wheels of a bus, then, two years later, she had pushed her mother down the stairs. And when that didn't kill her, she dragged her back to the top of the staircase, and pushed her down it again, just to make sure. There were shades of Lizzie Borden there, and I'd never have trusted her with an axe, of that I can assure you.

'Even taking into account her miserable home life, which consisted mainly of beatings and alcoholic rages, there was no need to resort to such desperate measures, but she's very independent, and likes to sort out her own problems. And so I collected all the little silver *objets*, and I hung them from that chain for her, so that she, too, could be reminded of her past.

'And Chef? He just liked, now and again, to dress up in ladies' clothing, so I thought I'd give him a little reminder of this, whenever anyone used his new name. All of this stuff kept them bound to me, but it wasn't a prison. I told them that if they made a reputation for themselves in their allotted jobs, I would release them from their contracts.'

'Contracts that existed only in your head, Grammaticus, for with those terms and conditions they would never have stood up in court; in fact, they would have put you in a very serious position with regards to their personal freedom. When I leave here, I want you to know that I've got your number, and I shall be keeping my eye on you in the future. You can't just use people like slaves and expect them to be grateful. Look at what employing Mrs Ironmonger did for your little business venture. Not only did she make an attempt on your life, but she killed two members of staff and a guest. How's that going to look when you're trying to entice guests to stay here?'

Grammaticus was up and out of his chair in a trice, shouting, 'That's it! That's it! I'll not advertise The Manse, I'll advertise 'Murder at The Manse'. Percy can alter the script so that we don't need to hire any fancy costumes. We'll still do a murder mystery dinner of course, but we'll get a clairvoyant in as well, and get her to sit in the exact places that the murders took place, and see if we can't work up a bit of a spooky atmosphere. We can use the attics for a game of 'hunt the murder weapon'. A few more buckets of dust up there, some spray-on cobwebs and a sound system that can produce creaking floorboards and doors, and the odd moan, and we shall have a real hit on our hands. I must speak to Percy. She should be home by now. And I know Jerome will agree to come in on it. With his brother's death, we each inherit a fifty per cent share of his part of the business, and he's not as soft-hearted as his brother was. Look at the way he tackled that foul old northerner over that piece of land. Yes, he'll be up for it, no problem.'

'Before we leave, did you have any trouble with your outgoing guests?'

'Them! They all demanded a full refund, of course, but I told them to claim on their holiday insurance, and managed to fob them off with a voucher for a fifty per cent discount for the next event; which they will find means absolutely nothing, as the full price is twice the discounted one, so they'll pay exactly what they paid for this weekend. No, I don't think I'll be seeing any of those characters again. It's onwards and upwards for this place, from now on. I'll have to get weaving, but let me see you out first,' he said, hustling towards the door of his office.

As they reached the front door, they met Alison Meercroft, standing just inside it, a costume over one arm, and a look of absolute fury on her face. 'Don't you dare try to avoid me, Jefferson Grammaticus. There's no point whatsoever slipping back into your office, because I've already seen you. I want a word with you about this costume the police have kindly released to me. Not only are there tears on the lace, where the gentleman fell down the stairs, but there are two – I repeat, two – holes in the seat of the trousers, and it's going to cost me to have that little lot put right. What do you propose to do about the damage? We have a contract!'

Pausing on the top step, Falconer and Carmichael shamelessly eavesdropped.

'I think that, if you take the trouble to look at the terms and conditions of our contract, you'll find that the hotel will only cover repairs or cleaning if the bill exceeds two hundred and fifty pounds. That is the specified amount of excess.'

'Two hundred and fifty pounds? How did you get that one past me, you bastard?'

'And as for any future events, again, in the terms and conditions, can be found a clause that allows me to go elsewhere to satisfy my needs, if the goods you offer don't satisfy the dress code for the event, and I shall make sure that yours don't.'

'You devious, swindling bastard! How dare you treat me like this!'

'It's only business, dear lady. Don't get so worked up about it. Now let me …'

But neither Falconer nor Carmichael waited to hear how he was going to talk his way out of this one. The man was as slippery as an eel, and obviously had no conscience whatsoever. They had three bodies waiting for them, and there were interviews to be done and reports to write.

'That makes my flesh crawl, now we know exactly where he was coming from,' growled Falconer, getting in to the car.

'He's definitely evil, sir, and he doesn't have any conscience at all. How can he live with himself?'

'I don't know, but if he takes one tiny step out of line in the future, I'm going to have him nicked so fast, his feet won't touch the ground. And I'll make it stick, no matter what it takes.'

As the car headed down the drive for the last time, they both took what they hoped was a final look at the impeccable grounds, and from the seat on a ride-on lawnmower, Henry Buckle raised a hand in a lazy wave. In his opinion, given the current renovated state of The Manse, business would go on here. It might go on with Mr G in charge, or it might have new owners with quite a different business venture, but one thing was for certain – the lawns would still need to be mowed, and the weeding done. With any luck, he'd see his days out working in the grounds of this place, and that didn't seem too bad to him, when he considered the size of his old age pension. He was a perfectly contented man, and he intended to maintain the status quo for as long as possible.

Henry waved, too, to Alison Meercroft, who shot out of the double doors like a cork out of a bottle, turning to shout something and wave her fist, before she got into her vehicle and sped away with an angry squeal of tyres. She didn't look best pleased, he thought, but that was Mr G's business, and nothing to do with him.

Back in his office once more, and lowering himself into his chair, Grammaticus' phone rang, causing his gentle descent into a seated position so as not to joggle his injured head, to end in an uncontrolled 'flumph'. 'Damn that bloody phone!' he expostulated, but answering it anyway. 'The Manse, Jefferson Grammaticus speaking. How may I help you?'

A feminine voice that sounded just a tiny bit familiar answered, 'Hello, Mr Grammaticus. My name is Penny Trussler. I'm a freelance journalist, and I was wondering if you'd mind if I did an article on the extraordinary events that have occurred recently at your fabulous new hotel? An interview with you should provide me with all I need to produce a story of real public interest. What do you say?'

Publicity! Just what he needed to drum up business, and the perfect start to the advertising campaign for his new ideas. 'I should be delighted to oblige, Penny. Shall we say tomorrow, at three o'clock? That will give us adequate time for afternoon tea a little later.' Mr Smooth was on the case.

'That would be most convenient, sir. I shall look forward to it very much. Until tomorrow.'

'Until then,' confirmed Jefferson, putting the phone down and yelling, 'Yes!' Life was good!

As Penny Trussler ended the call, she, too, yelled, 'Yes!' She knew the man would lap up the publicity, and that he hadn't yet sussed out who she was. She'd been shadowing 'Chef' since he'd been released, and had used the guise of a Frenchwoman to try to get to know him, already aware that she was safe, as he was English right through, like a stick of rock. And she already had some very useful notes on The Manse from her visits there in the guise of Alison Meercroft's assistant.

Now she had the opportunity of access to Grammaticus himself. If she lowered her voice a little tomorrow, and brushed her hair differently, maybe wearing sunglasses and different make-up, she'd have him done up like a kipper before he realised what was happening, and all her previous investigations would not have been in vain. She could see the headlines now – *Manager of Hotel of Death Admits he Employed Murderers*. Life was good!

Chapter Seventeen

Monday 21st June, – afternoon segues into evening

The rest of the afternoon was spent in the recording of interviews with the three people they had removed from the Manse 'on suspicion'. Falconer asked Carmichael and Starr to deal with Steve Grieve and Chastity Chamberlain, while he tackled Beatrix Ironmonger, with Merv Green in attendance. Aware of his apprehensions about the lady, Falconer couldn't help himself, when he chose the tall well-muscled frame of Green to stand in with him.

It was her similarity to Nanny Vogel that really unsettled him, and he had the feeling that Merv Green would deal with Nanny Vogel without mercy. To him, she would just be a slightly bossy woman, but to Falconer, she carried an air of nightmare, and of the nursery with her, and he didn't want to revert to being a little boy again while he was questioning her.

When she was brought into the interview room, however, she seemed to have been diminished, and Falconer realised at once, what it was that produced that effect. It was the absence of her chatelaine belt, which had been removed from her when she was taken into custody, which was no surprise really, as the *necessaire* that hung from it contained a murder weapon, as did the Georgian silver fruit knife, folded neatly into its own handle. They were both exhibits now, and would, at this very minute, be with the lab boys being tested for any evidence of blood, which he had no doubt they would find.

It may have been something, the wearing of which, had been imposed upon her by her employer, but he knew she enjoyed the noise it made when she walked, announcing her arrival before she was seen, and he also had no doubt that she had added a few little bibelots to it, of her own choosing. Without its talismanic effect, though, she was just another late- middle-aged woman in a long frock, and looked no more dangerous than any normal woman might, if she favoured her hemline very low.

The interview itself was a lot less traumatic than he had thought it would be (for him, that is), and Beatrix held back no details whatsoever.

'It's a very simple story, Inspector. Chef had been infuriating me beyond belief. I know little Cadence shouldn't have gone into the kitchen, but every time he saw her in there, he physically kicked her. There was absolutely no need for that. He could just have lifted her up and put her outside, but no, he had to kick her. And it wasn't a gentle kick either. He used to really boot her one. Sometimes she sat on my lap in the evenings and positively howled with pain if I touched a sensitive spot.

'The man was a beast; a perfect beast, and in the end, I just saw red. I guess you could say that the skin of my teeth lost its hold on the end of my tether. I made that quiche, and you've no doubt discovered my little jar of death? I collected those death caps last autumn, and dried them, and put them away – just in case, and Chef turned out to be the case they had been waiting for.

'With regards to Freeman, I was on my way upstairs on Saturday night, when I was dismissed from the dining room until later, and I saw one of the footmen going into the billiards room. I knew no one would be on the hunt for the "corpse" until another course had gone by. Now, I may be getting a bit long in the tooth, but I do my best to look good, and, boy, did *he* look good to me. I'd been admiring him from afar ever since I first saw those two.

'So, silly, deluded woman that I was, I followed him in, and I …'

'Go on, please,' prompted Falconer.

'Well, I'm ashamed to say, I made a rather crude pass at him, and put my arms around his neck to kiss him. And that was the end of my little fantasy. He pushed me away, then turned his back on me and ... and ... he actually wiped his mouth with his handkerchief, to wipe away the contact my lips had made with his.

'It was like a slap in the face, and I could already feel my hand reaching for the fruit knife dangling from my belt. Then he said he'd tell Mr Grammaticus, and that he'd throw me out on my ear for such disgusting behaviour. But I hardly noticed that bit. I told you how imprisoned I felt. It was the sheer insult of the thing. I used to be *paid* by men for all that, and I was beautiful once. To be called disgusting drove me into a fury. I'd already done for Chef, I thought, so what difference did one more make?

'The next thing I knew, I had the knife in my hand, and standing on tip-toe to get the right angle. Then I plunged the blade into his neck. The blood started to flow out at quite an alarming rate, and I pulled away as fast as I could, so that I didn't get my clothes splattered with it.'

'And then what happened?'

'I just went upstairs to my room and washed the knife. Then I lay down on the bed and had a little nap.'

'And Mr Newberry?'

'That happened a little later. I was coming downstairs from my little rest, and I recognised that Newberry as the one who had cheated me during that Goodwood Week that I told you about. It was quite a long time ago, but I couldn't mistake the jaunty way he walked, and the arrogant tilt of his head.

'What I did then, was purely an instinctive reaction, and more mischievous, on reflection, than with any real malice in it. I took out my little pair of scissors, crept up behind him as he approached the staircase – and poked him in the bum with the blades. I certainly had no intention of killing him, just of giving him a little sting, in a more physical way to the sting he'd practised on me.

But he must have been drunk. He yelled when I poked him

with the blades, and I made a cat-like yowl to cover that up, and slid out of sight as quickly as I could. He seemed to teeter there for ever, swaying back and forwards, and clutching at his buttock, then he just went too far in one direction, and tumbled right to the foot of the stairs. I can't say I'm too sorry; if he cheated me like that, he probably cheated hundreds of people.

'I hope you're recording this, Inspector. You can summon my solicitor whenever you like, but he'll have to make do with the recording, if you call him this evening, for I seem to be feeling inordinately tired. It's all this being released back into society. I'd much rather be in prison. At least I won't be worked like a slave, or dressed like some sort of Edwardian relic.

'The only thing I'm worried about is my darling Perfect Cadence. What's going to happen to her? They won't have her put down, will they? She's only young, and she's the sweetest cat that ever lived.' Beatrix was getting distressed, in a way that had never surfaced when she spoke of the consequences of what she had done to people.

'Have you got any room for my darling? You look like a kind man?'

'I didn't look any different when we were up on the attic floor earlier today, but you still intended to put a knife in me, answered Falconer, a cold shiver running through his body as he remembered the look in her eyes.

'I beg you to take her. If you've ever had a cat, you'll know how I feel. She's like one of my children, and I can't bear to think of her anywhere where she'll be unhappy. Oh, God, what am I going to do? How can I keep her safe and loved, if I'm going back inside?'

'Do you have a cat box?' The words where almost whispered, they were so quiet.

'Up on the second floor, in the room in the back left corner. I stored it there out of the way.'

'I'll take care of her.' Still the voice was barely audible.

'Do you know anything about looking after cats?'

'I've got three of my own. Might as well even the number up.'

'I'll get some money to you, somehow, to pay for her keep.'

'There's no need for that. She might as well join my ever-growing bunch. Don't worry; I'll take good care of her, and she'll fit in just fine,' said Falconer, horrified at the offer his mouth had made, by completely bypassing his brain.

'You're a darling man, offering my little kitty a home with yours. May God bless you,' she said, with real relief and gratitude in her voice. Beatrix Ironmonger – aka Ursula Freebody, and maybe aka a lot of other aliases too – smiled her grateful thanks at him. The vision of Nanny Vogel was immediately dispelled, and he just saw her as a sad and pathetic woman, getting on a bit now, and who had never really had the chance of a normal life.

Then, with a jolt, he pulled himself together. She had killed several people, and shown no remorse, as far as he could see. He'd get one of the patrol cars to pick up the basket *and* the cat, when they were in the area, for he had no intention of ever setting foot in that place again.

They were sitting in the new canteen at the end of a very long day, with cups of coffee and cakes. Falconer's plate held an apple Danish, as did Carmichael's, but Carmichael's Danish was accompanied by a doughnut, a square of lardy cake, and a giant treacle tart with whipped cream on the top. As they consumed this reward for another case solved, Falconer decided that he ought to give praise where praise was due, and said to his sergeant, 'This has really been your case Carmichael. Everything I've done has been a right cock-up, but you've shown real insight and logical thinking.'

'What, sir? I only did my job.'

'Well, if you carry on doing it at that level, I'll soon be calling you 'sir'.'

'Get out of here! We just make a good team, that's all.'

'That's very generous of you, Sergeant, and I do agree that

we do seem to click, despite our differences. And talking of differences, is that a fuzz I see, just making its appearance on your head?'

'It is indeed, sir. I got fed up with Kojak, so I'm growing it back, but it itches like hell,' the sergeant declared, reaching up both hands to give his scalp a good raking.

'So what are you watching instead?' asked Falconer, hoping to goodness that it wasn't *Cagney and Lacey*.

'*Columbo*! Oh, and sir, you won't believe it, but I've got this great old mac ...'

'Nooooo ...'

EPILOGUE

At exactly thirteen minutes past one, in the dark of the night, a grey cat slinked across the grand entrance hall of The Manse, as it had always done, and would continue to do, until the building was no more. It didn't mind the intruders who had moved in and out over the years, for he knew it was his home, his stalking ground, and he would continue on his nightly skulking in search of a spirit mouse for as long as it took.

THE END

An excerpt from

Music to Die For

The Falconer Files Book 6

Andrea Frazer

Chapter One

Let us open this story at the beginning of the events that led to the violent upheaval in the normally smooth timetable of the band's rehearsals, and the way in which these upheavals occurred.

At the moment, the band was without a musical director, and therefore without someone of sufficient training and experience to arrange and write parts out for new pieces they wanted to play. Its members, however, didn't want to spend any money on purchasing them, as they were a diverse mix of instruments, no two the same. Two out of the three previous musical directors were able to write for all tunings of instrument, whether in C, B flat, or E flat, could read and write for treble, bass, and alto clefs, and were, in consequence, sad losses.

A further complication meant that this also meant that they had no conductor, and to allow them to play without someone waving a baton, or their arms around, was akin to letting a lion perform un-caged and without its keeper.

The first of these previous MDs had suddenly had a whim to move to the Lot in France, and was gone within a few weeks. The next MD did exactly the same thing when her husband accepted early retirement, and they moved to the Dordogne. The third MD was also a woman, but she could not read either bass or alto clef, and could not cope with writing parts for transposing instruments, so for the best part of a year they had to make do with what music they already had and had had nothing new to tackle.

Two months short of the anniversary of this particular lady taking over the position, she announced that she and her husband had purchased a property in Normandy, and that they would be moving there in the very near future. 'What the hell did France have that England didn't?' many members were heard to mutter between themselves, but no open resentment was shown, and she went off on her adventure with the goodwill of all.

This left them all in the aforementioned dilemma, and when the vicar turned up at The Grange at their next rehearsal, and announced that he knew someone who had just moved to the village who had spent his whole life working with bands, it seemed like a miracle – although they'd have to ask him how he felt about France, before getting used to him and settling down again. To lose three musical directors to that country was catastrophic enough: to lose four would simply be calamitous and beyond belief.

Everyone knew, of course, that Wheel Cottage had recently been bought, but no one seemed to have any information about who now lived there. Granted, there had been a large removals van that had turned up one morning about a week ago, and unloaded a lot of rather fine furniture, but the new owner himself (or even herself) didn't seem to be present.

A few days later, there were suddenly curtains at the windows, and lights on in the evening, but still no visits to the village shops from whoever had moved in. Curiosity had nearly reached fever pitch, when the vicar announced that he might have someone to fill the void, and he would bring him – *him* – along to their next rehearsal, so that he could hear them play, and they could get to know one another a little bit.

Friday 25th June

It was the fourth Friday of the month and, therefore, it was rehearsal night for the village band in Swinbury Abbot. The members had gathered, as usual, in the home of Myles and Myrtle Midwynter. The Grange was a large residence situated

234

on Beggar Bush Lane, to the south of the village centre, and backing on to the terrace of dwellings known as Columbine Cottages. It had no near neighbours, and there was, therefore, no need to worry about complaints about the noise – either its volume, or its quality.

The players had assembled, as was normal, at seven o'clock, to commence with a glass (or two, or more) of wine and a bit of a chat. They knew that Rev. Church would be bringing round his mysterious stranger, as a candidate for the role of musical director, but did not expect the visitation until rather later in the evening.

When Myrtle Midwynter called them to the dining room at a quarter to eight, they settled themselves round the large table to an excellent meal of poached salmon, salad, and new potatoes, followed by a delicious strawberry trifle, still chatting with enthusiasm, and it wasn't until nearly a quarter-past-nine that Myles announced that he rather thought they ought to play a little something.

There had been a whole month of news and gossip to catch up on, and as only a few of the musicians had been nominated as the designated drivers, the other players had continued to imbibe, with scant attention to exactly how much they had drunk, Myles topping up their glasses whenever they showed any signs of having room for more.

The Midwynters made a good team, despite the disparity in their ages, with Myrtle being only thirty-six years old to Myles's fifty-eight, and anything they hosted, usually ran on oiled wheels. Every guest's needs were immediately noticed and catered for, and nothing was too much trouble; this was one of the main reasons why the band met there. Myrtle didn't mind either the time or the expense of feeding them all, and they all felt at home and welcome.

As Myrtle cleared away the dirty dishes, everyone assembled in the large drawing room, and began to get their instruments out of their cases, search for sheet music, and take on the monthly battle with the music stands – one which the music stands usually won, leaving at least two or three pinched fingers and, on one memorable occasion, a badly squashed nose, but that was more due to alcohol, than ineptitude on the part of the victim, and fortunately, didn't require any medical attention.

There was a sharp knock at the front door, as Myrtle was coming through the hall, still drying her hands on a tea towel, and she answered it before going into the drawing room to unpack her cello. Standing on the step, she found Rev. Church, and the person she presumed was the candidate for the position of Musical Director.

As Rev. Church introduced her, she took note of the small man with whom she was shaking hands. He was only about five foot seven, with white hair cut fairly short, probably in his late sixties – but it was his eyes that captured her attention, for he seemed to be looking in two directions at once. One of them stared her squarely in the face as they greeted each other, the other had an alarming habit of wandering around, as if in search of something just out of view, and she longed to turn round to see what it could be looking for.

Remembering her manners, she invited them in, and preceded them to the drawing room, opening the door and calling over the loud buzz of chatter and the sound of instruments being both tuned and warmed-up.

'Quiet everybody! Your attention, please!' She clapped her hands loudly, in the hope that this would penetrate the hubbub, then called again, a little louder this time, 'Silence! Be quiet! We have visitors. If I could have your full attention, please, I would like to introduce you to … Oh, I'm terribly sorry, but I never asked your name. Rev. Church, perhaps you would do the honours?'

'Of course, my dear,' replied the vicar, smiling fondly around at all those present. 'May I present to you Mr Campbell Dashwood, who has recently moved into Wheel Cottage. He has been involved in music all his life, both as an enthusiastic amateur performer and, later, as a professional.

'He has a great deal of experience as a conductor, and is

sufficiently multi-talented,' (here, the vicar made a small bow in Mr Dashwood's direction), 'to produce arrangements for all of those – oh, what do you call them, now? – transferring instruments.'

'That's 'transposing', Vicar,' interjected the newcomer, with a small, superior smile.

'Precisely, Mr Dashwood; just what I meant to say. Anyway, here is the man himself, and perhaps I could hand over to you now, Mr Midwynter, so that you can introduce him to all your players, and then, perhaps, you could find us somewhere to sit, so that we can listen in on your rehearsal, and just give Mr Dashwood here, a flavour of your playing.'

As Myles Midwynter put down his clarinet, Campbell Dashwood extracted a small notebook from the breast pocket of his jacket along with a minute pencil, licked the end of the latter, and stood, ready to take notes. Before Myles could speak, however, Campbell Dashwood was moved to verify some information.

'I understand that your performance later this summer is to celebrate the tenth anniversary of the forming of the band, and that it will take place in the church, with half the proceeds going to the church restoration fund, and the other half to a charity to which you regularly contribute.'

'Absolutely correct, Mr Dashwood.'

'Please, call me Campbell,' suggested the little man, but his smile never reached his eyes – either of them – and was somehow chilly.

'Right, Campbell,' continued Myles, 'may I begin by introducing you to the strings section of the band. Perhaps when I call out your name, you could stand, so that Mr Dashwood – sorry, Campbell – can identify you,' he requested, moving to the front of the assembled musicians.

'Let's start with first violin. May I present to you Mr Cameron McKnight.'

Cameron stood, still clutching his violin and bow, and made a small bow to Campbell. 'Very pleased to meet you,' he said, smiling, but as Campbell made no answer, he sat down again, feeling a little flustered.

Myles cleared his throat in embarrassment about the lack of response, but put this down to, perhaps, a bit of initial shyness on Mr Dashwood's part. Dammit, it didn't feel right calling him Campbell. He'd have to do something about that later; and he put his mind to finding a suitable ruse to address this enigmatic little man in a more formal manner; one that felt comfortable.

'Next,' he continued, 'we have second violin, Mrs Gwendolyn Radcliffe.' A short, dumpy lady with an iron-grey perm and more than a hint of a moustache rose to her feet, blushing, then sat straight down again, without even waiting to see if any response was forthcoming. Dashwood considered her to be in her early sixties.

'On viola, we have Miss Fern Bailey,' intoned Myles, and a slightly plump woman shot up off her seat and beamed round at all assembled. She wore a hairband and had a 'jolly hockey sticks' air about her that proclaimed her to be just an overgrown boarding school girl, even though she was in her mid-thirties.

Myles continued gamely, 'Now we have my own lovely wife, Myrtle, on cello.' Myrtle didn't stand, but as they had already met on the doorstep, waved her tea towel in the air instead, before folding it into a small square on which to place the spike of her cello so that there would be no damage to the carpet.

'I say, old girl,' called Myles. 'All this announcing is thirsty work, do you think you could do the honours, and top up all the glasses. There are a couple more bottles of white in the fridge if you need them, and a couple more red, breathing, on the dining room sideboard. May I get you a glass of wine, Mr Dashwood?'

This time, Campbell didn't correct Myles's form of address, and said, with a certain amount of smug pride, 'I never touch anything alcoholic. Not only does it damage the liver, but I am convinced that it rots the brain as well. I don't suppose I could have a glass of water, could I, if it's not too much trouble?'

'Got that!' called Myrtle, and disappeared in the direction of the kitchen.

'Moving on, we have Miss Vanessa Palfreyman on double bass. Stand up and show yourself, Vanessa. Don't be shy.' A tall, somewhat stout middle-aged woman with short-cropped dark hair, just beginning to show signs of grey, slid out from behind the camouflage of her large instrument, then ducked back out of sight as quickly as possible.

'Right, that's the strings dealt with. Now we move on to woodwind, starting with Gayle Potten on flute.'

'Overweight mutton dressed as lamb,' thought Dashwood, disparagingly. 'She could do with losing at least three stone, if not more, and if her T-shirt were any tighter there would probably be a very nasty explosion of flesh to be dealt with.'

'Geraldine Warwick, on piccolo and miscellaneous percussion.' Myles had dropped the use of titles; it was all too wearing to remember which of the women were Miss, Mrs, or Ms, when he'd already sunk a few sherbets.

'Mouse,' was Dashwood's only thought about the apologetic pixie, who had bobbed briefly to her feet in response to her name.

'Wendy Burnett, on oboe,' Myles droned on, stifling a yawn. Surely it wasn't that late.

'Methuselah's mother,' thought Dashwood, unkindly, as Wendy was a very spritely eighty-nine, and looked years younger than her actual age.

'And last in this section, but certainly not least, we have Lester Westlake, on saxophone.'

Dashwood observed a tall, slim man rise from the back of the room, bowing to all present, and grinning a smile that seemed to contain a great number of large and very white teeth. 'Lounge lizard!' His thoughts allowed him the luxury of a minuscule smile. He knew the type, all right. All looks, and nothing much of anything else. Well, he'd better play well, or he'd have his guts for garters.

'Oh, not quite last. I'm afraid,' Myles apologised. 'I've

forgotten myself. I'm on clarinet. The brass section has only one player, I'm afraid, but it is the unforgettable Harold Grimes, on trumpet.'

A fairly short, elderly man rose to his feet and, extraordinarily, to one who hadn't seen how much wine he had imbibed, did a little dance on the spot.

'The fool of the group,' was Dashwood's silent verdict.

'And our last member to be introduced is Edmund Alexander, who plays keyboard for us, and generally keeps us in line.'

'We'll see about that!' thought Dashwood. 'He'd better be good, or he's out.'

'Come on, woman; where's that glass of water? We've got a man dying of thirst here,' shouted Myles, with such volume that Geraldine Warwick was observed to physically jump in her seat.

'I've put it on the little table between the two red leather armchairs. Oh, and I've put a glass of red wine there for you, Vicar. I know how you like a little tipple.'

'You get yourselves sat down, and we'll just have a little discussion on what we're going to play for you this evening.' Moving back to his place in the band, Myles exhorted the others to wrack their brains, and come up with something interesting.

'Come along, you lot! Mr Dashwood and the vicar don't want to be sitting here all evening, while you bicker and squabble about what we ought to play,' he said, cutting across the babble of talk. 'I know; let's do 'The Teddy Bears' Picnic'. That's always a good laugh – at least it is for me. You know what my timing's like!' he finished, with a rich chuckle, drawing smiles from all the other band members, who did, indeed, know how erratic his timing was, and how many hilarious moments it had produced in the past.

After an enthusiastic, but wildly inaccurate fifteen minutes of fighting the chosen piece, Dashwood whispered something in the vicar's ear, then rose from his seat and left the room, dragging an embarrassed clergyman in his wake.

Once out in the hall, Dashwood turned to Rev. Church and asked, in a furious whisper, 'Have they really been together for ten years?' His rogue eye seemed to rake the ceiling, as if he were looking towards the heavens for an answer.

'Yes. The odd person has left, and another one joined, but they're basically the same people here now, who started it all.'

'And how often do they rehearse?'

'Once a month,' replied the vicar, now mortified after what he had just listened to in the drawing room.

'Well, that's going to have to change, if I'm taking over. It's got to be once a week. And tell me something else. Do they always start that late, and drink so much?'

'They have a meal first, and there's wine with that, and more during the rehearsal if anyone wants it.'

'Well, that's got to stop as well. And that drawing room's no use for rehearsing in – people sitting in low armchairs, and on drooping sofas. Would it be possible for us to use the old meeting hall on a Friday night?'

'I have no problem with that, Mr Dashwood, but who's going to tell them about the changes?'

'Oh, I will. They don't frighten me. If they want to be a decent band, then they'll have to learn discipline – and I'm the man for the job. I'll drop a note through Midwynter's door first thing in the morning, then I'll telephone him later, if you would be so kind as to supply me with his number.

'We can thrash it out between us over the phone. If we can get the rehearsals started earlier, there will be plenty of time for them to go for a drink afterwards, but, in my opinion, one mouthful of alcohol in the system completely befuddles the fingers, whatever instrument one plays.'

'Rather you than me, old chap,' retorted the vicar, his face a mask of dismay at the outcome of such straight talking, to a man of such entrenched habits as Myles Midwynter.

'Oh, it's not luck I need, Vicar, just determination and structure, tempered with an iron discipline. I'll soon have them playing like professionals. You just wait and see. They just need the alcohol-induced scales to fall from their eyes, and they'll realise what an appalling racket they actually make. I'll soon have them eating out of the palm of my hand.'

It had been one of those frustrating days for Detective Inspector Harry Falconer, with a very awkward moment with Detective Sergeant Davey Carmichael. The moment had occurred when they were both in the office, up to their eyes in paperwork, and Carmichael had suddenly said, 'John Proudfoot' [PC] 'said something very odd to me today, sir. He patted me on the arm and said, 'You're a very brave lad, carrying on working like this, and we're all very proud of you. You keep on eating those lollipops – they'll help to build you up. Now, I'll say no more.' What do you think he meant by that?

'And then, when I went to the canteen, the woman behind the counter gave me an extra doughnut, and then wouldn't charge me for it. She said I needed to keep up my strength and just carry on taking my medicine. I'm fair flummoxed. And I've had some odd, sad looks from some of the others working here – you know, the civilian staff? What the hell's going on?'

'That does sound odd,' Falconer replied. 'I've got to go down to the desk, so I'll see what Bob Bryant has to say. He's usually got his ear to the ground and knows just about everything that goes on around here.'

Ten minutes later, the inspector stormed back into the room, a look of fury on his face. 'You and your stupid Kojak look!' he exclaimed [see: Murder at The Manse].

'What about it, sir?' asked Carmichael, puzzled at the out-of-the-blue reference to his recently-shaven head.

'Proudfoot's only put two and two together, and made eighty-seven. He's been going around telling everyone how tragic it is that you've got *cancer*! They think you're having chemotherapy and still coming into work, despite the way you obviously must be feeling.

'Well, I bearded him in his den – asleep behind a

newspaper in the canteen – and I told him that there was nothing wrong with you, and that he'd better get round to spreading *that* good news. There never had been anything wrong with you, and now everyone thought you were ill. I said he also needed to apologise to you, personally, as you had no idea what people were thinking, and couldn't understand why you were being treated so differently.'

'You didn't tell him about Kojak, did you, sir?' asked Carmichael, nervously. He didn't want anyone extracting the Michael about his little fantasies.

'Oh course I didn't, you twerp. I told them you'd forgotten to put the spacer into your hair clippers, and after the first run across your head, you realised you'd made a mistake, and had to shave the rest of it off, to make it look acceptable, otherwise you'd have had a great bald stripe right across the top of your head.'

'Phew! Thanks, sir. I didn't want anyone to think I was a fantasising twit.'

'Even if you are – although not the fantasising bit,' Falconer muttered under his breath, so that Carmichael wouldn't hear. How things can be twisted all out of shape, if someone gets the wrong end of the stick, and just happens to be the station's biggest gossip and rumour-monger.

Harry Falconer was late finishing work that day, and it wasn't until seven o'clock that he packed up the paperwork he needed to take home, and prepared to leave the Station, but he wasn't to escape the building that easily.

At the foot of the staircase, he was hailed by the desk sergeant, Bob Bryant. 'Hey, sunshine, not so fast! There's been something left here that I don't think will keep overnight, so I'd be grateful if you'd collect it now and take it with you.'

With a puzzled expression, Falconer crossed to the desk, only to have his gaze directed to the floor just behind it, where a small grey-spotted cat nestled on part of an old blanket, in a wire cat basket. 'Oh, no,' he thought. 'I'd forgotten all about that.'[3]

'I seem to recall,' Bob Bryant went on, 'that you promised to take this tiny, helpless creature into the care and comfort of your own home. That fella from the hotel phoned the RSPCA to take her away, but fortunately, word had got around about your very kind offer, so one of their lads went and collected it, and here it is. I don't know whether it's a he or a she, but it seems very placid.'

'So did they say why it's taken so long to get her here?' asked Falconer, still slightly puzzled.

'Had to catch it first, apparently. It can run like the very devil, when it wants to. Anyway, sunshine, it's all yours now. I can't be having animals behind my desk. Gives completely the wrong impression to visiting members of the public, and the next thing you know, we'll be inundated with all sorts of waifs and strays. Here it is,' he said, handing over the cage. 'And good luck. You're going to need it with that snooty Mycroft of yours, not to mention the other two you took in after that affair at Stoney Cross.'[4]

Falconer took the cat basket with a sinking feeling in his stomach. After the first day or two, he thought everyone had forgotten his rash offer to give Perfect Cadence a home, then he had conveniently forgotten it too, making sure he didn't mention it to anyone, in case his spontaneity came back to haunt him; and yet here it was, much more substantial than a ghost, and liable to cause chaos with Mycroft (his seal-point Siamese), Ruby (a red-point Siamese) and Tar Baby (a huge, black, furry monster of a cat). Still, such is life! He'd just have to learn to keep his mouth firmly shut in the future, and not let his sentimental side get the better of him.

Placing the basket on the passenger seat of his Boxster, he carefully fastened the seatbelt round it, and headed for home, full of trepidation. The cat had woken up as soon as he started the engine, and managed to howl mournfully for the entire

---

[3] See *Murder at the Manse*
[4] See *Choked Off*

journey, which did nothing for his spirits.

Entering the house, three furry figures skittered out of the sitting room to meet him, skidding abruptly to a halt when they saw what he held in his left hand. They couldn't quite see what was in the cage, but they could smell 'cat', and it wasn't one of them. What was going on here? Why had he brought another cat home? Weren't they enough for him?

Before Falconer had even had the chance to close the front door, the three furry bodies had turned their backs on him in disgust, and gone about their business, feigning total disinterest in what he had brought home for them, for if it was a present, he could just take it away with him again, because they didn't want anything to do with it.

Fortunately, they had all stalked out of the cat-flap in a huff, to see if anything interesting was going on in the back garden, and he was able to set the flap to 'in only', and release Perfect Cadence from her prison. Setting the cat box, door still open, in case she felt she needed somewhere to retreat to, he filled a fresh bowl with food, and another with water, and put both down on the floor, on the plastic mat he used for the other feeding bowls, so that his kitchen floor did not get too dirty, for his pets had absolutely no table manners at all.

Reaching to the top of one of the kitchen cupboards, he retrieved a litter tray, removed the emergency bag of litter from the cupboard under the stairs, poured the latter into the former, and put it down near the back door for the new cat's use, until he felt she was at home, and ready to go outside, and still know where to come back to.

Perfect Cadence performed like a natural. She slunk over to the food bowl, eyes going from side to side, in case there were any of those other cats that she had smelled around, then lowered her head, and ate, making unnerving growling noises, as she made the food disappear. When the bowl had been licked clean, she took a dainty drink of water, then approached the litter tray with an intent look in her eye.

Falconer finally found the poop scoop about ten minutes

later, under a pile of old newspapers that he had placed under the stairs to take for re-cycling, and then completely forgotten about. Armed with this, and trying not to breathe through his nose, he set about cleaning the foul little present that his new house guest had deposited in the litter tray, tied the carrier bag in which he had placed it, and then stood thinking.

He couldn't take it outside to the dustbin, because she might get out, so he'd have to distract her, and shut her in another room, before he could discard his noisome little bundle. Oh, boy; was life going to be more interesting from now on, and he could only hope that his three other cats would accept her as easily as Mycroft had accepted Ruby and Tar Baby, last year.

Once free of his stinking little bundle, he went into the sitting room, and sat down in his favourite chair with his newspaper, only to find the little cat sliding gently on to his lap, purring like a little engine, and rubbing her face against his left hand as it held the pages of the paper up. 'You little darling, Cadence,' he crooned, already having shortened her name for the sake of simplicity, and, dropping his paper to the floor, started to stroke her silky soft fur. 'You're going to be no trouble whatsoever, are you, you little poppet?' he predicted.

Saturday 26th June

When Myles Midwynter came downstairs, a little later than usual as it was a Saturday, he espied an envelope sitting on the doormat which definitely had not been there the night before, and could not have come by post, as the postie never came before eleven on Saturdays.

He picked it up with some interest, slit it open with his thumb, and unfolded the single sheet of paper contained therein. As he read, his face grew redder and redder, and he began to shake with rage. 'Myrtle!' he shouted, loud enough to wake the dead, then charged back up the stairs again, holding the letter at arm's length, as if it were alive. 'Myrtle!'

he bellowed again, and found his wife sitting up in bed, rubbing the sleep out of her eyes.

'What on earth is wrong? And why are you making all that noise?' she asked, in a husky, just-woken-up voice.

'This – this letter! This bloody letter!' he exclaimed, thrusting it under her nose, before she had even had the chance to reach for her reading glasses.

'That bloody man!' he exclaimed, his voice rising to a shout again.

'What the hell has he – whoever he is – written, to get you into such a fine old state?'

'It's that Dashwood, the bounder! He's suggesting that we completely reorganise how we run our rehearsals, if we're to be under his baton. I'll give him 'under his baton'! He wants us to rehearse in the old meeting hall, so that we can sit on *suitable* chairs in our *proper* musical groups …'

'Well, the old meeting hall's just a few yards down the road for us, so that's not a real problem, but as far as musical groups go, that'll leave Harold rather lonely, won't it?' cut in Myrtle.

'Harold be damned! He's always sat with the sax. But – get this – he doesn't think it *appropriate* that we should be under the influence of alcohol when we play, as this obviously leads to inaccurate note-reading and an under-par performance. My arse! That's the way we've always done things! Who does he think he is, telling us what to do, when he's not even been in the village for more than five minutes?'

'Calm down, Myles. You know you need to be careful of your blood pressure.'

'And,' he went on, 'he thinks that a heavy meal before playing is also a bad thing. Dammit, we've been having a meal together before we've played, for the last decade.'

Myrtle had now located her reading glasses behind her nightly glass of water, and held the letter up to the light, the better to read it. When she had finished, she dropped the sheet of paper on to the bedclothes, and pierced her husband with a gimlet eye.

'We have been getting rather lax of late, you know,' she stated baldly. 'Why, on at least two practices out of the last half dozen, we haven't even bothered to play more than one or two pieces. And I can see his point in rehearsing weekly. The concert's only a couple of months away, and there's no way we can be ready if we carry on as we are, you've got to admit.'

'What are you suggesting then? That we give in and do exactly what he says, like naughty schoolgirls and boys being told off by the headmaster? Dammit! I won't be written to like that! I won't be bullied!'

'No, but you will be swayed by simple common sense. If we really want to do this concert for charity, then we're going to need to practise a lot more, not just at home, which I don't think anybody bothers to do at the moment, but together, and on a much more regular basis.'

'Traitor!'

'Don't be so childish! This is a perfectly polite and reasonable letter, and I think we should give his suggestions serious consideration. And, as for the food and wine, there's no reason why I can't leave out a finger buffet here, if I put cling film over the plates. He says here that he'd like us to start at seven. If we do that, and he runs it competently, we can be back here by nine, stuffing our faces and having a few glasses of the old vino. And if he doesn't run it well, we can tell him to sling his hook.'

'I vote we tell him to sling his hook now, and just go on as we are.'

'Now, you know that's not really an option. The vicar bringing him along, has at least opened my eyes to how much work we actually need to do, to be ready to perform in front of an audience, and I think we should give him a chance. If he can get us through this concert, you can do whatever you like after that, but it's been much more of a social club than a band practice lately, and you can't deny that.'

Myles sighed, ran his hand over his suspiciously dark hair, then used both hands to twirl the ends of his magnificent (and also suspiciously dark) handle-bar moustache, actions that indicated that he was thinking. 'You're right, of course, but I don't like admitting it. I'll do an e-mail for those who've got computers, and phone those who haven't, but they won't like it.'

'Then they'll just have to lump it, won't they. It's either practise like the very devil, or cancel, and we simply can't let the vicar down – or the church restoration fund.'

The Falconer Files

by

Andrea Frazer

For more information about **Andrea Frazer**
and other **Accent Press** titles
please visit

www.accentpress.co.uk